ALL *Your* FAULT

KRISTIN LEE

*To all the strong women, in particular, my niece.
She's the glue in our family, rushing around, doing more
things in a day than most people do in a week. She's been the
only girl in a sea of boys. I'm forever grateful that she
considers me a second mom.
Love you, Bug.*

ALL YOUR FAULT

Campus Stallions

Kristin Lee

Chapter One

Adalee

I AM READY.

During my three weeks in Alabama, I decided I'm ready to take the next step with my boyfriend. Chaz has been pressuring me for months. My inner voice keeps telling me to hold off, but I'm sure all college guys try to persuade their girlfriends for sex.

I'm back on campus and ready to fulfill my childhood dream of winning the SEC All Around in gymnastics. It would be the icing on a cake that I rarely eat.

Okay, Adalee. Quit thinking about gymnastics and focus on preparing for your date.

Slipping into a little black dress, I admire myself in the mirror. My hair is twisted up in the back. The plum-colored lip stain goes on smooth, then I *pop, pop, pop* like they do in the Hip-Hop instructional videos—just for a bit of fun. This is exciting. He'll be here at any moment to take me to an upscale hotel for dinner and a night together where our roommates can't interrupt us. Surprisingly, my nerves are steady and calm.

I sling my gym bag over my shoulder and skip down the hall before sliding on my black lacy criss cross heels, then I tie the ribbon around my ankles. My phone is sitting on the bar in the kitchen/living area. It lights up, and I glide my finger across the screen to answer Chaz's call. "Hey," I say cheerfully.

There's a pause. "Can you meet me? I'm already here and had a couple of drinks." His voice is flat.

"Yeah," I answer, attempting to squelch my disappointment. "Sure. Is everything okay?"

"Just get here. I need you now," Chaz demands.

I'm not sure if I even answer him. He has huge mood swings, and he's hard to handle sometimes. With my spirits dampened, I drive myself to the hotel. So much for being swept off my feet for our first time.

Baseball isn't going well this off-season. Chaz has been a bear since some guy transferred here from Illinois and is competing for the same spot he wants. Chaz is a competitor, teammate or not, he's going to fight for his position. And he told me that his new teammate is going out with other guys' girls.

When I enter the hotel lobby, Chaz isn't waiting for me. Why did I expect him to be? Why did I think three weeks apart would change his personality—he's never gentlemanly.

He's cocky and expects everyone to do what he wants when he wants.

Red flags start waving in the wind as I stare over to the bar and a woman is draped over his body. Her hand rests on one of his shoulders as she pushes back and then laughs in his ear. And my mother *fugging* boyfriend is eating-it-up.

I cross the white marble tile that's veined with gray and black. My heels click and echo in the decorative, arched room. I hate heels. Why did I dress like this? I'm used to running around barefoot and covered in chalk. I may not be comfortable but at least I know I look attractive as all eyes stare at me as I walk.

I clear my throat to give the woman with *pure* intentions time to peel herself from my boyfriend.

"Nice to meet you Jane," he says, and I swear to God he gives her his trademark head nod where his blond hair shifts over his forehead and to the side.

"Yeah, I'll catch up with you later," Jane says as her smile lingers on her mouth.

"Can we put my bag in our room?" I ask, hoping Jane with the double D's gets the hint that he's taken. The cougar looks ready to pounce but lurks off to monitor her prey.

He knocks back his crystal glass of what I assume is bourbon then slides it to the bartender. "One more."

He nods as he cleans a glass with a white cloth, then asks, "Anything for the lady?"

Chaz's response sends chills through me—and not in a good way. "No, she's a prude."

The bartender pours the bourbon into a new glass and moves it in front of Chaz, giving me an expression of pity—mouth closed, tilted head with a half-grimace.

My mouth has gone dry at Chaz's insult. "May I have some water, please?"

The bartender pours me a glass, and I sit down in the barstool beside Chaz. I take a long sip of my water and ask, "What's going on? I thought we were having a special night."

Chaz chuckles then sucks down the rest of his second glass of alcohol since I've been here, making me wonder how many he had before I arrived?

He's wearing dress pants and a blue fitted button-down that matches the color of his eyes. His hair is perfectly coiffed in a college guy kind of way. He styles it where the long part in front swoops to the side.

He's a handsome guy and he knows it. He's listed as five-foot-eleven in the baseball program but he's closer to five foot ten—not that I care since I'm a tiny gymnast. He has a sharp nose and square jawline, but tonight, his normally crystal-clear blue eyes are stormy and red. He's definitely had a few more drinks than usual.

Finally, he speaks, "Let's go up and do this." He taps his drink against the oak stained bar, stands, and heads toward the elevators without asking to carry my bag.

Is it asking too much for him to act like a man with manners?

We wait for the elevator in silence.

We ride up to the highest floor in silence.

We enter the junior suite in silence.

I glance around the room which has a king size bed and sitting area but only separated by one piece of furniture. The stark white comforter is tucked in neat, and an abstract horse painting hangs above the bed. The room feels sterile, and Chaz hasn't done anything to make it feel special.

Is that my job?

He begins to unbutton his shirt, revealing a lean, sculpted torso. My stomach isn't flipping. What's wrong with me?

He stalks toward me and says, "Ready?"

I shake my head.

"It's just sex with your boyfriend. You have had sex before, right?" He laughs rather maniacally.

It dawns on me that we've never had the conversation. I always said I wasn't ready and swatted his hands away or left angry that he'd pressured me to go farther and do more. Honestly, why am I considering this? The farthest we've been is second base—a little fondling and fingering.

I cross my hands over my waist. "Why didn't you pick me up?"

"Because I didn't fucking want to. I wanted to have a drink and relax before trying to have sex with my fucking girlfriend. Which, by the way, I knew you would flake out. Like you always do. You're a fucking tease."

Tears form behind my lids, desperate to push them down, I close my eyes and gather my emotions. It's a skill I've mastered over the years. So many disappointments when you can't hit a skill, no matter how hard you train, teaches you to push feelings like that away. "I'm leaving. I drove myself so don't worry about driving." I swat his hand as he grabs me around the wrist so hard it hurts.

"We're doing this," he says through gritted teeth and yanks my black lace dress so hard one of the thin spaghetti straps rips.

I try to wiggle away but he tightens his grip on my shoulder and hip. My eyes widen, my heart races and tension fills my body. He has been a butthole before but never violent. I snap back, "No, we're not. You were the one flirting and drinking when I got here. You won't tell me what's wrong."

"You really want to know?" He waits a moment. "*You*. You're what's wrong. I want a girlfriend that wants me. Do you know how many girls throw themselves at me? I definitely picked the wrong girl."

He speaks about us as if we're a product and not human beings in a relationship. My mouth goes drier than the Sahara Desert.

Chaz leans down and sucks the skin above my breast. With that opening, I push him away with the same strength I use to push off the vault and he staggers backward. "Stop. What is wrong with you?"

"Me? That's hilarious." He continues to ramble something about his new teammate while I hold my arms stiff to keep him away. Then in a cool sardonic voice, he says, "You're just like that fucking transfer... always thinking you can come in and call the shots."

"Wow. To think I was going to give myself to you. But you're the last person that deserves my body. And grow up, athletes come and go to make a team successful. You're the captain, and if anyone should be making a new transfer feel comfortable in a Stallion uniform, it's you. You can't stand it when someone else has the spotlight," I hiss.

His hands run through his honey blond hair as he cuts the distance between us in half. "He's a hotshot—a showoff."

Pot calling the kettle black. I don't know this transfer because Chaz has never mentioned him by name. Based on my limited knowledge, he sounds like a replica of Chaz.

He pushes me down on the bed. "We're doing this now or it's over." My eyes widen in disbelief. He crawls on top of me, but I pull my knees into my stomach and press my feet against his chest, pushing him off me and allowing myself time to run to the door.

"Fine. There was a little voice in my head telling me to hold off. I'm so glad I fugging listened."

Chaz cringed. "God, I hate you. You can't even say the word *fucking*. Little miss goody two shoes. And by the way, those shoes portray you as the slut you are."

He's so drunk, he can't decide if I'm a saint or a sinner. I yank my shoes off and storm out of the hotel room. He follows me down to the lobby where he continues to verbally assault me. I throw the fancy rhinestone shoes at him and he crosses his arms in self-defense. "Go *fuck* someone else. The cougar in the bar is more your speed."

There, I said it. But internally I say, "Fugg him," as I hand the valet my ticket.

Chapter Two

Hagan

The minute I stepped foot in the bluegrass, I knew without a doubt this is where I'm meant to be. Don't ask me why. Maybe it's the fresh air—no salt from the ocean or fog from the pollution. Or it could be the bounce of the bluegrass beneath my cleats.

More than likely, it has something to do with the abundance of beautiful women. A place like this can make me forget her. I'm a loser for letting a girl from the past rule my life.

A few weeks ago, I transferred to the University of Kentucky in time for summer workouts with the baseball team. I moved in with three football players because a friend of mine, Mac, plays both football and baseball. I decided to transfer here on the last day the transfer portal was open, so this living arrangement was the most convenient.

Life should be easy, so I try not to overthink my decisions. I talked to my dad and brother, and they supported the idea of me switching colleges. The Southeastern Conference is the best in baseball and being on a large campus is just what I need. Get lost in the crowd and not run into my ex around every corner.

Since all my roommates play football it leaves me with a bit of alone time to focus on baseball. Mac, Logan, and Pearse's schedules are packed. Poor Mac rarely has any free time. He's scheduled all day. Most of the baseball team is here doing voluntary workouts and Mac, like me, wants to bond with his baseball teammates, even though football is his priority.

Today, one of my teammates and I are working out with a private coach off campus. Joe Danke's a catcher and expected to be a big hitter this year. He's been texting with one of the girls on the women's gymnastics team. There's a party tomorrow night, and he's hoping she'll come.

The coach has us flipping tires, starting from a squat position, and ending the same way. It's important for baseball players to have strong quads. We go through a variety of unconventional exercises before we break to hydrate. I'm covered in sweat, my T-shirt clinging to every muscle.

"How did you find this guy?" Joe asks as he takes off his hat and shakes his hair out. Sweat flies off the ends of his hair, and stinky drops land on me. I take my towel, slinging it at his biceps.

"That's disgusting. We're not dogs." I take a big gulp of water then I do the same. My hair is much longer but because it's wavy it appears shorter. "I hope Ginger likes smelly men."

"Dude, girls can't resist me when I take a shower," he claims. "So, have you met anyone you want to ask out?"

The rest of the water flows down my throat as my heart squeezes. *Jesus, Julia, get out of my brain.* "Nah. Concentrating on ball." I look around the metal building with all the different training areas. I point to the hitting lanes. "I think we're over there now."

He lifts a brow, and says, "I saw you with some girls at the last couple of parties...heard you took one home."

I pull my batting gloves from my pack, stretching them onto my hands. Then, I take out my bat and use it to help stretch my shoulders as I twist, loosening my core before saying, "Things aren't always what they seem, but yeah, I took Erika back to her place."

 Joe gives me a quizzical glance but thankfully the coach interrupts. "Gather the balls, then we'll alternate twenty pitches."

"Yes, sir," I respond.

"Chatham don't call me sir. Coach or Latham. I'm five years older than you."

One thing boarding school drills into your head is manners. They don't care if you drink, smoke, curse like a sailor, or perform sexual activities in the dorms, but you damn well better address your elders as sir or ma'am—and it's a hard habit to break. "Yes, coach."

 Joe leans in, turning his back to Coach Latham and mumbles, "I repeat, where did you find him?"

"Are you sure you want to know?"

"Boys, you're wasting my time," Coach growls. "When your brother set this up, I thought you were serious about baseball, Chatham."

We hit for an hour and my swing feels good, but Coach Latham is a grouchy son of a gun. His voice booms with directions for me, before yelling, "Danke, how many times do I need to say I want a smaller step? It's physics. Have you taken physics?"

"Yes, coach. I'm majoring in engineering."

Coach Latham shakes his head, mumbling, "It was rhetorical. Pick."

This means pick up the balls. Training is over. When we finish, Coach calls me over, letting me know his schedule for the next week.

We load our gear and grab some food on the way back to campus. I miss my teammates in Illinois, but so far, coming here has been an easy adjustment. Logan and Joe invited me into their world and introduced me to nearly every girl on campus. Granted, it's summer, so there's not thousands. But still, I haven't met anyone to take my mind off Julia.

The only hiccup has been a teammate, Chaz, the captain of the team. I've played baseball and been around professional baseball my entire life, and I've never seen a captain be such an ass. They're usually the most disciplined and one of the best players on a team. They lead by example. But this douchebag is an egotistical asshole.

We play the same position and he's throwing attitude around the field during workouts. It's been several weeks, and the summer coaches are fed up.

Yesterday, he was pulled aside when we were on a water break.

Joe heard the head coach say to Chaz, "Chatham's faster, stronger, and God gifted him a naturally athletic body. Shape up off the field, and it'll relieve the pressure on the field."

Chaz snapped, "A fucking transfer is not taking my position. You're just taking his side because his dad owns the Kodiaks, and you want to please baseball royalty."

When Joe tells me what he heard, he watches as my skin turns an angry color red, which is almost impossible considering I'm dark complected. "Chaz used those words? I work for every homerun, catch, and steal. My dad made me sweep the concourse floors, take out trash from the concessions, and every other dirty job inside a ballpark. No one, especially my dad, thinks we're baseball royalty. I've missed time with my family to train. Hell, I left my twin to be here. That asshole doesn't know what sacrifice is."

"You're a twin?" he asks as both eyebrows reach his hairline.

I nod.

Then he says, "Chaz's dad is a senator."

"Aww, that explains it. He expects success without working for it."

Grease a palm.

Return a favor.

Make a call and it's done.

Evidently this off-campus coaching staff hasn't gotten the memo. They don't seem to care who either of us are.

Joe shrugs. He doesn't want to make enemies with the team captain. But Chaz definitely thinks of me as his enemy. I'll need to figure out how to turn my monster teammate into a friend.

"Does he have a thing for Erika?" I ask because it's possible he thinks I moved in on his territory.

Joe shrugs. "He has a girlfriend, Ginger's roommate, but word around campus is... he cheats on her."

My lips twist, thinking about if I've said or done anything other than baseball that would make Chaz hate me. "Alright man, thanks for the lift. Catch you tomorrow."

Chapter Three

Adalee

"You've got this, Addy Bug!" my teammates scream.

I'm attempting a new vault which is the most difficult skill for our team, and we'll need every point if we're going to eclipse Georgia this coming season. They're the gold standard in the Southeastern Conference.

Holding my arm up, signaling that I'm ready, I inhale and drop my arm on the exhale. I'm ready. I've got this. I've trained in a foam pit. I've come to learn that the most important part of gymnastics is sticking the landing. You can perform a perfect twisting layout in the air, but if you can't land it, it doesn't matter how beautiful it was or how high it floated.

With a furious run, my chalked feet pound against the floor. My arms are pumping as I focus straight ahead.

Hit the sweet spot.

My round off onto the springboard lands dead center as I back-handspring onto the vaulting table. My shoulders shrug up toward my ears, and I soar into the air.

Don't over arch. Twist. Twist.

I'm flying too high. Too much adrenaline. There's nothing I can do now but pray, and there's only a half second for that. Definitely not enough time. My heels jam, skidding into the pad as I cry out. My body keeps rolling, then I feel the coach's hands on me. I grab my knee with angry tears spilling over my lids. "My ankle."

The coach lays me down, and the trainer runs over. He gingerly pokes around my ankle. I sit up with the coach's help, biting my lip. "What's wrong?"

He asks me a few questions and then answers the original question. "High ankle sprain."

I can see the pity in his eyes. I'm out for weeks. I need four months to perfect this vault. The Stallions offered me a scholarship based on my vault, floor, and beam skills. The uneven bars are my nemesis. My shoulders slump as my hopes for the rest of the summer shatter, knowing it will put me behind schedule. It's a harsh reminder that an entire season can be defined by an injury.

My teammates clap while the trainer puts my arm over his shoulder and helps me off the mat. He carefully helps me onto a chair and begins to tape my ankle. The girls come over and pat my shoulder or give me a side-armed hug. In college, gymnasts are more of a team. And even though I don't like depending on others to win, in this instance, I'm glad I'm here—with these girls and with this staff.

It's a good thing my apartment is on the bottom floor; it'll make getting in and out easier. Ginger, my roommate and best friend, helps me hobble to my room. Sitting on the bed, I place a pillow under my ankle and make the dreaded call to my dad.

"Adalee, I'm in a meeting." His voice is brittle and perturbed as always. He's a manager at a local bank, not a CEO.

"Dad, I got hurt today at practice. I was trying—"

"Just tell me what I need to know," he says, cutting me off, annoyed at the interruption.

"It's a high ankle sprain. No need to worry." I know he won't worry about this anyways. I would have to have something broken to get his attention—something that would put my scholarship in question.

He mumbles to someone, and I hear his hand slide over the phone, causing a muffled noise. When he returns, he says, "Take care of yourself. I need to go."

"Okay, love you," I utter, not expecting him to say it back. I'm right again. All I hear is a dial tone.

It's time I realize that I have one family—the gymnastics team. Even the people I thought cared about me, like Chaz, were disingenuous.

I contemplate who designed popcorn ceilings while lying on my back. It's something I need to know. Like why? Everyone

I know has them, but fancy places have flat ceilings. I'm trying to think of anything except my ankle and what that means. I'll be at least two weeks behind for sure.

Falling asleep with the help of an over-the-counter pain pill and the whizzing of the air conditioner brings peace. But I wake in a cold sweat, my torso jerking up from the bed. I can't catch my breath. In my dream, I made it to the Olympics only to have it ripped away from me because of a torn ACL. I'm too old for the Olympics, but I still have dreams—or *nightmares*—about it.

Quit thinking about it, Adalee.

Outside my room, there's all kinds of commotion, but I'm too tired to hop out there. Ginger is slurring her words, and I hear a guy, or maybe guys. I'm hurt, and she invites people over? Picking up my phone, it reads ten-thirty p.m. I must have fallen asleep instantly because it's been four hours and it's time for another dose.

I take another pain pill and drift off, thinking about how badly I wish I had a guy to snuggle me and tell me it will be okay. Someone to call and tell them how I really feel. The voices outside my room, although muffled, are loud and obnoxious. I limp outside and see Ginger asleep on the couch but Joe and another guy watching Sportscenter. I'm half asleep, and ask, "Do you mind keeping it down?"

The other guy scoffs, "Are you the fun police?" He doesn't even turn his head to look at me.

Joe glances over his shoulder. "Sorry, we'll be quiet."

I pad back into my room, irritated. It's been a week since Chaz and I broke it off. I cried...but not over him. I knew I didn't feel any real connection down deep, but I loved having a boyfriend. I enjoyed having someone to talk to, but I was more of a trophy girlfriend to Chaz.

Of course, now, I regret the time I wasted. Time which would have been better spent chopping lumber or painting the faces on dolls. Yes, he was that bad. I guess sometimes you stay with a person because it's hard to break up. The confrontation is uncomfortable. It's easier to stay together, even though I knew in my gut he was all wrong for me. There were warning signals flying into the air from the very first date.

Mark my words—I will never date a cocky athlete again. I could never trust someone like him again.

When I wake up this time, it's morning. It doesn't matter what I do, my brain is trained to wake up at five-thirty every day. Gymnasts, like most athletes, are driven by a set schedule. College gymnastics took a while to get used to. Before college, I went to the gym from six to eight a.m. and then went to school at nine. Right after school, I went back to the training center for four hours, finally getting home around eight in the evening. Then it was dinner, homework and time to start my routine all over again.

The door squeaks open, and Ginger pops her head in. "I'm on my way to practice. Want me to wait?"

"No, I'll drive over." She gives me a curt smile, and I sit up with a throbbing ankle. I need the trainer to look at it, so I pull on a T-shirt and shorts. I slip on one shoe but the other foot is too swollen.

 Arriving at the gym, all the girls come over to see how I am. Shannon is the only one that doesn't give me encouragement. Instead, she says, "Hey Ging, I saw you with Joe getting all hot and heavy." Ginger smiles. She's had her eye on him for a few months. We went to every baseball game that didn't interfere with practice or meets. She'd paint his number on her cheek, trying to give him the hint. I didn't even do that for Chaz.

But then Shannon says, "No wonder you're smiling, two guys one night. I saw you left the party with Joe and Hagan."

Ginger's face goes taut, then her chin moves back and forth. "You're a vile person. I would never... just because you... oh, forget it." Rumor has it that Shannon hooked up with two frat guys at the same time last year, but she's never confirmed or denied it happened.

Since it's summer, we're working on our skills at a local gymnastics training center off-campus. Some girls left and went to gyms in their hometown since they had to move out of the dorms. There are six of us here for the summer, but Shannon's the only girl with venom in her veins. She's probably enjoying my injury and hoping it will give her an opportunity to sneak into the vault rotation.

The women's coach for this gym walks in and blows his whistle. All the girls but me line up on the mat for stretching. I take the tape off my ankle and put a bag of ice on it and then make an appointment with the athletic trainer on campus for after lunch.

As I sit on the sidelines watching my teammates, my best guy friend from freshman year slides onto the bench next to me. "What happened?" he asks as his fingers skim from my thigh to my ankle. I shiver because it's cold, but his lips turn upward as if his touch is affecting me.

Never again. He made a move on me and stuck his tongue down my throat. I've done my best to avoid him since, so it's been awkward. Why can't guys just be friends or take a body language course? We'll let them know when we want them to kiss us.

"Tried a new vault and couldn't stick the landing." My voice is monotone, like it doesn't bother me that he's asking. But it does bother me that he's asking, pretending to care about me. I tried to shirk it off and be friends, but he didn't want that. He said I led him on. That's why this is weird. Just another guy with a singular motivation—sex.

He asks me a myriad of questions that he already knows the answers to because all gymnasts have had high ankle sprains in their career. How long are you out? Does it hurt? I just nod my head. I don't want to hear the sound of his voice. But then he says, "Come on, I thought we were friends. I heard you and douchebag broke up."

Closing my eyes, I nod. That's why he's being nice—because he thinks he has a chance. "We did. I'm focusing on gymnastics. This year there will be no distractions."

None.

Chapter Four

Hagan

THE GUYS THAT PLAYED ON SUMMER TEAMS ARE BACK. This is the first year I didn't play in the summertime. The off-campus staff decides to scrimmage. This is how we can voluntarily practice together in the off-season—by using facility and coaching personnel not connected to the university. Of course, they know and follow the college baseball team and communicate with the staff.

The baseball organization we're practicing with is called Top-Tier Baseball. It's voluntary but guys want to advance their skills in hopes of making it to the big leagues. They divide the players into red and white teams, which is the color of their eighteen and under teams.

Of course, Chaz is on red and I'm on white, playing the same position. He gives me a threatening grin with his jaw clenched.

In the last few days, I've tried handing him a drink or throwing him a towel when he needed it, but he's iced me out for whatever reason. His entourage follows him around like he's the MLB MVP. But I actually know the league's most valuable player—and he'd be appalled if he saw this dickwad abusing the role the coaches gave him. Wilson Shepherd plays for my dad on the Chicago Kodiaks and he's disciplined, leading by example. For example, Tackett was the youngest guy on the team, and Wilson took him under his wing instead of yelling and demanding allegiance.

Both red and white are even skill wise, as far as I can tell. I just met some of these guys. Chaz yells as the redshirts take the field. "Let's see why the transfer is here. Does he have a bat? Or is it because his girlfriend broke up with him, and he was so upset he had to change teams? Watch out, Danke. I've heard you and the transfer have been spending a lot of time together."

I roll my eyes as I walk up to the plate. This putz wants drama. I'll give him drama. I visualize hitting this guy with my fist, but instead, I think about what Archer would say. "Baseball is about you. No one else. You have the power to hit the ball and make the plays, every single time."

I grip my bat while looking up at the barrel. Give it two rotations and step into the batter's box.

The pitcher's cold stare holds me in place for strike one. Then Chaz goads me about my bedroom skills. I swing—strike two. Stepping out of the box, I look to the third-base coach for his signals. The leadoff batter's job is to get on base. My stats on the other team were astronomical. Granted,

SEC baseball is a step up from my former college. But I understand Chaz's point that no one comes in and takes a fifth-year senior's spot.

I'm not going to take his position on the field because of my name. If I take it, it's because I earned it. I dig my foot into the red dirt and watch the ball into the glove for ball one. The count is two strikes and one ball. Everyone knows if it's close to the strike zone, I'm swinging. Lead off batters don't like to stay in the box too long. It makes us antsy. The pitch comes in on fire—a fastball low and a bit inside, my favorite fucking pitch.

I load up and make the perfect step and swing into the spinning orb, sending it flying over the centerfield wall. When I pass from second base to third, I say, "Winner of the longest home run buys the beer."

The guys on my team run to home plate, meeting me with congratulatory fists and chest bumps. We do it in style. If my time around the Kodiaks and Sharks taught me anything it's to give the crowd a show. This may be a scrimmage, but the few maintenance men deserve a good time, nonetheless. If I can't join Chaz, I'll beat him. End of discussion.

Chaz was two-for-three with a double and single and one error on the field. Joe's keeping track because he's never clicked with Chaz. I went three-for-four with two home runs. I'm not normally a home run hitter, but Baker had scorching speed today, and if you made contact, it was going to the outfield. Luckily, I had the extra umph in my swing today.

Several guys from the baseball house come up to me, making sure I'm coming to the party tonight. "The baseball house. We're cooking out at about seven, then we'll play some volleyball, and then party!" one of my teammate's shouts.

"Sure. I'll be there."

Chaz looks back and says, "See you there." I swear he has the voice changer from Darth Vader's mask.

A smile tears across my face because I'll beat him at any game he wants to play. I keep hoping that he'll come out and tell me what his problem is. If I unknowingly did anything to embarrass him or whatever, I'll apologize and put this wedge between us to rest. If he's not willing, there's nothing I can do.

"Can't wait. You owe me a beer."

Chapter Five

Adalee

"Come on, Adalee. It's summer and this party is going to be filled with Thor duplicates. Not just baseball players but football players, too. It's the last party before school starts. Besides, you can't let Chaz win." Ginger pleads with me, giving me her best pouty face.

Every weekend, she begs me to go to parties with her. There's a new guy on campus, and he's making a name for himself. "You should hear the girls," Ginger says. "He's so charming. He's hot."

Summertime is coming to an end, and students are moving back into off-campus housing, so this party will be *big* by summer standards. There's not much going on to talk about, no sports, no classes, so one new—supposedly hot—guy, is big news.

I nod my head, roll my eyes, and say, "Fine. But don't expect me to stay long."

"I wouldn't dare." Ginger pushes me into my room giggling. "Now let's find you a come get me outfit."

Pushing her away from my walk-in closet, I protest, "Not a chance in hell am I going to look like a bimbo. Where's the party?"

"The baseball house. You know they call it the home run house." Ginger's eyes sparkle.

I mumble under my breath, "Aren't they clever?" Chaz and I didn't hang out there very often because we dated during our athletic season.

Decisions, decisions. I tug on some skimpy orange shorts, but I pair it with a white flowy tank that shows about an inch of my midriff. I pull my long dark hair into a side ponytail and let it cascade over my shoulder. After a little mascara and lip gloss, I slip the boot on my injury and we're out the door.

The front lawn is littered with guys in athletic gear, their shirts stretching across their muscled chests. Maybe Ginger's right...I should come to parties more often. There are plenty of girls here with one inch and you're in dresses. The flowy ones are cute, but the spandex dresses leave nothing to the imagination.

Several girls from the swim team swarm us. They never get a break, swimming all year long. I guess none of us really do. We chat for a few minutes before Ginger and I make our way inside. I make eye contact with one of the football players, Logan Warren. He's a notorious playboy and the Stallions starting quarterback. And he's walking straight toward me in all of his bodily glory. He's way too big for me—I'm five-foot-two-inches on a good day. The smile that glides across his face as he nears me has me preparing for tropical force winds.

"Hey, look who came out of her cave." He hugs me so tight around my center, I might be popping out the top and bottom, like when you squeeze the middle of a balloon.

I manage to choke out a laugh while wiggling away. "If you were nursing a high ankle sprain, I know where your focus would be." I look down at my booted ankle and Logan's eyes follow.

"True." His smile fades as he considers the thought of being hurt or it might come true. "So that's why I've seen most of the gymnastics team without you—been rehabbing?"

"Yeah, the trainer says I'm about eighty percent." My voice is perky, knowing I'll be back in training for the winter gymnastics season. I add, "Plus, some of us have to work. Gymnasts don't get the same perks as the star quarterback."

I'm on scholarship but it only covers tuition. I still have to pay for my apartment and the costs that come with that. My dad gives me a little but says he can't afford more so I took out loans and work when I can, babysitting for our coaches.

He shakes his head in agreement, and I notice it's traced with a small shadow of embarrassment. Then, he throws an arm around me and says, "Come on Little A. Let's get you a drink."

I walk with him but decline a beer and opt for a Sprite. More hands touched Logan in that short walk than have ever touched me. The slaps on the back. The fist bumps. Then there's the ladies with their paws pressing against his chest and the kisses on his cheeks. "Don't you get tired of it?" I ask.

He gives me a quizzical glance. "No. I have little downtime and I can't think of a better way to spend it than with a pretty woman. You should try me some time," he jokes.

Snorting, my sprite comes out my nose, showering my shirt. "No thank you. I might be the only one you haven't slept with this at the party. And why don't you feel weird about it? What if they start comparing stories?"

He smirks but there is a loneliness behind his eyes. "They were all thoroughly satisfied. And there's only handful— you're exaggerating." He hands me a napkin to dab my shirt dry.

"So, who's that with Josie?" I ask, attempting to sound unphased by the specimen in front of me across the room.

Logan's eyes dart to the den, surveying the area. "Oh, that's my new roommate, Mac. He's a freshman wide receiver. He moved in with me so I can whip him into shape." He points to another guy in the room and says, "And there's Hagan, the baseball transfer. They came as a package deal."

I was definitely talking about Hagan, but Logan doesn't need to know that. So that's the guy that has Chaz's underwear in a wad. I should get to know him just to piss off Chaz. Not.

And now I understand why the girls on this campus have Hagan on their tongues and minds. He's gorgeous. He stands with one hand in the pocket of his athletic shorts while sipping from a blue plastic cup. His conversation with three girls flows easy like a stream running downhill. He maneuvers his eyes and smile with the flutter of their eyelashes, giving them each attention.

"Do you want me to make an introduction, Little A?"

What I want is for Logan to quit calling me Little A, but instead I say, "No. I've sworn off cocky buttholes. I saw some friends outside so I'm going to find them. Good to see you." I give him a sidearm hug.

"Find me later if you need me or if you change your mind about this." Logan points to his chest, and I can't help but laugh. I don't feel any spark with Logan, and I don't think he feels one for me, either. I'm an only child and my attachment to him is more like a brother. I know if I needed someone, he would be there for me without a doubt. But do I get all ooey-gooey over the Adonis of campus? No. Not one, single, heart melting thought.

Giving Logan a saccharine smile, I saunter to the front porch. Ginger is cozied up to one of the baseball players who lives here—Joe. They've been hooking up for weeks. They're sitting in the front porch swing, and she has her head on his chest. She looks up at him with her big green eyes and he kisses her forehead.

Maybe good guys do exist.

Suddenly, girls scream from inside, so we all flock to see what's happening. Two girls are fighting, pulling hair, and barking obscenities. Over what? "I saw him first!" one shouts.

Really? Are we in middle school?

Behind them, Hagan shakes his head, all while sporting a goofy grin that spreads across his face. What an ass. He sees me blazing a hole through his forehead. His smile fades into a seductive smirk with one corner of his lip tugging upward, raising his blue cup in the air, as if giving me a silent, *cheers*. And I feel the traitorous clench of my core in response.

Hagan seems bored with their antics, and strides toward the backdoor, stepping outside. I wander that way and peek out the screen. Outside, there are even more thirsty girls eating out of the palm of his hand. Erika included, one of the swimmers who lives in the apartment above mine.

I can't help it—I look him over. He isn't bulky, but he has well defined shoulders and his forearms are straight out of a baseball commercial. But why would a baseball player be living with Logan? Knocking me out of my Sherlock Holmes persona, Logan leans over my shoulder and whispers, "Who are we spying on?"

He sees the person in my sightline and his expression turns into a frown. I attempt to push him out of the way. He chuckles nice and deep, saying, "Damn, Hagan's giving me a run for my money." He playfully, storms out, leaving the screen door to rattle and slam behind him. Logan joins Hagan and the circle. Their bodies are different but both muscular.

Hagan catches me staring, and now, I can't look away. His dark, shaggy hair is perfectly messy. His body is tanned, and it might fit me perfectly. He looks to be close to six feet, maybe a little less. My body warms at his omnipotent gaze, like he knows my thoughts. This time, there's not cheers, just a slight movement of his left brow, acknowledging my existence.

My thighs shouldn't be tightening, and my mouth should not be dry.

I turn away and quickly walk to the bathroom. God, I hate guys like that. Think they can have whoever they choose, whenever they choose. If only there were guys that looked like a Greek God, but had a sensitive, romantic side. I'm not stupid enough to get stuck in a jock's web again. I need myself a STEM man. Someone with brains and a fair amount of brawn, not one that dips his stick in every hole that opens up for him.

After washing my hands, I stare into the mirror, seeking answers to the universal question, *When will I find someone to love me, truly love me?* I reach for the hand towel laying on the counter and think better of it. Opening the cabinet door, I pull out a clean washcloth. As I'm drying, I overhear a couple talking.

"I don't care how many girls you've been with." The girls' voice sounds familiar. When I unlock the door, the girl is on her knees in front of Hagan.

So it's all true. He pulls her up and hides her face. "This isn't what it looks like."

It doesn't do any good because I know the girl, she lives above me. I scoff, "It's none of my business. Erika, at least make him take you to a room."

Charging down the hall as quickly as I can in my ankle boot, a wave of jealousy hits me. Hagan's hair as he looked down at her was sexy and when he tried to explain, his eyes were a gorgeous golden brown. In my experience when guys get sex on their brain, their pupils dilate and even blue eyes like Chaz's darken.

Why am I attracted to bad boys? If I went to a therapist, I know they would say it's because of my relationship with my father.

Minutes later, I'm outside. Ginger and Joe are kissing under the tree in the front yard. His hands are cupping her jaw and I crave that experience. I want to feel like there's no one else in a room besides my partner, even when the room is packed like sardines. Hagan's face shoots through my mind. I know I need help.

I sit on the porch swing deciding what to do, whether to leave or stay for a bit longer. Since I'm not having fun and I don't want to bump into Chaz—or Hagan for that matter—I pull out my phone and text Ginger.

Me: Hey, I'm headed home. I have an early call with the trainer tomorrow morning.

She doesn't respond because obviously she's busy. Glancing over my shoulder, Hagan's smoldering eyes are on me.

This time he's alone.

Not a Barbie in sight.

They must be fetching his refill.

I need to get away. My skin burns from his gaze. It must be my hatred for players. Guys that think that just by flashing a smile, women will drop their shorts. Not me. Nope. Not for an insensitive jock.

It's dark and the clouds hover, blocking the light from the moon. I walk home, staying on loosely lit paths for the most part but the shortcut to my apartment is cloaked with trees. The height of the boot makes my gait a little awkward, but I walk as fast as I can.

I can't shake these feelings for Hagan, which is absurd because I haven't even met him. We've only exchanged a few glances and one short sentence when a girl was ready to worship at his throne. I shiver again recalling how my skin pimpled and how jealousy surged in my gut when he pulled her close to keep her identity hidden. I wanted to be her—not on my knees but with my head tucked into his chest. It would be nice for someone to be protective of me.

"Ahhh," I cry, stumbling over something on the sidewalk. "Oh God! Help!" I shriek, clutching my leg.

It's midnight and nobody's around. I hear the clatter of my phone tumbling from my pocket, but I can't find it. It hurts to even snake crawl across the concrete, using my hand to pat around until I feel it. I call Ginger she doesn't answer, then a few more teammates with the same result, so I have no other option but to call 9-1-1.

My stomach is nauseated, and dizziness drowns me. I've never felt pain like this before.

Chapter Six

Hagan

THIS SHOULD BE IN THE TOP TEN PARTY SCHOOLS. There's a party nearly every night and crawling with girls. I would say the girl to guy ratio is three to one. Good odds if you're me, but none of them shake my thoughts of the girl who cheated on me.

This party is no different. Girls. Girls. Eager Girls. There may be a *Girls Gone Wild* video in their future if they don't quit drinking. As the night drones on, they flash their tits or rub their butts against me and other dudes. I'm not saying I'm blind, because God, I'm not. Not saying I don't like the attention, because God, I do. But there's something about these girls that *screams I'm not choosy.*

For the second time tonight, I feel the glare of a brown-haired beauty. I watch her as she talks to my roommate, Logan. He wraps himself around her and she rolls her eyes but smiles. I get a peek at the smallest amount of skin between the hem of her shirt and the band of her shorts. It's bronzed and tight and when she twists, there's a flicker of defined abs.

Logan releases her and bursts through the door, and I shoot her an *I see you watching me* glance. My eyes hold onto hers and a twinge runs up my spine. An almost forgotten feeling sits inside my chest. I deny the feeling because it hurts when you really like someone, and they screw you over.

"Hagan, Mac is looking for you inside." Logan hints for me to take a hike. I understand bro code, and Logan has picked out one of these lovely ladies for himself. Or maybe all three. I've heard rumors.

I find Mac in the hallway on the phone talking to his girl. They're having some issues with long distance dating. They've been dating all through high school, so I imagine it's a shock for both of them to be apart for this long. He holds his finger up for me to wait a minute.

Mac and I met through his cousin, Patrick Callaghan, who plays for my dad's professional baseball team. When I told Mac about my coach taking a job at a Big Ten school, soon he'd convinced me to talk with the coaching staff here at Kentucky. My older brother, Archer, sent them a highlight reel and my statistics, and now everyone refers to me as the transfer.

I point to the other room to let Mac know where I'll be.

Out of nowhere, I'm assaulted by a girl I met last night. She jumps on me pulling my neck into her mouth. "I'm so glad you came. We can pick up where we left off." I can't remember her name, I've met so many people. She drives her head into my neck and starts sucking on my neck then nudges her way up and starts kissing me.

Making an excuse, I separate from the girl. Now I remember who she is. I talked to her last night at a different get together. She was so drunk. She basically fell into my lips, so I made myself scarce and went home to call my sister. My family, although somewhat famous, are down-to-earth, and they drilled into my head to never compromise myself with a girl that has had too much to drink.

The music blares and a game of flip the cup rages on the porch. That's where I see the brunette sitting on the porch swing. I watch as she lifts her legs and tucks one under her thigh while kicking the one with the ankle brace out to the side. My mind drifts to how her legs would feel wrapped around me. How bendable she looks.

Wind catches in my chest at the sight of her. But as quickly as her eyes dart toward mine, she traipses off, phone in hand and a medical boot on her foot. With that body and tight abs, she's more than likely an athlete. She's probably meeting a guy because there's no way she's not taken.

I wanted to explain what she saw was nothing. Erika had too many shots and fell at the exact moment the brunette that was hanging out with Logan left the bathroom.

Mental note: Ask Logan if she has a boyfriend.

I find Logan making out in an Adirondack chair with a volleyball player. If they were to have a baby, they would be a professional athlete without a doubt. This is one hell of a mixture of people. All we need is someone from the basketball team to show up. Clearing my throat, I say, "Hey, I'm headed out. I have an early workout tomorrow morning." I'll have to wait to ask him about her. He's tied up, literally with the longest limbs I've ever seen.

Logan scoffs, "It's twelve thirty."

"Yeah, I have to be there before the sun comes up. My job isn't cemented like yours. We all can't be Logan Warren."

He rears his head back, laughing. "True. It's good to be me."

I text Mac that I'm heading out and within minutes he catches up to me. "Is everything okay with Marley?" I ask.

"For so long we've been by each other's side. Games, family dinners, parties and now we're doing it all alone," he says, his voice quieter than usual.

His feelings aren't lost on me. Even though Julia and I weren't long distance, I understand the loneliness of not having that *special* someone by your side. When Julia broke it off, my body went numb. I couldn't control any aspect of my life except baseball. But then my coach, who recruited me, called a team meeting, and the next day he was leaving too. It was the punishing final blow to my gut and heart.

Betrayal from the girl I loved and the coach I loved was almost too much. I slap Mac on the back and say, "You've got me, and you can spank that monkey anytime you want—in your own shower."

He shakes his longish hair and sports a sideways grin. "You know, you should slow down. Don't want to go through all the girls in the summer."

"Now what's the fun in that?" I laugh. I haven't done anything other than kiss a few girls, but I can't stop the rumor mill.

Upon entering our house, Mac heads straight to the shower and we both know what's happening. I sit down on the couch, turn on the television to *Everybody Loves Raymond* reruns. I've seen them all so if I fall asleep, I haven't missed anything.

Looking at my phone, I swipe through all my notifications. Five are from girls that I've met recently asking me to come over or back to the party.

But my conversation with Mac makes me think of Julia, and she's the last person I want in my head. I lean my back on the tan, plush couch, staring at the ceiling. Why can I still feel her twisting the knife? She took a wrecking ball to my heart and my life. I was so happy—I loved her, loved my coach, team, and friends. She was the first brick to fall, and the rest came tumbling down.

Stay positive. This is the right team, and the right woman will come.

For some reason, my mind wanders to the gorgeous brown haired beauty in the boot.

Chapter Seven

Adalee

My life is on a downhill slope. I had surgery on my ACL, but the boot is off and replaced by a brace on the other leg. Thanks, Hagan. It's his fault I fell. In fairness, I know he didn't push me and actually cause the fall, but his smile and laugh were like watching a comet streak through the sky—hypnotizing. For some reason the cocky guys just stick in my mind. Possibly because I'm inexperienced and their confidence is appealing. In the beginning, Chaz had that same easy cockiness but somewhere along the way, it turned into aggressive behavior.

Unfortunately, I had to miss the first two weeks of school so today is my first day of the semester, and my brace slows me to a turtle's pace, but eventually I make it to my second class, which is all the way across campus. A thin sheen of sweat blankets my forehead as I try to catch my breath. I've been reduced to needing an oxygen tank to walk a mile. I'm exaggerating, but my body is usually in tip-top shape, and it sucks waiting for someone to open the door for you. When no one comes, I hobble up to the entrance, but it opens from the inside.

"Adalee, how are ya doing?" Joe asks. He pushes the door open wide and waits until I'm clear. Joe is Ginger's regular hookup, although they function like a couple but refuse to put a label on it. I find them spooning on our couch a few times a week.

"Honestly, I don't know...tearing my ACL sucks. I've done so much to my body over the years, it's inconceivable that I would hurt myself by doing an activity as simple as walking."

I'm out of breath from maneuvering inside the doorway. He helps ease me into a seat in the back row, so steps aren't an issue.

"Hate to beat a dead horse but you should have asked me to take you home. You never did say why you left in a rush." He sighs. "Wait for me and I'll help you out after class," Joe suggests. He raises his eyebrows, waiting for me to answer.

 "Okay. I saw Chaz and didn't need for him to make a drunken scene," I lie. I did see Chaz handing Hagan a beer, so are they suddenly best friends?

The auditorium is curved, and Joe takes a seat next to some other baseball players, and I can't help but notice the electricity surrounding Hagan. He's magnetic with guys, too. He's telling a story—his mouth moving and hands gesturing wildly. Joe and the guys burst out howling. Hagan's lips spread and I'm mesmerized by his panty-dropping smile. But when he throws his head back, cackling—it's the happiest sound I've ever heard.

What it must be like to be happy and free. I've spent my life in gymnastics with every minute scheduled for me. And now, I'm lost not knowing what to do with my time, and it's one hundred percent Hagan's fault.

If his eyes didn't drill into my soul.

If his smile didn't make butterflies inside me spread their wings.

If he didn't have girls hanging on every word. If he didn't raise his glass to me. If he didn't try to protect Erika. If my stomach didn't do a two and a half twisting somersault when I was within twenty feet of him—I would have been paying more attention to my surroundings and wouldn't have torn my ACL.

"Ugh," I accidentally say out loud. I realize it's not rational to blame Hagan if I lose my scholarship or can't compete by winter but blaming him is a way to keep me from falling for the panty-melting baseball player.

This is a senior level engineering class, but I had so many credits combined with summer school that I'll be graduating this year. My family is one of those that doesn't have enough to pay for college but earns too much money to receive grants. My hope is to start graduate school next year if I still have a gymnastics scholarship.

The professor's voice booms in the small auditorium. "Welcome. We're lucky that a major company has agreed to partner with us for some hands on learning. The downtown revitalization project is underway, and I'll be pairing you up to work on solutions to problems they've already encountered and solved on paper."

This is fantastic.

I hate—absolutely *hate*—working with others. I'm not a team player, which is why I participate in an individual sport like gymnastics.

Erika sits beside Hagan, running her fingers at the nape of his neck, fingering his curls. He tilts his head away, but she continues. Her blonde hair is streaked with glimmering strands of the quintessential swimmer. Last year, she and long-time boyfriend, Bryan, broke up. He was drafted to play baseball for Washington, but I think he's currently playing in the minors.

I guess Erika is trying to pick up where she left off with Bryan with Hagan.

I'm exhausted, and it's going to take me longer than ten minutes to get to my next lecture. Class ends in five minutes, so I decide to slip out the heavy wooden door. It makes an obnoxious squeak and smacks itself shut.

I struggle on the uphill slope, so I sit down on a bench and open my backpack. The banana I pull out is covered with brown spots and it's mushy. It's not what I want but I need energy to get across campus.

Erika and Hagan come out of the lecture hall talking before going separate ways. But then I see Chaz come out of nowhere and grab her arm. He's yelling at her, and the words "fucking transfer" echo in the quad. What? Why does Chaz care if Erika is flirting with Hagan? They argue until they're out of sight.

Three hours later, I'm in the athletic trainer's office. He takes off my brace, inspecting from my thigh to my toes, and gives me a list of activities to do this week.

This weight room is scheduled a few hours a day for specific teams, and right now the baseball team is occupying it. I stay lying down on the training table until it's gymnastics time.

When I reach the weight room, I see Hagan and Joe chatting it up with Ginger and some of my teammates. I've not even met him, but for the life of me can't get him out of my head. Joe gives Ginger a quick kiss before the guys walk out.

 The coast is clear as I limp to the weight room door. A burst of air hits me as does the solid smell of sweat and virility. A large hand latches onto the bar on the door, pulling it open. "After you," he says in a genteel manner.

I give him a quick glance. "Thanks."

"I'm Hagan. Adalee, right? Logan told me that you had surgery. What happened?"

I'll tell you what happened. You snapped my ACL.

"Yeah," I mumble. "Freak accident." It was a freak accident. I'm a freak for thinking about an easy going baseball player with a laugh that sounds like a song in a kids movie. Right now, I'm thinking about how his laugh put a smile on my face and will never be erased from my memory. But in the end, I'm not getting caught up in another athlete.

"That sucks. Let me know if I can help you with anything. Being in a brace must suck—just follow your doctor's directions," he says, his caramel brown eyes staring into mine. He waits for me to say something and when I don't respond, he places his hand on my back. "Lean on me. You shouldn't be putting too much weight on it."

Don't play your knight in shining armor routine on me. I know your type—all gorgeous and self-absorbed.

I jerk my body away from his touch—sizzling through my Stallions Gymnastics tank.

I felt nothing. Don't smile at me. You're just like Chaz. But is he? I never had these feelings with him.

He smiles then says, "Sorry, I shouldn't have touched you without asking if you wanted my help. I was brought up to help. If you were my sister, I would want someone to help her."

Now I really hate him. He's nice. He takes two steps backward, sporting a smile that could melt a snowman. It's that bright and full of life. He slowly swaggers out.

As I adjust the weight on the shoulder press, I notice a phone lying on the floor. I pick it up and push the side button and a picture of Hagan and a girl pop onto the screen. She's pretty but her appearance isn't the same as the girls he's been hanging out with on campus—blondes have been his scene.

I look around and the baseball guys have left. So, I tuck the phone into my athletic shorts and begin my workout. The whole time I'm exercising, I think about Hagan's gentle touch and his manners. But then I remind myself—no more athletes.

An hour later, I arrive at Logan and Hagan's house to return Hagan's phone. I don't know why I'm here, I could have given it to Ginger to give to Joe, but my gut wants to see him in his environment, by himself.

Luckily, Hagan answers the door and not Logan or I would never hear the end of it. His eyes widen at the sight of me. He leans against the door frame. "Hey. Logan's at practice."

I chew on my bottom lip. "Umm, no I came to see you."

His dimples make an appearance but then fade to a half-smile. "Oh. Do you want to come in?"

"No." I hold out his phone. "You left this behind." When he wraps his hand around the phone it surrounds my hand. The pads of his fingers skate against my skin, producing an unexpected hunger in my gut.

The sound of his voice sounds miles away like we're in a storm and I can't hear him over the thunderous pellets of water striking a tin roof. Except it's not water beating, it's my heart.

His raspy voice taunts me when he says, "Thanks, you could've given it to your roommate."

"Ginger was going to the baseball house; it was easier for me to bring it to you," I claim, as I notice the way his body fills out his black athletic shorts and how they stretch across his thighs when his knee crosses over the other. "Bad things happen when I go there."

A concerned look spreads across his face as he finally slides the phone from hand and into his pocket. "Well, I appreciate you making a special trip. I can't believe I hadn't realized it was missing. Can I buy you an afternoon snack at the cafeteria to thank you?"

I laugh. "That's not repayment, the food is already free for you."

"True, but we could talk and I could explain..."

Cutting him off, I say, "You don't owe me an explanation about what I saw at the baseball house. I have to get home. I'm babysitting for my coach tonight, but thanks for the offer."

He smiles. I smile, but my feet don't move. He seems content to let me walk away first, so I swivel around on my good foot, limp to my car, while arguing with myself about why I can't *do* athletes.

Chapter Eight

Hagan

It's game day. All my roommates will be taking the field today. Of course, Logan is the face of the entire athletic program. He's not only the quarterback but the leading candidate for the Heisman Trophy. We're only three weeks into the season, but if he keeps up at this pace, he'll demolish the record books for the Stallions.

Mac is only a freshman, but Logan has been working with him so much outside of practice, the coach told him to expect to play today. Mac says his first love is football, but baseball is a close second. The dude can ball.

Joe knows I'm into Adalee so we come up with a plan so I can spend more than five minutes with her. I drive over to the home run house to pick up Joe, Ginger, and hopefully Adalee. She told Ginger she was a firm maybe. What is it with this girl? She's not like anyone I've met before.

It's been a few weeks since I officially met her in the weight room and she returned my phone, but over a month since I first saw her face. When we talk after class or in the weight room, she does her best not to let her gaze meet mine, but when she does, I see fireworks in her eyes. She likes me because two things always happen—she blushes, and she breathes more rapidly.

Knocking a few times, another baseball player answers the door. "What's up, Chatham?" Athletes have a pension for calling you by your last name.

I ask, "Are you going to the game? Happy to give you a ride."

"Nah, my girlfriend is sick, so we're going to watch it here. Come on in."

I walk in and he steers me to the back patio where all the Adirondack chairs circle a fire pit. I haven't been here since the night of the party.

"Hagan, have a drink with me!" Joe yells.

"Can't. Driving about a hundred thousand dollars' worth of scholarships to the game," I insist and get a few laughs. I clap my hands and rub them together. "Is everyone here that's riding with me?" I look around and Adalee is nowhere in sight.

Ginger speaks up. Her hair is a dark fiery red and straight, neatly tucked behind her ears. She's a little taller than Adalee, and Joe has been fucking gleeful at fall camp. "Adalee is using the restroom."

I nod like I could care less, but the truth is my dick springs to life at the mention of her name.

"There she is," Ginger says, jumping up from her seat. "Let's go."

My body swivels and I see her. Adalee is as graceful as she is gorgeous as she waltzes into the room. Her brown hair is all the way down. She has on a royal blue knit dress that ties around the waist, and cowboy boots with her leg brace. I can't help the upward turn of my mouth. She looks good enough to marry.

Wait, I mean eat.

When she sees my apparent approval, her eyes roll so far back in her head, I have to turn away. The whites of eyes gross me out after my older sister made me watch *The Walking Dead*. I'm a pussy about Halloween and scary movies.

It's okay. I like a little challenge. It distracts me from Julia's gut punch.

As we stride out of the house, I walk a half pace behind Adalee to make sure she's steady descending the steps. She appears annoyed, shaking her head. She says, "I'm fine," at the exact moment she stumbles. Being the nice guy, I am—I envelop her in one arm, so she doesn't fall. Her head rotates to the side and with a slight uplift of her chin. We deadlock.

"What the hell is this?" Chaz marches up to us, glaring at Adalee. "Are you going out with him to get back at me?"

What? Chaz is Adalee's ex?

I asked Logan if she was dating anyone and he said no. He didn't think to mention she dated the only guy on my team that hates me. Ginger or Joe never mentioned it either. It seems like an important detail since he's my teammate.

Adalee snaps back. "It's none of your business. Come on, Hagan."

What feels like snow flurries tickle my stomach right now as she slips her arm around me, squeezing. Adalee's not refuting Chaz's claim. I know it's fake, but I would be lying if I said I didn't love the feel of her embrace.

"Transfer, you're dead. I'll turn the team against you."

I throw my head back as I hoot. "You still owe me a beer. And by the way, Adalee's not a possession, not yours or mine. But I can assure you, I'm more of a man than you'll ever be. I can satisfy her in ways you never could." I'm so fed up with this guy, and it horrifies me that Adalee and Chaz were a couple. Is my judgement that bad?

"Hagan," Adalee growls.

My jaw tightens. "And pencil dick, don't threaten me again. In case you haven't noticed who the team is hanging out with... it's me with the exception Ned."

We stare until Joe says, "Let's go. We don't want to be late."

I help Adalee into the Rover. Traffic is awful so it takes fifteen minutes to arrive at the stadium. I keep peeking at her in the rearview mirror. She's smiles until she sees me looking at her.

"How did you get this parking space?" Joe asks as I whip into the second row reserved for Platinum Level Stallion Fund members.

 I put the Range Rover in park, and steady myself for Little Miss Attitude's reaction. "I called my dad."

Adalee mumbles, "Of course you did."

I give her a curt look in the mirror before continuing, "I told my dad that a friend had ACL surgery and asked if he could get a good parking location."

She doesn't respond but keeps glaring at me. Ginger screams, "That's so sweet of you. Isn't it, Adalee?"

She utters, "Yes. Thank you." And then I see her lips continue to move and I think I hear, "I wouldn't be in this mess if it wasn't for you." Maybe she's talking about Ginger. I know she had the accident on the night of the baseball party when Ginger and Joe were getting to know each other better. Clear throat. I was there when she walked away, minutes before she blew her ACL out.

The football team is crushing it today. But it seems the only guy Adalee likes is Logan. She waves her pom-pom and screams his name after every complete pass and touchdown.

At halftime, I ask if I can get her a drink or snacks. She declines but I bring back two different drinks hoping she'll like one. Ginger and Joe are still in line, so I take the opportunity to try and steal a few moments with her. See if I can get her to ease up a little. She's wound tighter than a corkscrew.

"Hey, I bought you a drink anyway," I say as a peace offering. I don't know why she hates me but I don't mind a challenge and I have a feeling she may be worth it. "Lemonade? Or Coke?"

She shakes her head. "No thanks."

God this girl. I chuckle as I pull out a bottle of water from my pocket, offering it to her. "Here. Every athlete drinks water. So, unless you're a badass alien man killer, you'll take it."

She rewards me with a sweet smile and it looks a lot like I may have won this round, but she'll fight harder in round two. I unscrew the cap and hand it over.

Adalee looks onto the field where the marching band plays the *Star Wars* theme. I watch her watching them. The music fades and all I see are stray strands of her silky brown hair blowing in the gentle wind. The way her hand swipes it out of her face. She brings the bottle to her lips, and then I watch her gently swallow.

Finally, I shake those warm fuzzies off and ask, "Why were you walking home by yourself the night of the baseball party? I'm sure Ginger or Joe would have taken you home. Hell, I would've taken you home."

"In your dreams."

"Maybe. But maybe you're waiting around on Logan," I hypothesize attempting to gauge her interest in my roommate.

Her head slowly swivels to mine. "You think I would ask you to take me home? Mr. Transfer who's had his lips and God knows what else *on* or *in* dozens of girls since he moved here two months ago? Logan and I are friends, only."

Ignoring the part about Logan, I ask in surprise, "You know when I moved here?"

She rolls her eyes. Does she know any other expression?

"You don't know me, but let's go over what you know for a fact. Tell me what you know about me."

There's that smile again like she's going to win this round hands down.

"Well, you're a player."

"Yes, I'm...a baseball player.

"Let me rephrase...a playboy." I don't interrupt. Wow, does she have me all wrong. "You're a rich daddy's boy."

She has me completely wrong. I'm a twin which trumps parents. Harper is the person I turn lean on. "My parents are wealthy, and yes, I'm my dad's youngest son."

She huffs so loud I can't even hear the band for a second. "See. You're one of those guys that has an answer for everything. You think you are everything to everyone, exactly like Chaz."

Adalee knows how to deliver a punch to a guy. No wonder she doesn't date, except for Chaz. How long were they together? How could she put up with that guy?

"Wow, that's low, considering your obvious opinion of him. What else do you think you know about me?"

Chapter Nine

Adalee

I KNOW YOU MAKE MY THIGHS CLENCH AND MY stomach flutter.

But I can't admit that to Hagan. My brain races, searching for something I know for a fact.

"You've been with Erika, Darrah, and Shannon," I spit out with too much venom for someone that doesn't care.

His eyebrows shoot up. He opens his mouth, then closes it and moves his head ever so slightly from left to right. The sun shines against his caramel brown eyes and it looks like rays of sunlight bursting through his irises.

"Well, it seems like you have me all figured out. Except you left out every fact that you were there to witness. I helped you into the weight room. I went out of my way to get a parking spot today, so you wouldn't have to walk in your condition. I bought three drinks to keep you hydrated," he states in a candid but bitter voice. "And I made dickwad believe you've moved on from what had to be a one-sided relationship."

He takes off his royal blue Stallions baseball cap and runs his fingers through his wavy brown hair before replacing it on his head. His jaw tenses as he says, "Do you want to know what I see?"

I twirl a section of hair around my finger, letting it glide off and bounce before I re-wrap it. I know I'm being difficult, but I can't give another man a chance to let me down. My dad. My best friend. Chaz and I won't add Hagan to that list. They don't want a sweet and innocent girl. They want partners to spread their legs at the drop of their dirty little baseball caps, like Chaz.

 "I see a beautiful but judgmental woman sitting next to me. One that doesn't care if she has the facts correct as long as they support her opinion." He stops and does that thing with his hat again. He pops his lips when he says, "You know what's sad? Now you have me hating you as much as you hate me... and I've never hated anyone. I don't even hate your ex, even though I probably should."

Hate? I don't hate him.

The stadium erupts in cheers as the band does their traditional power K exiting the field.

Ginger and Joe come back all talky and telling us who they saw down on the lower concourse. Hagan hands Joe his keys.

"You can drive home. I'm going to go turn some accusations into facts." Hagan's tone is full of anger. When he glances over his shoulder, my eyes shift away as the players return for the second half.

I watch him take the stairs two at a time and I yell his name, but he doesn't look back. Ginger nudges me and throws her arms in the air, palms up like *what the hell?*

Hagan did do all of those things for me, but the underlying reason is he wants in my pants. I'm the only girl not giving him shameless accolades. It's a game with these guys. It's always a game, and I'm not playing again.

Joe and Ginger barely speak to me the rest of the game, but Joe says, "Whatever someone else did is not Hagan's or any other guy's fault."

I know he's right, but I can't seem to stop protecting myself from more hurt but it's coming off as rude which isn't my nature at all. Yeah, I'm a little sarcastic, but I'm making an ass out of myself.

After the game, I change into comfy clothes, while visions of Hagan run through my head and his red-hot stinging word. *Judgmental.* My phone pings with a message as I sit on my bed.

Logan: Can you come get me at the stadium?

Me: Why me?

LOGAN: BECAUSE YOU'RE THE ONLY I KNOW THAT probably isn't partying right now.

Me: Okay.

Logan: Walk of Champions entrance.

Me: Be there in ten.

Logan's waiting. He's definitely Adonis material—freshly showered, slightly damp hair and...wow, that body. When he decides to settle down, he's going to make one lucky lady very happy. He plops in my Camry and the car sinks. "Thanks, Little A."

"What happened to your car?"

He sighs. "Flat tire."

"Did you call a tow?"

"Nah, Hagan has a small air tank in his car, so we'll come by tomorrow, pump it up and then he'll follow me to the tire store. How 'bout that game?"

I ignore his shameless request for praise, instead asking a question I need the answer to. "Why didn't Hagan come and get you?"

He reaches into his pocket and unwraps a few pieces of bubble gum. "Said Joe has his Rover for some reason and since I was the last to leave the locker room, I needed a ride."

Did Hagan walk home after leaving the game? Ginger and Joe dropped me off at our apartment before they went to Joe's house for the party. I'm sure Hagan is there too. "So, do you want me to take you to the party or to your house?" I ask.

Please say house. I don't want to get within fifty feet of the baseball house. Even though I do love the porch swing.

"Home. I ordered a big ass pizza and I want to eat before I head out," Logan says.

His house is only a ten-minute drive, and though he could have walked, I knew after playing a game he's too tired. I pull into the driveway and park in front of the dark, empty home.

Logan quickly adds, "I don't want to eat alone. Come in and eat with me."

I pause and consider. I am a little hungry, and if I go home, I'll just make myself crazy thinking about Hagan's words. "Sure," I answer. "I could eat a little."

He jumps out, not thinking I need help out of the car. I press against the door and gingerly get out. The brace is on my left leg, which means I can drive, but it also means I have to place weight on that foot when I get out of the car. Finally, I follow him inside. He flips a switch that turns on a dim over-head light in the front room.

"I'll be right back. Make yourself at home."

He takes his duffle bag and lumbers against the hardwood floor as he walks upstairs. It's a typical guy's house. Modular furniture, very little décor except framed photos of the foot-ball team for the past three years. Above the fireplace is a large screen television.

I walk into the kitchen, and I'm blown away. The kitchen is all new with custom cabinetry and appliances. Logan must be doing well with the new NIL agreements in place. It effectively allows student athletes to earn money from businesses using their name, image, or likeness. One opportunity came my way in the winter during the gymnastics season. The local cheerleading gym asked me to do a commercial, so I made three thousand dollars.

But Logan must make hundreds of thousands. He's predicted to go number one or two in the NFL draft, so he's not only getting local commercials but national ones, too. He did one for a local horse farm because they make money off of breeding their stallions, and I've seen one for a national hot dog.

He probably got that one for being such a hot dog on the field.

No one should begrudge student athletes from getting paid. Most students don't understand what we have to give up— during the season, there's little time to do anything more than train, eat, and sleep. There's barely time to study, and definitely no time to work so the money we bring in from NIL agreements is sometimes all the money we athletes have to live on. We do get time off after our games or meets for that night only.

But for most athletes, we're fulfilling a dream of competing at the college level, and it makes the struggle worthwhile. Which brings me back to why I'm mad at Hagan.

I was thinking about his molten gold-ish brown eyes and his laugh when I fell that night. I've thrown twenty years of gymnastics away over a guy. The thought that one or two piercing looks from a hot jock is altering the course of my dream and career makes me sick to my stomach. It may sound unreasonable, but a gymnast dedicates her life from an early age and to destroy my future over a guy, is a Muhammad Ali left handed jab to the gut and to the heart—because I like Hagan.

Muffled noises come from upstairs. I look around and there are no bedrooms on the first floor. I guess Logan is on the phone.

There's a blue sticky note on the fridge that says, *Hagan, Harper called. Needs you.*

I bet she does.

Quick footfalls come down the stairs and when they hit the bottom step, I hear giggling.

Four people live here, so surely it's Mac or Pearse. The footsteps grow louder and the man taking up so much of my headspace rounds the corner.

When Hagan sees me, his laughter abruptly ends, and his jaw clamps closed. We both stare at the other. The air is full of nuclear energy—like Chernobyl amount of energy. The kind that will not only burn you, but one that will decimate your life.

He lifts his phone back to his mouth. "Hap, I'll call you back. Yeah. Whatever you need. I've got ya. You know that."

He moves in slow motion, tapping his phone to hang up, letting his arm fall to his side. Hagan moves around with ease. "Well, look who's here with Logan," in a decidedly snarky tone.

"He needed a ride," I say as I shift my weight.

His jaw ticks and a sly smile covers his face. "What are friends for?"

Closing in on me, he backs me against the fridge, placing his palm on the stainless steel and the other on the curvature of my waist. My heart pounds against my rib cage. It's so loud, my eyes are vibrating.

He drinks me in, looking into my eyes, then they travel down my neck. I'm wearing a midriff sweatshirt that hangs off of one shoulder. His eyes skim my bare shoulder, then to my hips. His breath is heavy, and my airways constrict. I drink him in, too. It's impossible not too—he's breathtakingly handsome.

"Like what you see?" he asks in a raspy whisper. His hair is slightly damp and curling at his nape and usually clear brown eyes are anything but clear. His pupils are dilated.

Oh, I like what I see, but forming words are way down the list for my brain—it's too busy producing a boat load of dopamine. My head feels concussed—dizzy from his woodsy scent, his wintergreen breath, and his wet, raspberry-colored lips. I nod my head involuntarily—it's like I have no control.

"That's what I thought. You like bad boys. Nice guys finish last, don't they, Adalee?"

His words breeze across my ear and under my jaw. My legs feel like overcooked noodles. He's melting me with his svelte voice and proximity. He presses his body against mine then raises his hand to my neck, using two fingers to roam the length of it. His tongue peeks out between those perfect lips.

I'm about to explode. I place my hand on his muscular abdomen, moving it upward when he grabs me by the wrist. He turns it over and blankets the sensitive skin with a kiss as gentle as a falling leaf.

 A throat clears in the distance. Hagan lowers my wrist and swipes his thumb over the same spot. Back and forth. Finally, I exhale. The corner of one side of his lip tugs upward into a knowing grin.

"Am I interrupting? Because I need some milk and you two are... umm... blocking the fridge." Logan mumbles.

Hagan steps back slowly and says, "Nothing going on here. She hates me. Right, Adalee?" Each breath is harsh whisper. He turns and knocks on the steel fridge twice. "I'll let you two get to it. Erika's waiting on me."

I snap the postie note from the frig. "Wait, you have a message. Who's Harper?" I stride toward him, holding it out as he snatches it from my hand.

He cackles. That's it, but this time his laugh makes my heart plunge into deep depressing waters.

The pizza delivery girl is standing outside the front door when Hagan pushes it open. He hands her cash and throws the pizza on the coffee table before walking out the door.

Logan pours himself a glass of milk. "Do you want one?"

I nod.

"You going to tell me what's going on with you two?"

Ignoring his question, we walk into the living room. I grab a piece of meat lover's pizza, taking off half the toppings while Logan has already consumed a whole piece. We eat in silence, and he turns on the news to watch highlights of the game on the local channel. Logan will be able to go pro after this year and he'll be the face of an NFL team, the one to breathe life into a struggling franchise.

I watch him watching himself talk. He leans forward like he's totally interested in what he has to say. "You are a class A narcissist," I joke and poke him in the side of his ridiculously hard obliques.

"Little A, if you don't love yourself, how can anyone else?"

I find myself nodding. "Will you please use my name?"

"Nah, you love it," he claims. "Now tell me about Hagan."

My feet are on the coffee table, which has a metal top and wooden legs. I rub my palms over my jeans. "I don't know, and that's the truth."

He gives me the side-eye. "That's not the truth."

"We got into an argument at the game. I took things a step too far, in his opinion. I called him a player." We've only spoken a few times, so he hasn't done anything to me.

He laughs. "I've been called worse."

"I'm sure you have, big guy."

He turns the television to Sportscenter, I'm assuming to see what the national analysts are saying about him and the Stallions.

"Logan, why don't you settle down?"

He pats my leg. "Because no one has ever given me that feeling. The one where your stomach is all tied up in knots. Well, I take that back, Natalie Ostensky. She took my breath away in fifth grade. After three weeks of hanging out on the swings at recess, I got bored and went back to playing football."

I laugh because it would be tough to outrank football in Logan Warren's eyes.

Logan holds the last piece of pizza above his head and makes an airplane noise as he stuffs it in his mouth. "Why do you think Hagan's a player?"

"I have, on excellent authority, a list of girls he's been with. Plus, he's just all charming and knows the right thing to say and do."

He half-chokes on his slice. "Huh, I never knew pinning a girl against a fridge was considered charming," he says while doing air quotes with his fingers.

Touché.

Chapter Ten

Hagan

ADALEE SHOULD LISTEN TO THE OLD SAYING "TO ASSUME is to make an ass out of you and me." She assumes to know who I am. I don't flaunt that my dad owns a major league baseball team. Other than my roommates, my teammates are the only ones that I've told.

Most guys figure it out and recognize my name because of baseball. All of us have been memorizing baseball cards and stats since we were six or seven years old. We eat, sleep, and breathe baseball on repeat. The Kodiaks won the championship two years in a row so my dad, George Chatham, is well known.

But I don't brag about it, and it doesn't mean I don't work hard. Every day, I spend time watching games of opposing pitchers we'll face this season. This is in addition to the weight room, training sessions, position practice, and team practices. Fall camp isn't as hard as it is during the season, but it's still busy.

My brother, Archer, drilled it into my head that you become the best by studying the best. You beat your opponents by learning more about them than they learn about you. I can assure Adalee; she hasn't studied me and yet assumes she understands me.

Until I went to college, I dated, but nothing serious. Then Julia came along. The men in my family never prepared me for her. She grew on me until I didn't know where I ended and she began. But it all came to a screeching halt when she cheated on me. I didn't say it was over—hell, I was willing to work on our relationship. Now I see how unhealthy I was when we were a couple.

Julia was the one to cut me in half, when she said, "I'm not happy with you, anymore." Fuck, it still hurts.

The few times I'd been around Adalee, I thought she was different. She always smiles when she speaks to everyone but me. She never shamelessly flirts with anyone. I also noticed she never drinks. So, on Thursday when Joe asked if I wanted to go to the football game with him, Ginger and possibly Adalee, I said yes, almost too fast. He can feel the underlying current between Adalee and me.

So now, I'm walking around on a Saturday night trying to shake off the aftershocks of Hurricane Adalee. It's the same type of feelings that I had with Julia, only different. With Julia it grew slowly.

My stomach churns thinking about Adalee and the memory of my fingers sampling the skin of her neck and the taste of her delicate wrists on my lips. That's what is different about her—she hit me like a line drive in the chest. I'm in deep without the first kiss being exchanged, much less a relationship. Sometimes I tell myself over and over again to quit thinking about her.

When I backed her up against the cold stainless steel, the heat radiating from her skin urged me on. Our breaths were short and shallow. But her eyes, God, those eyes were globes of desire. She wants me, even if she doesn't like me. If I could figure out why she hates me so much, I could explain.

If Logan didn't walk in, our lips would have met, and our tongues would have danced. My fingers would have skimmed the skin on the small of her back while pulling her tightly into my body. It would have been a moment she couldn't forget.

When I look up, I'm at the baseball house. I told Erika I would meet her here because I need to lick my wounds. Erika isn't who I want or the type of girl I want but I agreed to meeting her anyway. I decide it isn't right to make her think there's a chance for us, but as I turn around to head back home, she flies off the porch, slinging her drunk arms around my neck.

"Hey," is all I can say as she spills her drink down my back. The beer soaks through the shirt and trickles down from my shoulders to the waistband of my pants.

Erika slurs her words into my neck, "What took you so long? You've made me wait weeks."

"I was talking to my sister. She's having a hard ti—"

Erika cuts me off by attacking me with her lips. Her beer breath is awful, like she's eaten hot wings mixed with a lager. I pull my head back, separating us. There's no denying that she's beautiful, but I'm not feeling it.

She mumbles in my ear, "I want you to fuck me. You've been playing the field, and that's okay. But I want what you're packing." She can't keep her eyes open, and she believes it's a perfect time to have sex. I shake my head in disbelief. "I've heard stories about your package." Erika doesn't have to throw herself at me—I like her when she's not drunk. But only as a friend.

Whatever she's heard, someone made up. My dick has stayed firmly in my pants.

Women have been forward with me before, but nothing like this. It should be a turn on, but all I can think about is Adalee. The way she didn't have to say a word to make my heart explode in thunderous beats like a racehorse in the final stretch of the Kentucky Derby.

"Dude, you love slopping up my seconds?" Chaz laughs. "She's a clinger and a talker. I'm sure Adalee would love to see this." He takes out his phone and snaps a picture, practically skipping as he heads inside the house.

I push Erika away, but she goes limp, and I have to hold on to her waist to keep her from face planting in the grass. A few people stop by, and I ask who she came with, but no one knows. I slip my phone out of pocket with one hand and text some of my teammates to see if she's here with friends.

Finally, Joe comes over. "Hey, when did you get here? And I see you're making good on your promise to make some rumors come true." He half-snorts as he takes a drink.

"Ten minutes ago. If you and Ginger are going back to her house, take Erika home."

"Can't man. Ginger is in my room, sick. She's been puking since we came back from the game. The hot dog didn't look good. It was dark gray, but she ate it anyway. Those redheads, when they make up their mind, there's no stopping them. I had to hold her hair and wipe her face. It's tough shit, man."

I smile because Joe's in love. "Yet you took care of her like it's a badge of honor." It's my understanding, they haven't exchanged those three scary words, but he's definitely all-in. Joe's a great guy. Parties one or two nights a week but not heavy and never gets wasted.

He nods. "Yeah, I love taking care of her." He looks up at the sky as if he's listening to the universe speak to him. "If taking care of her is the last thing I do on earth, it will be a life that is worth living."

I smack his arm with my free hand. "Damn man, that was deep. How many have you had?"

"Just one. Here's your key back, if you want to take Erika home." He dangles the keys and drops them into my palm. "I parked around the corner."

I shake my head in disgust. "Why me?"

"Because we both know you're one of the good guys," he states with a sincere tone. "Plus, you might see Adalee. That girl is different when you're around; it's like she tightens up when she's in Hagan Chatham's vicinity." He takes a pull of beer and then continues. "She either has it bad for you or she really hates you."

Tell me something I don't know.

I raise Erika up a little because she was slipping from my grip before I say, "She's with Logan at my house." I emphasize the word my.

Joe's eyebrows shoot up his forehead. "Like with him, with him?"

I shrug. Logan told me they were just friends, and if she thinks I'm a player, she has to realize he actually is one. "I don't know. I don't think so. He called me to pick him up at the stadium, but you had my car, so I guess he called her. Can you help me get Erika to the car?"

Joe sets his beer down in the grass and pulls one of her arms over his shoulder. We have our arms around her waist as we head to my car. He helps hoist her up into the seat and buckles her in, then closes the door. I slide into the driver's side as he slaps the window. "Be safe."

A few minutes later, I'm carrying Erika to her apartment. I knock and ring the doorbell, and no one is home. She's been passed out since Joe and I were talking at the party. I check her pockets for keys with no luck.

It's frustrating because I have fall camp early in the morning for position drills. She must have come with someone and I'm the one taking care of her. But I always think what if this was my sister? What if this was Hap? Somebody better handle her like she's a crystal wine goblet at Buckingham Palace—with *keep your fucking hands to yourself* gloves. So, I wait and wait while Erika sleeps and snores on my shoulder.

An hour passes and I'm thinking of hauling her back down and taking her to my place when a car stops in front of her building. Hopefully, her roommates have returned home. I pick Erika up and walk to the balcony, but it's not Erika's roommates—it's Adalee.

She has this little pink leather wristlet wrapped around that same silken skin that my lips caressed only hours ago. She's singing something. The words get lost as they drift through the air, but her lips are moving. She's singing to herself. I wonder what her favorite song is, whether she likes pop or country. Is she from Kentucky? There's so much I want to learn about her.

Her apartment is underneath Erika's on the bottom floor. She steps over the curb and is startled by Erika moaning. Fan-fucking-tastic. Just my luck, she would spot me with Erika in this condition. She looks up and her sing-song smile dissolves into narrowed eyes and lips pressed together in a thin line.

I don't have a choice. I have to ask for Adalee's help. "Hey, can you help me out?"

Even from ten feet up, I can see the way her face tightens. She may need a mouth guard the way she's grinding her teeth. Then she gets a smirk on that pretty little face and that cute button nose scrunches up a little.

"I'm not into three-ways, except for chili."

I do like her sarcasm. Trouble is, I can't figure out if she's flirting or just hates life. "Adalee, whatever you think of me. I'm not the bad guy here. Can you please help your *friend*, Erika?" I stress the word friend.

She huffs. "What do you want me to do?"

"I've been waiting for her roommates to come home for an hour. Can she sleep at your place?"

"Ugh, bring her down." Adalee blows out an exaggerated breath.

This time I pick Erika up, honeymoon style, and carry her down the steps as I wait for Adalee to unlock the door. She holds the door open wide to let us in.

"Just put her on the couch." She slams down her wristlet on the bar.

"I can put her in Ginger's room. Joe said Ginger was sick and staying the night at his place."

She thinks about it for a minute and then says, "Her room is on the right."

I go in and lay her down on the bed, take off her shoes, and set them beside the bed. Adalee peers in through the doorway. I walk toward her, and she doesn't step aside. "Thanks for letting her stay."

She lets me pass and then follows me to her front door. "I guess neither of us got what we wanted tonight."

She has no idea what I want, and it's certainly not Erika. "Nope I didn't. Maybe you did. I can't compete with Logan Warren."

Adalee bites back a smile at my admission that I want to compete for her attention. "Logan and I are just friends. You've probably never been just friends with a girl."

"Is that what you want us to be? *Just friends?*" I take two strides and our chests are mere inches apart. I purposefully talk soft and low because it turned her on, earlier tonight. "One thing I don't understand is why you love being friends with a notorious playboy like Logan, but it's like pulling teeth for me to get a smile from you. I promise you, Logan's been with more women in the three months I've known him than most guys in three or four lifetimes."

I run my knuckle over her lip. "But maybe you're biding your time, hoping you'll be the last woman standing in Logan's eyes. The one that let him sow his oats then tamed him. His friend turned wife."

The result of my comment is a stare off. She shivers with a sound rumbling from her chest. Her eyes widen as she looks at me through her lashes. I kiss her on the corner of her mouth. My lips touch just enough of hers to know that I want more, but I'm the one that needs to bide my time. Deep in my bones I feel how much she wants me to claim her, I'll wait her out. This may or may not be love, but it's something. And like the preacher said at all my siblings' weddings, "Love is patient." I've waited my turn my whole life, being the youngest in a large family, stuck somewhere between much older siblings and grandkids.

So, dear Adalee, I'll happily play the waiting game.

I grab the knob and walk out. I faintly hear my name, but she needs to understand how this waiting game works. I have a strange thump inside my chest, and with every single beat, it tells me she's worth the wait.

Chapter Eleven

Adalee

THE LECTURE HALL IS HUMMING TODAY. THE PROFESSOR made attendance ten percent of our grade, so it's packed with students. I'm still sitting in the cheap seats. It's easier with the brace not to do steps. Joe stops and talks for a few minutes before heading down to sit with Hagan and a few other friends. Erika sits in the same row, although this time, Hagan's on the other end sandwiched between a football player and blonde from the Kappa Delta sorority. Judging from the way he's ignoring Erika, he's tired of being her caretaker.

When Erika woke up in Ginger's room Sunday morning, she didn't remember even seeing Hagan Saturday night. She said he called and told her he would meet her, but then never showed up. I filled in the facts about how he brought her home and waited for her roommates to come home. She was embarrassed and apologized repeatedly. Hagan was telling the truth about just bringing her home.

Saturday, Hagan proved to me, beyond a doubt, that I want him to kiss me. He left me so hot and bothered that I needed relief. His dimples kept appearing in my head—and so did the way he took care of someone that isn't his girlfriend.

The professor hits his palm against the lectern two times, and the loud chatter slows to a few murmurs. He fingers the microphone on his button-down and says, "Thanks for showing up today. Scan this QR code for your attendance." A huge QR code flashes up on the smart board. "The company the university is partnering with is ready for the student infusion. You'll be working with a partner of my choosing."

The class lets out a universal sigh. People like me want to make sure I'm getting a student that will pull their weight.

"I've taken an extensive look at each of your strengths and weaknesses and have put together teams that will complement each other," the professor claims.

He goes on to explain the project and how each pairing will have a different problem to solve and is required to give a minimum of two solutions. Our assignment is to give solutions to a specific problem the design team has encountered. The company already has the answers but it's a way of testing our intuition, current knowledge, and our critical thinking skills. At the end of the class, he asks us to check our class app for details.

I scroll through my phone on our university app to find this class. There are approximately one hundred people, so that's fifty pairings. Before I've located my partner, Hagan knocks on my desk twice.

"Looks like it's me and you, kid," he says while grinning, and I get caught up in his golden flecked eyes, charming little dimple and teeth that would make a toothpaste model jealous.

He shows me his phone, showing me proof that we're partners. "Great. With our schedules, he should have paired us with students that have less hectic lives."

The guy sitting beside me chimes in, "Just because we're not athletes doesn't mean we're not busy. I work two jobs and go to school full time."

Hagan jumps in to defend me. "She didn't mean it like that. Adalee just doesn't want me as her partner. Sorry man."

The tall, lanky guy purses his lips as he scans the room for his partner saunters off. Hagan slips into his seat and his clean, fresh scent wafts through the air. He has a white Stallions baseball cap on today and his brown hair curls up under the edge. Sometimes he's boyish like today, and other times, like after the game—he's all man.

Hagan snaps his fingers, which startles me. "Earth to Adalee." Then he starts singing Frank Sinatra's, "Fly Me to the Moon." Geez, is there anything this guy can't do?

He pulls up the requirements on his phone, places his arm on the back of my chair and scoots in.

"Hey, it looks like our professor organized this with our coaches."

He extends his hand so I can get a better view of his phone. I lean down and read the schedule. I feel a slight tug of my hair and I notice Hagan's looking at my hair while barely touching the ends. Goosebumps travel across my skin as he flirts with me. No one has ever touched my hair so gently and made my pulse race so hard from a simple gesture.

Is he flirting with me?

"So we'll meet at the job site tomorrow?" I ask.

"No, I'll pick you up." I open my mouth to protest that I can drive, but Hagan starts shaking his head. "Before you say no, let me remind you that there's very little parking downtown during the day. Plus, I'm going to prove to you that I'm a good guy." He pauses, "Now come on, I'll take you to the weight room."

"How did you know I have weight training today?"

"Adalee, never underestimate me."

He's wearing me down with that smile and that boyish grin that holds so much happiness. He grabs under my elbow and helps me through the door. We talk about class and the project on the short walk to his home. By the time we arrive, my leg is swelling. The house is quiet; his roommates must either be in class or in bed. As I plop down on the couch, I raise my leg, resting it on the coffee table. The sight of my brace reminds me that I'm in this condition because of Hagan.

Once he returns from his room in a tight white tank with the Chicago Kodiaks logo stretching across his chest, I almost forget that my resolution to not date athletes. He gives his car keys a little toss and catches them back in his palm, moving it quickly in front of him, reminding me of playing Jack's by myself when I was young.

"Do you play Jacks? The way you caught your keys makes me think you're good with your hands," I state, trying to maintain a straight face. It doesn't work. The expression on his face is priceless. His eyebrows practically reach his hairline, eyes are as open as I've ever seen them. A goofy yet bashful smile appears, briefly showing teeth. But it's the dimple that makes my knees weak.

"Yes," he squeaks out, but instead of a sarcastic remark about how good he is with his hands, he asks, "Ready?"

It feels good to catch him off guard. I dip my head, feeling a little flirtatious before glancing back up at Hagan Chatham, and thinking of all the ways he could turn me inside out. "Ready for what?"

Chapter Twelve

Hagan

Take a deep breath and just be yourself. It's easier said than done. After Adalee's flirty words yesterday, I've thought of having her in every position imaginable. She's fucking beautiful even when she's hating on me. Honestly, I feel her sadness in my bones just by the tone of her voice. She has barbed wire keeping her heart safe but if she would give me a chance, I'll prove I'm worthy.

When we went to the weight room, she saw the trainer while I was lifting. My hopes died when she didn't enter with the rest of the gymnastics team.

I hope her leg is okay. I didn't know I said it out loud because I was waiting for my sister to answer the phone. She called me in a panic so I'm returning her call at the most inopportune time.

My sister asks, "Whose leg?"

I stammer, "Oh—a—no one. Are you okay? Your message sounded like you were..."

I'm picking up Adalee to ride to the jobsite together. As I swing my leg to get out, Adalee appears on the sidewalk. Her brown hair is in a ponytail, swishing and shimmering from the fall sun. She's petite perfection.

Harper fills the void. "Freaking out. You can say it. Why is it that you can do life without me, but I can't do it without you?" Hap's voice is full of discontent. "Are you even listening to me?"

No. I'm watching the woman I'm going to marry walk down the sidewalk.

Adalee pulls the door open, and I run around helping her up, holding my cell between my shoulder and cheek. My reward is a slight grin. Her gift is the burn marks my hands must leave when my fingers touch the delicate skin on her wrist.

I hold up a finger, gesturing to Adalee that I'll be off the phone in one minute and stay outside talking.

"Sorry, Hap. You need to find something that you love to do. I've always had baseball, and I've loved every minute that you tagged along, but I want you to be happy."

My sister quickly says, "It's all your fault, you know, taking up more food and fluid inside Mom's stomach."

I react like I'm hurt. "I didn't."

"You did. The doctor told mom."

"Are we still having this argument twenty-one years later? Tell me what's wrong."

As I get into the Rover, the line goes silent, and I hear little sniffles that tug at my heart. I hate that I'm living my dream and Harper feels abandoned. I want to support her, but I also need this alone time with Adalee. I'm going to prove that I'm one of the good guys on campus. "Hap, I start a building project today and I just picked up my partner. Can I call you back this afternoon? I promise three to five is all for you."

Adalee's eyes go wide. She knows how valuable an athlete's time is. To give someone two hours in the middle of the day is a huge compliment. I glance over again, and her brows are pinched, so she probably has the wrong idea.

Harper finally agrees. "Okay. Love you."

"Love you, too."

I put the phone in my console waiting for the question from Adalee about who I was talking to, but it never came.

Campus is less than a mile from downtown, but the petite brunette reads off the directions from her phone, telling me where to turn. I know where we're going but I'm not feeding into her misconceptions about me being a know it all.

Some of my friends might disagree, like Tackett. He's one of my best friends and plays for the Atlanta Braves. He hates when we play trivia because I give him a run for his money. This tiny thought gives me an idea—Harper should talk with Tackett. His season just ended, losing the first round of the playoffs so he'll have time.

When we pull into the parking space, I grab my phone and text him to give Harper a call. He texts back immediately and says he will. He's engaged and the four of us spent most of the summer together. Harper and I were there for Tackett and Talynn when they hit a rough patch. But Tackett and Harper have as strong of a friendship as I've seen.

Adalee and I walk slowly to accommodate her gait in the brace. But I'm so much taller, my feet are in slow motion. She'll need to power walk once she's my girlfriend. Yes, I'm a positive thinker—she'll be mine one day.

Most of the class surrounds a man in a suit with a construction hat and our professor. We step into the circle with some of our friends. They pass out the yellow hard hats and vests. Adalee takes off her backpack, handing it to me, and slips on the vest. I smile inwardly because things are looking up. We have a few minutes before they divide us up with the project manager, so I talk to Joe, and Adalee talks to Erika—and Jayce, who's on the men's swim team.

Out of my peripheral vision, I watch how laid back she is with everyone but me. With me, she's as tense as a fishing line, like when you have a fish on the hook desperately swimming away. I'm deep in thought about how I'm going to reel Adalee in—it may take a while, and she might fight it, but we have chemistry.

The person overseeing us gives a tour and tells us about our problem:

The columns were designed according to the construction documents but a change in design on the upper levels means a change in the structural load. What changes are necessary? What are the structural options and the costs associated with each?

Then leaves us alone to start the work he gave us. Adalee removes her portfolio and three different pens.

I laugh, asking, "Why do you need three pens?"

"If you must know, Blue is for suggested solutions. Pink is for questions that need to be answered for each suggestion. Green is for the cost of implementing each one."

My whole body shakes, and I can no longer hold back, grabbing her by the waist. Her initial reaction is to wiggle from my grip but then our eyes lock before her lids fall, hiding the windows to what I want to be my world. "Do you know how sexy you are right now?"

Her body softens into mine as she looks up and under her short, thick lashes. And this hard hat is turning me on. It's the combination of strength, intelligence and softness. I'm almost a foot taller than her, but somehow it seems we're an engineering masterpiece. She feels so right against my body.

After we've looked at each other for a long time, she asks, "How sexy?"

I love how she's coming out of her shell with me. Her tongue caresses her bottom lip, leaving a trail of possibilities. I can't think—watching it like a video in slow motion. Our mouths are so close. Our chests meet when we inhale. I don't have words for how sexy.

Just do it—fucking kiss her.

Adalee stays firmly in place as my head falls to meet hers. This girl already has me tied up in knots. My lips tremble as our mouths touch. It's more like a graze as I move my lips left and right over hers. She tastes like honey flavored lip balm.

I tease her over and over, but in all honesty, I've never kissed a girl like this—it's tentative because I don't want her to scare her off. I need to understand if she wants this as much as I do. How long will it take to register that we're kissing?

One of Adalee's hands glides between my safety vest and my plaid button-down. Even with fabric between our skin, her hands leave a trail of accelerant. My body lights up with something more than desire. She catches my bottom lip between her honey flavored flesh and a short hum rumbles from her mouth to mine.

She unwittingly answers the question in my mind. She wants this chemistry experiment that's happening between us. The way our lips release and catch, I have a sneaking suspicion that our relationship is about to change for the better.

Our moment is over when her hair sticks between our mouths. We're ten stories up on this skeleton of steel beams and a strong gust of wind causes me to tighten my hold around her waist. I take my finger and remove the errant brown strands. Her forehead leans against my chest as we both exhale.

She clears her throat as she pushes away. "I think we should get to work."

We should because I may have a heart attack.

Nodding, I pull out a black leather notepad from my pocket that has a small pen looped inside it. She chuckles. "That's very efficient."

"Sometimes, small is good," I add, raising my eyebrows, indicating I love her petite frame. That earns me a fleeting smile with both cheeks rounded.

Our project manager comes up an hour later to look at our progress. He gives us further instructions, and thirty minutes later, I'm dropping her off. The gentleman in me opens the passenger side door, helps her out, and walks her to her apartment. I want another kiss or maybe ask her out. I slide my fingers from her shoulder to her hands, but she doesn't latch on.

Great. She's already reconsidering the kiss and me.

"Thanks for driving me and umm... we should exchange numbers since we're partners and all." Her voice is faint, and her eyes narrow slightly. She holds her cell as I type in my contact information.

"Call me."

I turn the knob and push it open. Adalee closes the door behind me with a nod.

The ball is in her court. I've only reached my car when she calls and immediately hangs up, ensuring that I have her number.

Baby steps.

Chapter Thirteen

Adalee

Hagan Chatham. His lips floated over mine like they were weightless. Using my index finger, I skim my lips, memorizing the feeling, but it's not the same. When he said I was sexy, my ovaries burst open, ready to have his children. No one has ever described me as sexy. God, it sounded so smooth coming from Hagan's mouth. A little part of me is in denial—refusing to believe that Hagan could want me and no one else.

That's where the trouble is—him wanting me, as in exclusive. Guys like him aren't into monogamy.

I change into comfy clothes. Nothing feels better than a pair of old, thin yoga pants and a T-shirt with bursting holes at the seams. Staying the same size is a perk of being a gymnast.

I make a snack and sit on the couch to work on an assignment for a different class. Concentrating on a research paper isn't happening though. I check my phone ten times, hoping for a text from Hagan but then I remember, he gave me his number.

I chuckle inwardly at how he knew just what to do to make me putty in his hands—the soft, lingering kiss, the gentle caress of his fingers.

He gave me his number—pitching me the ball—it's up to me whether to swing.

Me: This is Adalee. Wanted to remind you to call Hap. 3-5 is Hap time.

Hagan: Thanks, getting ready to call her now.

Me: Oh, okay. Good.

Hagan: You. That kiss. Needs to happen again.

Me: You shouldn't have done that when you obviously have a girlfriend.

Dots disappear and reappear. Yeah, Hagan let's see you explain this one.

 Hagan: Nope, no girlfriend.

Now it's my turn to sit and stew on his line of dishonesty. You don't call a girl and talk for two hours if she's not your girlfriend. Finally, I text back, noticing it is 2:58 and there won't be time for much back and forth.

Me: You never answered me when I asked, "How sexy?"

I can't believe I'm being forward, but he brings it out in me.

Hagan: Come over, I'll tell you.

Me: You're such a Casanova. Can't anyway because you're busy for the next two hours.

Hagan: I'll order food from that all natural place. Hell, I'll come get you at 5.

Me: No can do. One kiss doesn't make us a couple.

Hagan: No, it doesn't. I have to make that call.

Now I'm more confused than I was when I sat down. This person is obviously important to him. Old flame? Long distance girlfriend? Old girlfriend trying to rekindle their relationship? It's the second time I've heard bits of a conversation with her. It has to be a girl—he used a caring tone he wouldn't use with his mom. So yep, he has a girl back home.

Asshole.

Ginger busts through the door like a mountain lion is chasing her. She's breathing hard and bends over to catch her breath. Her red hair curled up around her temples from sweating.

"What's up Ging?" I ask.

She snaps, her voice straining. "I saw Joe getting out of a car with another girl. They looked all cozy and he hugged her."

"What kind of a hug?"

Tears fill her eyes as she slumps and takes the cushion next to me. Ginger has never had a jealous bone in her body until she started dating Joe. "The kind that lasts too long when your girlfriend is watching."

"I'm sure it was not what it looked like," I say, trying to reassure her. "Was it Josie? Because they're partners in class."

Ginger grabs a tissue, blowing her nose, and shakes her fiery redhead tendrils. "Tell me something to get my mind off Joe."

I'm not sure if I want to disclose the kiss between Hagan and me. At least, until I know if I'm going to act on my feelings to take it farther, I prefer to keep it to myself.

Instead, I say, "Hagan and I didn't kill each other today." I pause thinking about how I could feel his hard body through his shirt. He had on khakis and a thin-weight flannel button-down. It was smooth and probably expensive. "He was actually helpful today. He's smarter than I gave him credit for."

She pats my leg, straightening her back. This is Ginger fighting back her tears. "When are you going to let someone in? It's been over two months since you and Chaz broke up. And you were never really into him anyway."

"I'm just focusing on rehabbing and getting back on the mat," I say, lying to myself and Ginger. I'm scared to death.

I'm not like most girls in college and because I don't drink and spread my legs. But then I gave Chaz a chance because I was lonely, only to be cheated on and chastised. Ginger's right—I wasn't in love with him, and I didn't *need* Chaz, but I did like hanging out with him and other couples.

But Hagan and I have a surreal connection. When he backed me up against the fridge, I saw the I'll-take-control Hagan. His tone was commanding, and his breath was hot and spicy against my skin, those damned peppermints.

Then today I saw the I'll-take-it-slow-and-leave-you-begging-for-more Hagan. Both arouse me to the point of wanting more right now.

Today he grabbed my hand and pulled me into him play-fully. Then I asked a question that I never got an answer to. This time, he was vulnerable and soft. Knowing Hagan has all these different dimensions makes me want to get to know him better.

Hagan Chatham could destroy me if I let him. Plus, and I can't quit telling myself this enough—he's the reason I'm injured and can't do full-out practices with the team.

Joe bangs on the door, "Come on, Red. Let me in." Two more knocks. "Please, it's not what you think."

Yeah, it's always what we're thinking. Stop. Joe is a nice guy.

It's a good thing the door is five feet from the couch; I only have to hobble a few steps to open it at Ginger's refusal. He looks like hell. His eyes are swollen red, and his hair is a mess. His fingers make pathways through his thick maze. Gesturing for him to come in, he slides past me to the couch. The tenderness he shows, tells me he wasn't cheating, flirting maybe.

Not wanting to be in the way, I go to the gymnastics training center and chalk up. I miss the strong smell. I wouldn't be surprised if ten percent of my body is made up of chalk, I've been inhaling it for so long. All gymnasts have little hand movements and dips of our body as we turn that signifies the skill we are pretending to perform. I perform one-handed cartwheels landing with only one foot. At least my high ankle sprain is healed.

I scroll to the music on my phone, select my favorite playlist which are all the songs from the show *Hart of Dixie*. Then I grab the resistance bands and start working out. It's serene and I get lost in the music while exercising my upper body.

By the time I return home, Joe and Ginger have made up and are cooking dinner. After showering, I join them for some Chicken Tikka Masala. It's out of a jar but Joe did bake the chicken before tossing in the creamy tomato sauce. I used more energy today, so I make a salad to go with dinner and set our small four-person table—for three.

"Set four places," Ginger states as if we always have guests for dinner.

My eyes widen in curiosity. She and Joe act as if they don't hear me when I ask who they invited. Much to my chagrin, Ginger invited Hagan, celebrating that we didn't kill each other earlier today. He's Joe's new best friend and she wants him to be able to hang out here. The next thing I know I'm sitting next to Hagan at my kitchen table.

Hagan eats four pieces of Naan bread. It's not fair that men can eat whatever they want, and women have to watch carbs.

Butterflies be damned—I'm eating. I worked it off so when he grabs the last piece, I slap his hand. "Mine. All mine."

Hagan's lips curl up, flashing that hopeful, boyish grin, releasing the warm bread, before he responds, "Yours, all yours."

God he's handsome.

Chapter Fourteen

Hagan

Campus feels small when my chest is puffed out like I'm freaking Superman. I'm sky high for Adalee. When she said, "Mine, all mine," last night, something snapped inside me. Sure, she was talking about bread, but desire rippled through me. She said it like it was a double innuendo. The air thickened so much that Joe and Ginger went to the den.

Adalee and I discussed our engineering project. Neither of us mentioned the kiss, or any topic related to dating. She didn't even ask about my two-hour phone call. Unfortunately, Joe and I had to leave because my brother Archer and his wife Megan are in town. We went to play escape games with Mac, Archer and Megan. Logan had a friend coming over.

Archer's a sports agent and so far all of his clients are former baseball players of the Sarasota Sharks. He used to be the President of the team but gave it up for his wife.

But this weekend, he's here to watch the Stallions predicted first-round draft picks—Logan and Pearse—my roommates. They play number three Ole Miss, and everyone is jacked for the game.

Archer and Megan pick me up early for lunch. "Where to?" I ask.

"Wherever you want, but a friend suggested The Jugger Joint. Have you been there?"

"Nope but everyone raves about their awesome chili," I say.

The restaurant is what I call southern gourmet. White linens cover the inside tables and are paired with mismatched chairs. Painted shiplap adorns one wall with exposed brick on the other three. It's swanky, which is why I haven't been here. It's not a place a bunch of guys go—it's more of a date place or business lunches.

"Hey, can you go see Harper before heading to Chicago for the playoffs?"

Archer's eyebrow shoots up. Even though he wanted me to transfer to Kentucky, he was visibly unsure about Harper staying at Illinois A&M without me. "We'll do what we need to do."

Megan's eyes narrow. "What's wrong?"

I butter the cornbread and place it back in the plate. "She's a nervous wreck. Hap isn't happy. I'm such an ass for leaving. Some things are more important than sports. I'm sorry I didn't realize how difficult this would be for her." I shake my head, hating myself for leaving Harper. I don't want to alarm them, but I end up sharing my two hour conversation with Harper.

Megan scoots her chair around and puts her arm around my shoulder. "Nonsense. She's a strong young woman and just needs her friends and family to help her."

"That's just it. My friends have always been her friends. She never really had to make friends on her own. If you're not a twin, it's hard to understand."

Megan's eyes dart to Archer's. They speak telepathically because there's a long silent stare between them before Archer says, "We'll leave right after the game, but Hagan, you aren't responsible for her happiness or her anxiety. I know you both joke about it, but it's not true."

"I'll get Tackett and Talynn to go see her for a visit, too. The four of you spent most of the summer together and there's no way someone can be depressed when they're around," Megan chimes in with a knowing smile. She's the new President of the Sarasota Sharks and one of the smartest women I've ever known.

"Okay, but I can't stand to hear her cry. It's not her fault she was born a twin or into this baseball family. She needs to find something of her own."

We all agree, and my heart feels a little less tight knowing that Harper will be comforted with company for the next week. Megan is so efficient. She's already messaged her sister, Talynn, planning for all of them to be at the Kodiaks first round playoff game.

"Hey what about me? I want to come to the playoffs."

"No can do. You have that big project for the next few weeks. Our plan is for you to be the project manager for the new Kodiak Stadium in five years—if you're not playing on the team."

I frown, dipping my French fry into honey mustard. When you're an athlete, you give up time and important moments in life. It's a constant battle in my head. Archer says there are scouts interested in me, but do I want this life for the next fifteen years? One thing I'm certain of is I'll finish my degrees first. "If the Kodiaks make it to the championships, I'm missing class."

Archer taps his knuckles against the table twice. "Knock on wood."

Baseball players are superstitious. I look under the white tablecloth and laugh. "It's wood veneer. Does that count?"

Archer chuckles and says, "Okay, fingers crossed."

"So, I hope you don't mind but I'm going to skip out right after the football game. There's a huge party at the home run house. The baseball players have parties during football season and vice versa."

"It wouldn't be college without parties. Are you meeting up with anyone special?" Megan asks as she smirks.

I scoop up a big spoon of chili and swallow. "Hope so."

The waiter comes by dropping off the bill. Archer picks it up, takes out the pen and taps it on the table a few times. "Are you dating someone?"

"No. I think she hates me. She definitely hated me until yesterday," I volunteer.

"Why would she hate you?"

"She thinks I'm a one-nighter, a playboy."

Megan cackles and Archer coughs. "What?"

I give a little tilt of my head and shrug my shoulders. We stand up to leave, and Megan takes me aside while we wait for the valet. I absolutely look up to her and want my daughters to be like her one day. She reminds me of an older version of Adalee. Megan's only four or five years older and is also petite with brown hair.

"Hagan, she must not know you at all if she thinks you're sleeping around. Show her who you really are. Sometimes your confidence comes off cocky and that's fantastic on the field, but it intimidates the average girl. I think I had this same conversation with Tackett." Archer agrees. They grin at how they already feel like parents of all us twenty-somethings.

"Nothing about her is average and she's a gymnast. I should forget about her. It would never work with both of us being athletes, but we kissed yesterday. I'm playing the waiting game to give her time to catch up to my feelings. I just don't know how to date since Julia. She messed me up, and every time Adalee rejects me by making untrue statements..."

Archer joins us and when we get into the car, he says, "Hagan, be yourself and don't force it. She'll come around if she's worth it."

I mumble to myself, "You don't know how stubborn this girl is."

They both laugh as Archer snakes his hand around Megan's waist. "If she's anything like this one, I do." Then he bends down giving his wife a chaste kiss. "But there's *not* one thing I would change about Megan, except the clicking of her pen."

They married in the spring at home plate of Kodiak stadium, and they're always touching and kissing.

My family is filled with people to admire. Not because they're all successful but because they love like a home run blasted over the centerfield wall—deep. My oldest brother, Reagan, is a world renowned chef, and when he told my dad that he didn't want to work in baseball, he was fully supported.

When my sister, Sarah Jane, wanted to be a stay at home mom, the Kodiaks gave her projects that she could work from home on. Archer used to be the President of our minor league team and Megan was the Financial Analyst, so Archer became a sports agent and Dad promoted Megan, so they could be together.

Now, Harper and I are the only single siblings.

The chemistry between Adalee and me is amazing, but there's a wall around her heart, and it's my mission to find out why. Was Chaz as terrible a boyfriend as he is a teammate?

Energy is popping off my body, and I need a release. "Do you mind dropping me off at the gym?"

Chapter Fifteen

Adalee

As I turn the corner, hiking home from the gym, Hagan steps out of a car. I put my head down and keep right on walking. He says, "Adalee, Adalee." He's fifty feet away but runs toward me. "Hey, let me give you a ride."

"Someone dropped you off. How are you going to drive without a vehicle?" I ask, poking my hip out with my brows diving into my nose. The trainer told me that I need to see the doctor on Monday. I'm frustrated and nervous energy flows through my body, worried about my scholarship for next year.

He slides his fingers over my forearm and my polyester gymnastics jacket almost melts.

"It's my brother. We'll take you home, so you don't have to trek that far."

"That's okay, thanks."

Hagan's face drops and his eyes hold disappointment. "Adalee, come on," he says, clearly frustrated.

"I need to be alone right now. I want to walk." I pause, realizing how harsh I sound, so I soften my tone. "But I appreciate you asking."

With that, I make a beeline to my apartment. The least I could do was go thank his family for the parking space at the football game, but I'm home with self-pity rearing its ugly head.

I've never had an injury to this extent or been out this long. And all because I was thinking of the guy with the liquid caramel eyes, his boyish charm and never-ending confidence make him even sexier if that's possible.

But it's also why Hagan and I can never be. As much as I'm attracted to him, I can't be with someone that's capable of dazzling me into dropping my panties with only a dimpled smile, and I came close at the job site. I won't spend my life worrying about another guy being unfaithful to me, if he doesn't get sex right away.

And that pisses me off as much as my injury because I want to learn more about Hagan Chatham. Kiss Hagan Chatham. And why should I care as much about NOT dating him as I do about my gymnastics career?

I wish my mom was here. Her words would heal me—motivate me.

By the time I'm home, I realize I should have accepted the ride. Why am I so stubborn? I did need the space to clear my head and find the determination to push through the pain.

Ginger is at Joe's. The baseball team and the girlfriends bought a section of tickets to the football game tonight. School spirit is a top priority. As an athlete, I perform better when the crowd is standing room only, but the way my leg is throbbing, climbing the ramps into the uppers where the available students are located isn't possible.

It's cramping and swollen because I've overused it today. I lay down on the couch, propping it up on the rolled arm as I pop some Motrin tablets. Ginger and I always have it handy because it relieves the pain in our muscles. My phone dings with a notification.

Logan: You coming to the game tonight?

Me: No, I'm resting my leg. I've been on it all day.

Logan: Kickoff isn't for five hours. You have to come. I'm giving you my ticket up in the suite. I'll have my sister Kaylee pick you up. She'll be in there too.

Me: Are you sure you don't want to give it to one of your one-nighters? It will probably earn you a blow job.

Logan: No, this ticket is reserved for my friend.

Me: Okay, thanks Logan. Kick Ole Miss's butt tonight.

Logan: No doubt.

I like his last text. When it comes to football, Logan is the cockiest guy on campus. What am I saying? He's cocky all the time, especially with football—and the ladies.

After napping, I throw on jeans, a royal blue sweater, and a blanket scarf with a houndstooth pattern, hoping it will be enough to keep me warm. I detest carting a coat around the football stadium.

There's a knock on my door two hours before the game. As I open it, I introduce myself. "Hi, I'm Adalee. Thanks for picking me up."

"Kaylee, Logan's older sister," she replies as she chuckles. "Whenever we're together, people think I'm younger because he's enormous—six-foot-five."

Kaylee's visibly pregnant and probably in her mid-twenties. She and Logan share the same eyes and hair color, but there's a huge disparity in their height.

We talk all the way to the stadium about my torn ACL, when the baby is due and that she has a daughter who's already at the football field with her dad. She pulls into a primo parking spot that says, *PRESS*. After a short glass elevator ride, we step into a gorgeous gray hallway adorned with framed pictures of former Stallion players in their NFL gear. A gold sconce is placed between each image, giving the long walkway warmth.

"Here we are," Kaylee says.

I've been at the university for three years but have never had a reason to hobnob with the connected Kentucky Blue-bloods. Logan has set me up in a suite, and I'm not complaining. I hope he doesn't think I'm interested in him. One girl will hit the jackpot when he tires of his one-nighters.

An extremely handsome man in a suit, stroll toward us with a swagger and confidence. He's not huge but wears his suit well. His black hair is slicked back, and his grin grows as he reaches us. My eyes dart down and see a pretty little toddler with a dark complexion and honey brown hair.

He kisses Kaylee. "Hey sweetheart." He pauses, "I'm Nic Mancini, Logan's brother-in-law."

Another couple, also dressed in professional attire, join our circle as I'm saying, "Hi. I'm Adalee." The couple glances over their shoulder and then back to me.

"Nice to meet you."

I stare at the two men in front of me. They both look oddly familiar. "Did either of you play football or something? Where would I have seen you before?"

"I'm a sports announcer, working in the booth today," Nic says.

I feel my eyes go wide because recognition hits me in the face that he's on ESPN. I fangirl and say, "That's how I recognize you. I'm on the gymnastics team."

Then the taller one extends his hand as his clear brown eyes flicker. "Hi, I'm Archer Chatham. You may know my brother, Hagan."

Yes I do. I'm staring at an older version of Hagan. Yes, I'm salivating—they're both hot.

His hand is warm, and I shake it a little too long. How did I not spot they have the same I-can-get-lost-in-you golden brown eyes? I swallow hard. "Yes, sir. Is he here?"

"Yes, he's down with some of the baseball team. So, are you *good* friends with Logan?" He stresses the word good. A lady walks up beside him. "This is my wife, Megan."

We exchange pleasantries and I can see where Hagan gets everything—his looks, his smooth sophistication, and his self-assuredness. It's as if they seep sexy from their pores and like icing on a hot doughnut–a perfect glaze.

I don't understand why all of these beautiful people are here, so I ask Nic, "Are you calling the game? I bet that's hard since you're related to Logan."

He rubs his chin like he has to think about it. "It is, but today, I'm providing color, so it's not a big issue."

The gymnastics team isn't going to believe I met Nic Mancini and why hasn't Logan mentioned Nic is his brother-in-law. "So, you're the one that tells the stories and brings up their stats?"

He nods and all four of them look impressed by my knowledge of sports broadcasting.

As I grab sparkling water, I focus on Archer and Megan's interaction. They keep each other laughing and he can't keep his hands off her in a PG way.

Then Hagan pushes open the all-glass entrance with Josie in tow. Jealousy rumbles up my spine because Hagan brought her as his date.

Josie fills her plate while Hagan saddles up to the bar, his mouth moving, trailed by a smile and dimples. Why is he bringing a date? Does he not remember that kiss? The flirtations during dinner?

Why do I care? And why do I keep asking myself that same question, repeatedly? No athletes. Right? Maybe.

The bartender sets the drinks in front of Hagan, offering Josie the vodka cranberry. While he fills his plate, Josie scans the room, locating me. She stalks over to me in three leggy strides. What I would give for those long legs. No, if I had granddaddy long-legs, I wouldn't be a gymnast, so I'll keep my short, muscled ones.

"Adalee, didn't expect to see you here," she says, narrowing her eyes.

"I'm surprised as you are, but Logan invited me, so here I am," I say. We're acquaintances but not friends. Josie and I run in the same sports circle because one of her friends dated Bryce, another gymnast during my freshman year. But the past year, she's been hanging with the baseball crowd and since I was with Chaz, we'd run into each other.

She grabs the hem of her shirt and fiddles with it. "Oh."

Hagan's crosses the suite, eating filet medallions on one skewer and veggies on the other. His teeth sink into the meat as he slides it off and I swear to God my thighs squeeze. He exudes pure masculinity—the way his teeth skid slowly over the bamboo. My sight settles on his lips before I finally form words. "Did you two come together?"

Hagan's hand flies up to his mouth as he coughs. "No, she's Logan's date for the afterparty."

She grabs a skewer from Hagan's plate. "Yeah, Hagan brought me up to eat and then I'm headed back down. Logan didn't offer me a VIP ticket."

From her expression, she wants more than a one-time hit at an afterparty and she's worried that I'm Logan's long term goal. Does Logan like me, like me? I hope not. Did Hagan tell him about our kiss?

Now it was my turn to say, "Oh." I nod my head. "We're just friends."

Josie kisses Hagan on the cheek. "I know, Adalee. Hagan, thanks for the grilled chicken fingers. I didn't want junk food. Hopefully, Logan and I will see you at the party. Together, right?"

I start to say no, but Hagan interjects, "Yeah, we'll be there."

"It depends on how my leg feels."

Hagan walks Josie out. Before she leaves, he hugs her, and I'm confused. Logan invited her, but Hagan is being attentive and caring.

Logan also invited me. Has Josie slept with Logan before? He has a one-time rule and doesn't go out with someone twice. I make a mental note to ask him about it later.

Hagan's eyes meet mine from across the room. He's talking with Nic and Archer. God, if Archer is any indication, Hagan will be stealing hearts—forever. Hagan loads up another plate and walks my way, making my skin pebble.

"Have you eaten?" he asks as handing me a plate of the same food he had eaten. "No carbs."

I bite back a grin because I saw Archer make his wife a plate. Hagan pays attention to how he treats Megan, then does the same. It's thoughtful, but I can't help but push his buttons. "I ate at home."

"Jesus, why do you hate me?" he asks quietly with a slight dip of his head. "I've never been around someone that flip flops like you."

"I don't hate you."

I'm keeping a wall between us, knowing it will crumble faster than a sandcastle in a windstorm. I have one protector and that's me. It's the push and pull going on inside my brain. No man is trustworthy.

Seeing his jaw quiver and the lines on his tanned forehead, I regret goading him immediately.

He puts the plate down on the table beside us and turns away. I reach for his hand, pleading for him to look at me. "Hagan, I was joking." My body aching to continue looking into his eyes but he shakes his fingers loose and finds an outside seat in the front row.

Archer sits beside him, places his arm around Hagan's shoulders. They're clearly close and I wish for that. I must be in a daydream state because I'm startled when Megan says, "Their family bond is unwavering. Their sister became one of my best friends in college and I was always so jealous of their closeness, yet they always made me feel right at home. Do you have siblings?"

I sigh. "No, unfortunately not."

"That explains a lot," she says directly but pats my leg twice. "When one of them sets their sights on you, they'll do anything to take care of you. It's just how their family rolls."

A comfortable silence ensues when a man announces, "Taking our field for the first time in twelve years, the number three ranked, Ole Miss Rebels." Their fans yell and ours boo. That would never happen in gymnastics.

"Please get loud for the number six ranked team in the nation. Your Kentucky Staaaaallions."

The crowd, including everyone in the suite, is on their feet clapping and cheering. Logan's niece, Dani, yells, "Go Uncle Lolo." How cute is she?

White pom-poms wave throughout the stadium, to our fight song. The teams fill the sidelines. The Stallions are wearing their charcoal gray uniforms, white jerseys with their bright blue chrome helmets.

The public address announcer asks us to stand for Kentucky's anthem. I follow the words on the big screen with my hand over my heart. I'm captivated when I glance down at Hagan singing "My Old Kentucky Home."

But my heart swells when I see how excited he is when Logan and Pearse come out for the coin toss. Hagan's bouncing on his toes, screaming their names. "You've got this. Let's go, Lo!" We win the toss and elect to receive the ball first in the second half.

Kentucky fans are shouting "Defense." And on the second play of the game, Pearse intercepts the ball and runs it in for a touchdown. Hagan can't quit yelling, "That's my roomie!"

He really is a loving person underneath that cocky exterior. I need to apologize. Maybe I can show him I'm a loving person too, if it wasn't for all the pain. My mom. My dad. Even Chaz. The wall I've created around myself is made of bomb shelter material.

Chapter Sixteen

Hagan

We don't speak during the first half. I'm so fucking angry that I can't figure this girl out. I don't know how to be nicer or more helpful. Maybe I need to be a dick—girls like that these days. They want guys to treat them like meat and they keep coming back. Logan is the exception; he only hooks up with girls that also only want a one-night stand. Sure, some of them leach on but he reminds them of their agreement.

Realization hits me, I'm the girl and she's the dick. No. Not happening. Operation Dickface starts now. One, she deserves it. Two, I'm willing to try anything for a chance with this girl.

Crossing the room during halftime, I find Logan's parents who are here from California. I met them earlier in the year when they came to babysit for Logan's sister. His mom has Dani in her arms, and it looks like a damn Hallmark movie.

Other than playing baseball, creating a loving large family like my own is the goal. Of course, I need to find the right person first.

When Megan asks to hold the baby, Archer whispers to her, "I want us to have a baby, Beautiful." Often, I catch him calling her Beautiful like it's her name. I don't want to wait until I'm in my thirties for the love they have. I want it soon, very soon.

A smile creeps across my face as Adalee flashes through my mind; she's holding our child in a hospital bed. Lone brown strands stick to her forehead as she admires our baby's hand curled around my finger. *WTF?* At the same moment, a small hand lands on my bicep.

I know it's her.

"Hey, can we talk?"

"Nothing to say." I slip my phone out of my pocket and pretend to send a message. "Excuse me." I take the elevator down and enter the crowd of people where I can get some fucking air. Being around Adalee suffocates me. I can't breathe. So even being packed in like a can of sardines is better than being in a suite with Adalee right now.

I find some of the baseball guys and hang out until the third quarter starts.

Entering the suite, I grab some popcorn and scan the seating to see that the only place left is beside Adalee. How is my mission to be a dick going to work if I have to sit by her?

Reluctantly, I take the seat and she gives me a faint smile then asks, "Did you see Joe and Ginger?"

"Nope." I pop the P.

"Oh, she texted me and wanted to make sure we were coming to the party."

Nodding, I respond. "I might have other plans." I don't, but this isn't going as planned.

Stay on mission. Be a dick.

"I intended on heading to the party, but I guess I'll just go home after the game." Adalee's voice sounds small and far away as the word *game* is almost a whisper.

Fuck. I want to console her and not be an ass but I'm sticking with my plan. While throwing a few kernels into my mouth in a smug manner, I simply state, "It sucks for you that Logan's going with Josie."

Out of my peripheral vision, I see her slack-jawed, unable to think of a single smart-ass remark. I'm throwing her off her game. Would she have come if I invited her? I didn't want to take the chance, so I made a deal with Logan that in exchange for him extending the invitation, I'm on dish duty on his chore days plus a roommate only trivia night at The Bearded Otter.

Adalee bumps her shoulder into my arm. "May I have some popcorn?" Her smile drifts from my hand to my face and it's blinding. I try so hard to say, No, there's some inside the suite, but because this asshole thing comes unnaturally to me, I freeze. I'm mesmerized by her gorgeous face.

Holding the bag of popcorn in her direction, her fingers crawl until she finds the perfect pieces before nibbling each buttered kernel—one at a time. My dick jumps thinking about her frisky fingers holding me—taking her time with me.

 Shake that thought.

"Hey, isn't that your roommate Mac coming in?"

I must look like a deer in headlights because Mac's a freshman and never around. How would she know his number?

"Yep. Let's go, Mac."

The team lines up with forty-three seconds remaining in the game, and we're down four points. A field goal isn't an option. We need a touchdown to win. Mac settles in his stance on the edge closest to us. I watch his finger move back and forth in anticipation. The same thing I do when I'm stealing a base. The fans are on pins and needles. The stadium goes silent as we hear Logan's cadence, and the ball is snapped. Mac streaks down the sideline and Logan throws a fade to the corner of the end zone.

Get there, Mac. You've got this.

It seems like the ball hangs there forever. Mac has grown two inches since the summer. He jumps and the ball is perfectly thrown to his back shoulder. Mac's arms extend as he catches the ball for a touchdown. I jump, knocking over the popcorn by my feet. Adalee flies into my arms, hugging me in celebration.

Fuck the plan for a few seconds. This feels too good. The scent of her shampoo saturating my senses. Her body pressed against me but her breath on my neck is a jolt to my heart.

She looks so cute in her scarf and her brown hair spilling over her shoulders. Then our arms fall to our sides. I regain my composure, watching the festivities on the field. The fans swarm the field in victory, and I lose sight of my friends in a blanket of white dots.

Adalee shudders from the cold. She should have bundled up —that scarf isn't warm enough. We ended up in the outside seats for the rest of the game. I don't offer her my jacket and catch Archer's sharp gaze as he shakes his head in disappointment. He doesn't understand that I'm trying the opposite approach and it seems to be working.

We make our way inside with everyone chatting about the game and what it means for our football team. We're likely to move to at least the number three spot, possibly higher.

Adalee sticks by me, I guess because I'm the only one she knows. Archer says, "We're going to dinner with Nic and Kaylee. Do you need a ride to the party?"

"No, I drove."

"Hagan, do you mind if I ride with you?" Adalee asks.

The hushed tone of her voice and her heart shaped upper lip almost makes me cave, but I have to stand my ground. "Sorry, my car is full." It's obvious that Adalee wants a bad boy or a guy that treats her like dirt, being she dated Chaz.

I would exchange my left nut to take the hurt off of Adalee's face. Her eyes squeeze as her mouth opens slightly, not expecting that response. But before I can reverse course, she chokes out, "Oh, Logan's sister picked me up and…I'll find a ride." She leaves walking to the bathroom.

Archer's fingers fold tightly around my elbow and jerks me over to the side. Steam is coming out his ears, and I know why. He shoots a dagger through my eyes with his glare.

Just say it.

"I never thought there would be a day when I was ashamed of you." His voice booms in my ear. "But I am at this moment." He waits for an explanation and when it doesn't come, he continues. "Adalee is the girl you told me about?"

I nod.

"Then what in God's name are you doing?" he asks as he loosens his grip before completely letting go.

I cover my nose and mouth with my hands before slowly stroking my jaw. "She's so damn frustrating. With everyone else, she's sweet and lively. With me, she's snarky or runs hot and cold. Why can't she just run lukewarm?"

Archer's eyes glint in omnipotent way. He tries to hold in a smile off his smug face. We're the same height now, although he has thirty more pounds of muscle than me. We stare eye to eye, and it's like looking into a mirror. Even my twin doesn't look this much like me.

"Brother, you don't want a lukewarm woman—lukewarm doesn't heat you up in the winter. You want a woman that makes you want her so bad you need to rub one out in the middle of dinner. If she's hot and cold, then there are feelings that she's trying to reconcile. Be patient.

"Megan was dealing with so much damn stuff. I'm surprised that I ever truly broke through. Hopefully Adalee's walls aren't as high as Megan's but no matter what, it might take a while to deconstruct."

"Okay, enough. My cup is overflowing with brotherly love and advice."

Archer pulls me into a hug, and it feels good. My family is so close that it feels weird not having seen them for a month or more. He's right. She deserves my best, not my worst. If she likes guys that treat her like she's shit, then I'm not her guy anyway.

I walk over to Adalee and she's rocking back on her heels, twisting her bottom lip while biting it. "Hey, ride with me. My vehicle is suddenly empty."

She presses those fiery lips into a thin line, and my muscles tense as I prepare for an incoming bomb strike. "Thanks for changing your mind."

She's called off the strike, and maybe I should call off Operation Dickhead.

"But I called Bryce, and he's meeting me at gate nine."

Strike confirmed straight to the heart. And who the hell is Bryce?

The score: Hagan—1, Adalee—1

Who's going to break first?

Chapter Seventeen

Adalee

He looked like he was going to explode when I told him Bryce was picking me up. What was I supposed to do? Wait until everyone leaves the stadium and then call an Uber? I don't think that would have happened, but I'm not a charity case and there's no way I could hold my head high if Hagan's brother had to talk him into giving me a lift.

The Stallions recognized the men's gymnastics team for their charity work with a summer boy's camp. Since he was at the game, he was my only choice. Ginger didn't answer her phone. The stadium has 80,000 people trying to use the wi-fi and cellular so sometimes the calls fail.

Bryce and I stand in the front yard of the baseball house. Affection should be his middle name. His hands need to be in motion. He's fixing my scarf and touching my hair. He's had one beer and talking up a storm.

As I scan the yard for Hagan, Bryce grabs my hands, gripping them so hard it hurts. People don't realize how strong male gymnast's hands are. "Who are you looking for? Please tell me it's not the new baseball transfer."

"Actually, I am. We're partners on an engineering project."

His eyes roll so far back in his head that he may fall backward. He's handsome, but not when his eyes look like eggs. "Girl, it's your business, but haven't you had your fill of bad boys?"

"You just want him for yourself," I joke.

"Maybe, but Addy Bug, you deserve someone that has the same values, that won't pressure you." He wraps me in a hug.

I give him a faint smile. He's one of the few people that knows Chaz continually pressured me to be intimate. It's embarrassing that I'm twenty-one and haven't had sex. "Thanks."

Suddenly, the most sought after jocks on campus are standing in front of us.

"It looks like your plans didn't quite turn out." Logan laughs as his eyes dart between Hagan and me.

"Adalee, glad you made it here, safe," Hagan claims as he stuffs his hands in his denim pockets and rocks on his heels.

"Hey."

Logan scans the area before asking, "Who's your friend?"

Hagan answers for me. "Adalee's date." Then he peers down at mine and Bryce's hands clasped together. "I'm going inside." He spins, unable to get away quick enough. My heart drops because I like Hagan, more than I've let on. It's time to make this right.

I jerk my hands from Bryce. "This is my friend Bryce." I turn to Bryce. "Thanks for the ride. Are you staying?"

"Yeah, I told a friend I'd swing by. Have fun." Bryce wiggles his eyebrows.

Logan throws his arm around me as we walk up the driveway. I don't glance back.

"So, who's the friend?"

"Bryce is on the gymnastics team. I needed a ride here because—" He pats my shoulder in understanding.

Did Hagan tell him that I was awful today? "Did you know scouts were watching you?"

He grins, "Hagan's brother doesn't count. He came to see Hagan—I was an afterthought." He knows that's not true. "I have to say, I thought you would ride here with Hagan."

"Why?"

He looks down at me and ruffles my hair like I'm a toddler. The Adonis is a softie at heart. "You are clueless, Little A. His family bought the suite. Our families know each other because of Nic being a sportscaster."

"I don't understand."

"Hagan arranged it all. He asked me to invite you because he knew you wouldn't come if he did."

"Then why did your sister pick me up?"

He tilts his head, making this goofy face. "Same as above. If you aren't into him in the I-want to-jump-your-bones kind of way, then just friend zone him. Don't lie. He told me about the kiss, so don't act like you're not into him. Well, I guess he could be a terrible kisser, but Hagan thought it was... I think the word he used was special."

My jaw drops like a slow moving elevator. Logan puts his finger under my chin and closes my mouth. "He said it was special?" He nods. "I like him, but it scares me."

"Don't tell me, Little A. Tell him." He gets lost in thought then says, "I want to look at someone the way he looks at you."

This time, my jaw practically hit the floor. This is a huge revelation. It's one thing for Hagan to set today up, but it's surprising that Logan wants more than one or two nights with someone. "Does Josie fit that description?"

"Nah. We're superficial friends with benefits."

"What does that mean?"

"Just like with Hagan and some of the other athletic stand-outs, women want us for what may happen down the road, NFL, MLB, NBA." Nodding at his claim, I do understand. Some of Logan's teammates fist bump him on their way in. "You should find Hagan and apologize for whatever you did."

"Why do you think it was me? I asked for a ride, and he refused."

"Keep playing it through your head. I haven't seen Hagan mad or upset one time unless you had something to do with it." Logans smirks and his demeanor changes like a light switch. "I'm off to find Josie."

I'm about to return advice, but with his long stride, he's gone in three seconds. I'm left standing alone in what is fast becoming an out-of-control party.

I walk into the house and see my roomie lip locked with Joe. They're adorable. We had so much fun eating dinner together the other night. I need to find Hagan and talk. I'm not sure I have anything to apologize for—I'd eaten. I was joking around but maybe this was where Hagan drew the line. A person can only be rejected so many times before it's no longer worth their energy.

I was jealous of Josie and nervous that he wasn't feeling the same way I did regarding the special kiss, so I lashed out, obviously lacking in dating etiquette.

When I crossover into the next room, Hagan's shoulder is leaning against the wall talking to a blonde. They have blue cups in hand. She says something that makes him laugh and she beams, which makes her even prettier. They bump their cups together and she takes a large swallow while he takes only a sip.

His gaze drifts over the room like he senses my presence. His eyes lock on mine, expressionless, and my chest aches. I see the twitch of his lip from here before he motions for her to follow him.

Resentment travels through my body, leaving a torrid trail of nausea. I may be too late. Did Hagan decide I'm not worth it? We need to clear the air, but I can't exactly insert myself between them.

Some girls from my freshman dorm run into me giggling, asking what happened to my leg.

Hagan happened, not only in thoughts but now my mind and body are on the same page.

I give them the short version—and not the part where I was thinking of the transfer. They invite me to sit with them outside, so we fill our drinks, mine non-alcoholic. Joe knows I don't drink, so he keeps a stash of flavored carbonated waters under the sink. One of the girls, Kimber, is dating a guy on the team, so we file in around him and his friends.

Hagan sits in the circle around the firepit. Blondie, although not a Barbie, is on one side of him, talking to her friend. He glances my way, and as soon as our eyes meet, he drops his head and takes a drink. But even his short gaze heats me from the inside out. A simple glance tells me that I've hurt him, turning him into something he's not.

I catch up with my friends while waiting for my chance to speak with Hagan alone. When he stands up, rubbing his palms against his thighs, I'm hoping this is my chance, that his cute blonde sidekick doesn't follow him.

His voice sounds strained when he asks, "Adalee, you need my seat?"

God, he has the best manners. "No, thanks." He shakes his head and walks to the fence. His hand on the gate lock. "Hagan, wait."

My brace is not keeping me from talking to him tonight. He runs his hand through his hair and his other hand starts to put on a phantom cap. He must do it so often that it's a habit. There's no smile adorning his dark complexion. He pulls the wrought iron handle to the gate, but not before I make it to him and jerks the wooden fence. "Fuck."

Gripping his finger, blood pools out of his hand. He sucks the blood and I'm wishing it was my finger he was sucking on. This is how Hagan Chatham short circuits my brain. It concocts scenarios and feelings that are for mature audiences only.

After I quit fantasizing, I grab his wrist. "Hmm. This looks bad." Blood flows from his palm too. He either sliced it or that is one huge splinter. He rubs the blood on his pants and pulls out his phone for better lighting.

I reach out and he turns his body sideways. "I'm trying to help."

"Why do you want to help me? You hate me." He folds the hem of his shirt around his hand, then rips the T-shirt to use it as a bandage. His broad shoulders rise. It's a few seconds for them to fall as he expels a breath. His tone is harsh, and I know I put it there earlier today.

I erase what distance there is left between us. I don't know what I'm doing. My sixth sense takes over. Hopefully my instincts are better than my well thought out plans. "I... I," my voice is scratchy, and my instincts aren't telling my mouth what to say, so I say nothing. I stutter again, then lay my palms on his cheeks. I press up on one toe and lift my other leg off the ground, so I don't apply pressure, and I kiss the corner of Hagan Chatham's mouth.

His breath smells like peppermint and as I move to cover his full lips, there's no response. No kiss back. No hand running up my arm. Nothing, he just stands there stoic. I'm doing my best to show him my interest.

He steps back and my hands fall from his face. "Answer the question."

"I don't hate you. I'm scared of you. You make me feel things I've never felt before."

My heart constricts as I wait on him to speak. "Adalee, I'm a simple man. Most of the times we've been in each other's presence, you've copped an attitude for no apparent reason."

He turns to walk away, and I yank his arm—not the bleeding one. "Do you want to know why I pretended to hate you?"

He half-snorts. "Yeah, I would." He throws his arms up in frustration. This time he manages a couple of steps away but stops.

Clutching his arm, I admit, "It's all your fault I tore my ACL and may lose my scholarship."

Chapter Eighteen

Hagan

My fault? She has to be joking.

I freeze. What the hell is she talking about? I stop in place and take a breath the size of the Goodyear Blimp. I can't do this to myself. I've spent so much time thinking about her and trying to figure her out—showing her I'm a good guy—that my stomach is in knots. I wasn't this tore up when Julia slept with another guy.

I take a tentative step in her direction. My heartbeat is only two inches away from her face. My jaw is clenched tight, and my teeth are grinding. Frustration kicks me in the chest. A short sound somewhere between a sigh and a laugh escapes my mouth. "Why are you playing games? Damn, my girl-friend-radar must be broken. I thought you were different. You project yourself as polar opposite from most girls on campus, but yet you still play games."

Adalee sucks her lip inside her mouth, and then her tongue peeks out, swiping the seam of the prettiest lips. She stutters again. Her body trembles, either from nerves or the cool autumn weather. The baseball house sits in a little valley and the wind gets trapped.

"Just spill it—whatever you have to say," I snap.

She places her hands on my chest, and it burns like a hot iron. The gentle movement of her hands, back and forth a few inches, makes my dick stiffen. My chest expands, almost meeting her. This girl gives me wood no matter the mood or circumstance. Before we met, I got hard just seeing her from across the room.

"I left the party that night, and all I could think about was you," she stammers.

A familiar but stronger emotion snakes up my spine. She was thinking about me from the very first night we laid eyes on each other.

I'm stunned. Why is she touching me like this? She was thinking about me.

My left hand drifts slightly above her elbow. Softly I utter, "I want the truth." My stomach churns while my heart yearns for the simple truth. Hate and desire must be closely related because she's drawing me in, blazing a fire over my chest.

She licks her lips and my gaze is drawn to them once again. Then she looks up to me under her dark brown lashes, flashing me her almond eyes and shocks me when she says, "Because I wanted you to want me."

"I did." The short sentence strains against my throat as desire and confusion compete for control. The bridge of her nose pinches. "I do," I say as it rolls off my tongue, and I'm unaware that my hand has moved up her arm to the back of her neck.

"But I'm not a one-night kind of girl."

My fingers massage her hairline at the nape. I pulse in anticipation before the space between us disappears and her mouth parts. And when our lips touch, hers are so fucking soft. I treat them like my most cherished possession. Gently, I wrap her lips in mine, stopping and slightly sucking them into my mouth. She responds by sliding her hands around my back and pressing my shoulder blades, and there's no longer air between us.

"Good, because I'm not a one-night kind of guy." She shudders as my tongue caresses her lips before seeking entrance. "I've got you," I mumble into her mouth. I know I shouldn't be kissing her. She just blamed her injury on me, but she just let out the sweetest, most irresistible moan. We kiss until my dick is so hard, it's hard to mask.

Backing her up against the fence, without breaking contact, my hands roam over her tight, rounded ass. Adalee's breath hitches from my touch, and I pull away just far enough I can see her eyes.

She pleads, "Don't stop."

Stopping is not something me or my dick want but my brain wants an explanation about why she blames me for getting hurt. I back away, giving us a moment to think about what we're doing.

Pulling away, I say, "I have to—it's called self-preservation." I cannot be jerked around like Julia did to me. I can't do the on-again off-again relationship, not that we have a relationship, but her kissing me, then pulling away isn't something I can keep doing. I am the exact opposite of a playboy, not having a one-nighter in my repertoire.

I scan the lawn to see if anyone is sitting in the hammock at the edge of the yard. Yep, it's taken by a couple dry humping. At least I think they're clothed. There's no privacy here. My hand stings when I reach over her and unlock the gate.

"Are you leaving?" she asks.

"Yeah. Your place or mine?" I see the panic in her eyes and the tremble snaking up her spine. "We need privacy."

Suddenly, she fidgets with her scarf and folds her lips over her teeth. I need to understand what's going on inside that head of hers. It hits me that I said *your place or mine* like sex after a date.

"Adalee, I want to get to know you. I need to understand why you blame me for your injury. I'm not trying to get into your pants. I just want to talk in private."

I interlace my fingers with hers. They're so small compared to mine, but to me they fit perfectly like I'm the leather glove on her hand.

"Just tell me what you want." My fingers thread through my hair as I walk through the gate this time. "If you're ready to leave, I'll take you home, walk you to the door and stand outside until you tell me…" My voice strains and cracks. "How I caused you to tear your ACL. I wasn't even there."

Her brown eyes water as she stares at me and I swear there must be a magnet on my hand because once again, I'm holding onto her. She follows me to my Range Rover, and I give her a little lift inside.

She whispers, "Okay, let's go to my apartment."

The quick ride is quiet, and the unknown permeates my consciousness. Yes, I want to kiss her more and often. Thoughts of her are derailing my Fall Baseball Camp. Coach knows I'm distracted and off my game. So, when I turn into a parking spot in front of her apartment, I spill my guts.

"Adalee, I'm not good at living in the unknown. My parents have always been planners, schedulers. They had to be with five children spanning more than a decade. I can't live in chaos." She sneaks a peek at my profile before looking out the window. "Ever since I saw you, I've been twisted tighter than a rope. You've been hurt and so have I, but the difference is I'm moving forward and willing to trust the right person."

My fingers strum against the steering wheel, hoping she'll just start talking. I leave the truck running because the temperature keeps falling. The temperature difference between inside and outside fogs up the windows. Anyone that comes upon my vehicle might think something is going on. Pushing the defrost button, I ask, "Do you want to talk here or inside?"

She answers, "Here."

Her demeanor has changed from the girl saying *don't stop* to wanting to talk in the car instead of her warm apartment. Trust must be an issue for her. "Do you want the seat warmer on?"

She nods, so I press the switch on my steering wheel that activates her seat. I watch her picking at her royal blue nail polish, prompting me to ask, "Did you paint your nails blue for the game?"

I looked up her gymnastics pictures online. Her nails were painted in our school colors, sometimes embellished with a stallion or rhinestones. It's out of character because she doesn't wear much makeup, but she takes the time to get a manicure on game day.

She spreads her fingers, looking at them fondly. "Yeah," she says, pausing. "Why did you ask Logan to invite me to the suite instead of doing it yourself?"

Inspecting her jeans, I put my hand on her thigh. "The odds were better if my new bestie asked, since you're so fond of him." I tip my head and raise my brows. "Honestly, I knew if he invited you, you'd come. My goal was to get you there and then work my magic. I must be rusty."

Adalee half-laughs. "You still have it—don't worry."

SILENCE FALLS AND THE FLICKERING LIGHTS FROM passing cars illuminate the confined space. We've danced around the issue long enough.

Why is she confident in some situations? And in others, almost innocent? The moon glows, framing her face. The straight but delicate silhouette of her nose is gorgeous. It feels like we're in a movie that's too dark but it intensifies the scene.

"Talk. Tell me why you're blaming me for your ACL injury."

The windows begin to fog.

My voice strains. "How did I hurt you when you were thinking about me?" I ask, desperately trying to understand her logic. I reposition myself so I'm open to her, one knee bent in the seat with my back against the car door. "Adalee, please."

She pulls her feet onto the black leather and surrounds her knees with her arms, clasping her hands in front. I finger her brown hair, placing a tendril over her shoulder. She sighs. "I couldn't get you out of my mind. Your dimples, your smile, and your black waves... ugh, I love your hair." She rubs her palms together repeatedly. "It's your best asset."

That earns her a smile and another light touch against her arm. She shuts her eyes and inhales a short breath.

"I assure you—it's not even close to my best asset." There. My bravado is back—not the fake Operation Dickhead but my confidence. Julia ripped that from me for a while, but this summer, Talynn convinced me that I would find my girl at the right time.

Is it my time?

She peers down between my legs, eyeing the zipper over my semi. And I watch the twitch of her lips before folding them into each other.

"Anyway, I was walking home that night, already nursing a high ankle sprain, my heart was racing." I reach for her hand and rub my thumb over her smooth, dainty hands. "You were taking a huge portion of space in my mind without even meeting you. It was dark; I tripped, felt a pop and knew immediately it was a major injury. It hurt so fugging bad. My phone fell out and I had to crawl to find it to call an ambulance."

I gently pull her legs into my lap with her brace laying over my groin. She doesn't flinch, a good sign.

"I'm sorry that happened to you, but you don't truly blame me." It's more a question than a statement.

Adalee lays her hand on the back of mine letting it linger. "I was trying to convince myself that I wasn't attracted to you. Chaz expected more than I could give. It was my way of punishing myself for getting derailed. I've worked my whole life for gymnastics. I wanted to be the first in the SEC to perform this big difficult skill and hopefully win the conference all around, or at very least the vault title. One little glimpse of the Transfer, and I'm just as thirsty as every other girl on campus. It's not how I want to be known."

I lean forward to grab her other hand. "Let me relieve any doubts you may have about yourself. No other girl compares to you—on any campus—in my eyes."

A pink blush washes over her face. It's like a beautiful photograph a professional photographer would capture. Her back against the window with the moonlight outlining her hair, and a shadow creeping across her face but in the middle of it all—a light pink soft petal. My heart squeezes.

"I've been swooning with the rest of the female population...ugh."

"Adalee," I scoff. "If that was you swooning, you need to practice your swooning skills. I thought you were ready to string me up by my—"

She smacks my hand, interrupting. "When I heard you laugh that night, something happened. Add in your easy going swagger and that was all it took to get into my head—to turn my attention away from gymnastics."

Trying to lighten the mood, I hold my palms up, I notice the cotton material I have wrapped around my hand is stained with blood. "What can I say?" An exaggerated grin stretches across my face. It's so gigantic, my muscles hurt. Her comments make me feel fan-fucking-tastic. Too bad she doesn't seem to share my enthusiasm.

She attempts to slip her hands from mine, but I hold steady without gripping too hard. The last thing I want to do is squeeze overly hard and break a bone. I'd be in the doghouse for eternity.

"Hagan," she rasps.

My dick jumps at the sexy hum of her tone saying my name. "Adalee."

Her voice is barely above a whisper when she says, "I've never lost focus before, and I blamed you for the injury because you were all I could think about. And after Chaz, I vowed no more cocky athletes; that's why I've been fighting this." She looks down, tenting her nose and mouth, releasing a heavy sigh. "But that's not all. I've never been truly cared for, and I built a fence, insulating myself from more heartache. Gymnastics is the only love I've ever had in my life," she says with so much pain in her moonlit eyes.

I press the button on the door that scoots my seat back. The sound vibrates between us, and the heat whirs in the background. Then I grab her waist and gently set her on my lap, slipping her brace leg through the console opening. Our clothed bodies meet and press into each other.

"Do you wish I didn't exist?" I ask while roaming my hands over her thighs, and up her back.

"Hagan, I'm glad you exist."

Chapter Nineteen

Adalee

"Good to know." He shakes his head while his coy glance bounces off me.

I get lost in the confidence his smile holds. "This isn't me. I don't make out with random guys." I say with a ragged breath. The tension subsides when I let my thigh muscles relax. My center falls against his groin. The hard bulge feels so good against my pelvis. I thread my hands around his neck.

"I'm not random and you know it." His breath caresses my face. "We've danced around our connection long enough." His hands slowly crawl up my arms. His fingers twiddle with the fragments of thread on the edge of my scarf. The back of his hands are roped, and his knuckles turn white as he grips it tighter, pulling our faces together.

"I don't let my mind wander. I stay focused."

He laughs but it's broken. "I won't let you get distracted."

I utter softly, "I like you."

He moves his hands to my waist, gently moving me over his erection. The intensity of his gaze is sweltering, and my natural instincts kick in. I begin grinding myself against his hardness and the rough texture of jeans. And that zipper. Holy moly.

His tongue darts out, sweeping over his lips. He gives me one last look for consent, and then he claims me. This kiss isn't hesitant—it's dominant. His pulse races. I can feel his heartbeat in the cushion of his lips. Then he mumbles, "I like," he pauses as his tongue explores the depths of my mouth. "You."

My heart rattles against my rib cage. My body presses into him and pleasure snakes down to my core. He kisses me and as we grind. My panties are soaked. Hagan's thumb rubs circles over my jeans while digging his fingers into the slope of my hips.

Desire bursts from my body as my hips roll faster. His kiss drives deeper, taking everything I have. I've never been kissed like this. When we kissed the first time, it was the best, but now this has replaced it. How can he keep getting better?

The kiss ends way too soon as my orgasm hits without any skin to skin contact. I moan, "Oh dear God."

My lids finally open to his sexy smile and his hoarse voice. "Not God, but the next best thing."

Embarrassment heats my face, but he cups my cheek then lands a peck to my swollen lips.

"Come on, let me walk you to your door."

He helps me off his lap and holds his finger up for me to wait. He comes around the Rover with his finger tracing his own lips.

Did he love it as much as I did? Should I invite him inside?

Panic climbs from the pit of my stomach. What do I do now? Butterflies flap their wings taking over my body. He opens the door giving me one hand to climb out. I don't see many guys being gentlemanly these days. His brother was the same way with his wife. From what I've seen he has a good family. A good support system. Sadness creeps into my thoughts before Hagan breaks me free as we reach my apartment.

"I better get home." But then he adds, "We have a lot to think about."

Hagan's hands hover over my hair, bouncing them against the long strands sticking straight up from static electricity. He pulls me into a hug, snorting when my hairs tickle his nose.

I press my hands against his hard chest and all I can think about is what lies beneath his clothing. Of course, I've seen him without a shirt for a moment at his house that night, but I mean lower. I'm wondering what is lower. What's underneath that zipper? Suddenly my confidence soars. "What's there to think about?" I ask as I raise my eyebrow.

"That kiss—Adalee. Damn, I'll be thinking about that in the shower tonight."

His smile gleams like moonlight shimmering on the water. Hagan walks backward two steps before turning around. I swear I hear him mumble, "Maybe forever."

Sleep eludes me because Ginger and Joe return home from the party, and they're going at it like rabbits. They're in the den having sex. How do I know that? Because our cheap Ikea couch is scooting across the faux hardwood floor. Instead of being upset, I'm happy for them. I hope to have a relationship like that with Hagan. Giving myself completely to someone never felt right.

I've been so worried that Hagan is like every other cocky athlete on campus that I didn't see what was right in front of me. I lie back on my bed, grabbing my pink fuzzy pillow and pulling it into my chest. Do I dare dream?

I close my eyes and my mind roams to Hagan in the shower—thinking about me. My core clenches. A need so powerful consumes me. I decide to take matters into my own hands. My fingers slip inside my panties, rubbing in circles...but it's not enough.

Maybe if I could hear his voice?

I can't get there. Frustrated, I stop and slam my hand against the floral sheets. I look at my phone on the white nightstand. Snatching it, I look up pics from his social media posts. I see a picture from Archer and Megan's wedding. They have enough money to get married anywhere, and they choose a baseball field.

I want a love like that. One that is so consuming that nothing else matters as long as we're together. The kiss Hagan and I shared tonight felt that way.

There's a post from the summer with another guy and two girls at the beach. I wonder who they are. Why aren't they tagged? Does he know how social media works?

One thing is clear, Hagan is cut from stone. Dark delicious stone. Adorned with unusual golden brown eyes, and a smile that could light up New York City and dimples that frame it.

Hagan's name lights up on my phone. Think of the devil, and I mean that in the dreamiest way. It's two in the morning. "Hey."

"Did I wake you?"

"No." Feeling brave, I hit the video call option. It fades and then his face appears with a broad, ear-splitting grin on his face. As if he recognizes how that kiss affected me and turned into me dry humping him in the parking lot when there was a perfectly warm and spacious apartment twenty feet away.

"Miss me already?" he asks, then winks at me.

The answer is obvious. I'm up at two in the morning and needed more than just a voice. I need him to fill as many senses as possible. I'll have to settle for just hearing and seeing. "Yes," I say before biting my lip looking away from the camera.

He makes me feel powerful, waiting on me to steer our conversation. The jumbled bundle of nerves in my core throbs just hearing his scratchy, *I'm in bed* voice. Tonight, I'm burning up wanting more from him and with him. Feeling gutsy, I ask, "How was your shower?"

He visibly gasps and his mouth hangs open for a second before he regains his swagger.

"Hot." He licks those raspberry lips. "Wet."

His arm is bent with his hand behind his head and cocksure of what his dirty mouth is doing to me. I grab my nipple through the thin camisole I'm wearing. Rubbing. Oh jeez. What am I doing?

"Painful... Hard."

My legs clamp together and my knees. I can't satisfy this urge. It's so strong as his voice milks me for more.

"You played a starring role in my head. I came so hard."

Frantically I pinch and pull my drawn-up buds. They're small but sensitive.

Little puffs of air escape my lips as I desperately attempt to open my eyes.

"I might come again just watching half of your face flush and listening to those moans, pleading for me not to stop."

I'm fueled up on dirty talk and can't hold my arm up and touch myself at the same time, so the phone drops to my side.

"Pick the phone up, Adalee. The first time I see your body isn't going to be on a video call. Show me your face and lay on your side. Prop the phone against the headboard. Slide your eager, blue painted fingers across your abdomen and find the spot that makes you want to move faster."

Nothing computes except his commands.

"You're soaked thinking about what I'm going to do with you. Slow down. Just move to the sound of my voice."

"Oh, Hag—Hagan." I pant over and over, finally falling against the pillow.

"That's my good girl."

His words spin in my head. He called me his girl. Am I his? Are we dating? If not, then this is embarrassing. What am I talking about? I masturbated while Hagan listened.

"I've never seen or heard anything sexier. Adalee, look at me. You're beautiful, especially when you're coming with my name on your lips."

Slowly, I look into the phone and he's on his side with his head on his palm. A sated and satisfied grin plastered across his face.

"I can't believe I did that. I can't look at you," I say. "This isn't me."

"You keep saying that, but I think it is. Maybe you just needed the right man, and I'm that man, Adalee." He lets out a whispering hum. "I wish I was with you. To reassure you of how gorgeous and sexy you are. Unfortunately, I need to take another shower." His dimples deepen and we burst out laughing. I cover my face before he says, "Now we're even."

Does he mean we both performed a little self-pleasure? I ask, "Even—how?"

"Well, tonight I hyper-*sextended* my throwing arm in the shower. Coach is going to ask me how I injured myself."

"Don't you dare, Hagan Chatham." I chide.

The easy back and forth banter between us comes naturally —like we've known each other all our lives.

"Don't worry—a gentleman doesn't masturbate and tell." He throws his head back amused with himself. "When can I see you again?"

Hagan is one of those few people that puts me at ease without trying. Now that I'm a sex kitten, I tease him. "Soon, if you're lucky. Goodnight."

Chapter Twenty

Hagan

THE BALL SAILS OVER THE RIGHT FIELD FENCE. COACH is making me work on batting left-handed, and it's my job to get on base as the lead-off batter. Left-handed batters have the advantage of being at least one step closer to first base.

In twenty pitches, I hit twelve home runs. Confidence is an extra skill. When you have it, your swing is smoother, and your body works in synchronicity. It's fall camp and we're all vying for positions in the starting lineup. Chaz is in centerfield, and I didn't hit a single one to him. It either went over the fence or to Vasques in right field.

Joe states from his crouched catcher's position, "I hear you finally landed Adalee."

The smile that spreads across my face could light up this field at night. Talk about unexpected—last night was incredible. Her pinkened face. The way she moved her hips over my jeans. I felt like I was in high school again with one difference. I care about Adalee.

In high school it was all about getting yourself off. I learned with Julia, even though I hate to think about her in the same sentence as Adalee, that it's about pleasing your partner. Obviously, I did a poor job at keeping Julia happy or she wouldn't have slept with another guy.

"What the hell are you doing, Chatham?" Coach shouts from the dugout.

I didn't see the ball coming. I'm frozen in my batting stance when the ball hit Danke's catcher's mitt. "Sorry, Coach."

He spits and turns his back to me, scraping the red dirt with his cleat. Five more pitches and five more solid hits and then it's time to change batters. Joe and I walk toward the dugout together so I can unload the helmet and retrieve my glove and so Joe can take his catcher's gear off.

"Adalee told Ginger that you two made out. Her exact words were 'Adalee was swooning.'" Joe laughs.

I chuckle too thinking about how bad she is at swooning. "I'm not sure she was swooning. Aren't girls supposed to bat their eyelashes and have big doe eyes?"

"Brother, she's not like most girls. She doesn't party or date much other than ass-wipe."

We both down a bottle of sports drink. We ran three miles before hitting practice, and we'll follow it up with a scrimmage. Joe grabs his bat and puts it on his shoulders rotating his torso from side to side, stretching.

I lean against the blue painted concrete wall. "That's what has drawn me to her. I can't anticipate what she's going to do or say. When we were in the suite, I was ready to give up."

"She's not worth it, Transfer," Chaz heckles. "I was in there for months and believe me, she's fruitless. She should be called the Ice Queen."

I push off the aluminum bench, charging him. "You motherfucker." The whole time he's laughing like the freaking penguin from *Batman*. It's maniacal. I push him to the ground and rare back to swing as Joe jerks me off the ground.

Coach's eyes dart between us. "Chatham, shower and see me in my office in thirty minutes."

"But—"

He gives me an icy glare, and I shut my mouth. I gather my gear and sling my backpack over my shoulder. I should have ripped him apart. Everyone likes Adalee. What happened between them?

I tap out a message to Adalee.

Me: *We need to talk.*

She still hasn't answered after I've showered and changed. I knock on Coach's door, and I hear a gruff voice. "Come in."

Coach's office is filled with photos of him playing for the Cobras. Then accolades from his coaching career. He has a baseball in his hand and tosses it back and forth between them...left to right.

The motion would have been hypnotic if my mouth wasn't as dry as cotton. Coach took a chance on me and I'm causing problems on the team. My hands sweat as I rub them against my royal blue baseball pants.

Just say something, Coach. Put me in my place.

"Hagan. I'm in a precarious position. I can't have my players fighting. He did nothing and you pounced on him like a lion."

"Sorry, sir. But he was talking about my girlfriend." Did *girlfriend* just come out of my mouth?

Hell, am I fighting over someone that *isn't* my girlfriend?

Coach puts his elbows on the desk, clasping his hands together. Then he straightens his fingers and rubs then up and down before pushing them together in a triangle. I've seen my dad and Archer do this. It's a power move—letting me know he's in charge.

I notice his baseball cap is on the desk. Mine covers my wet hair, so I take it off in respect of being in his office and hold it in one hand, tapping it on my knee.

Finally, he speaks. "Coaching fucking college turns you into a therapist." A grin threatens as the corner of his lips trend upward. "My understanding is that your girl is Chaz's ex-girlfriend. Are there not enough beautiful girls on this campus? You just had to pick the same one?"

He has a point. "Coach, I didn't pick her. It's been months since they dated. We're working on a class project together and Joe dates her roommate."

"Ginger. Yes, he's mentioned her."

"He's in love." I laugh because he's all about her. Ninety percent of our conversations have been about Ginger in the last couple of months.

"Are you?" he asks.

I don't know how to answer his question. I loved Julia but this is different, stronger, almost like I require her to breathe.

"Surely you don't threaten to beat up your teammates over a girl you don't love?"

I roll my lips in and process his words. "I'll apologize to you and the team but not to him. He doesn't deserve an apology."

He mulls it over and presses his fingers to his temples. "Listen, I know he's a less than stellar teammate, but he does have a few guys that will back him up. This better not split our team. You have the ability to go the majors. Is that your goal?"

"Sure." People expect you to want to go professional when you play a sport, and I did when I was eighteen and nineteen years old. But the percentages aren't on a collegiate player's side. I have no idea if that's what I want because I have firsthand knowledge of how much time players spend away from their families. I used to sit and draw buildings wherever we were—stadiums, skyscrapers, the drug store and I'm loving my structural engineering class.

"If you don't love her, don't let a girl and her ex stand in your way. You can't play if you're suspended from the team." He pauses and it seems like he's staring into my soul. "If you do, then keep going to bat for her."

We sit in silence as I watch the digital clock on the wall change minute after minute. Is he done? Does he want me to figure out right now if I love her?

Adalee pushes my buttons, and it makes me want her more, but is that love? I loved Julia. I said I did anyway. I was torn up when she cheated but was it love or wounded pride? Probably both.

Coach watches me with a slight grin on his face until he clears his throat. "I have to punish you. Chaz didn't retaliate so he's in the clear, but I'll keep a close eye on him. Chatham, you're going to be on clean up duty for team meals this week. You're in luck, there's only two this week."

"Yes, sir. Is that all?"

He stands and extends his hand. "Yeah. I've done a little homework and found out she's a gymnast here. That's going to be tough finding time being together in a couple of months."

I shake his hand. "One day at a time, Coach. I promise it won't interfere with baseball again."

"Alright, get out of here. And Chatham, good job hitting the ball today," Coach says as he replaces his hat on his head.

As soon as I exit his office, I check my phone for messages. Zero messages. Did I just get in trouble over a girl that can't make up her mind?

Last night, I've never felt so at peace, like I could watch her facial expressions forever. Not just when she's pleasuring herself but God that was hot. And I didn't see any of it. Why did I say don't show me? That sounds like I'm a goody two shoes.

When I get to the house, I make an early dinner while Joe and I wait for our roommates to get home from their film session. Simple spaghetti and meatballs. My mom taught me to make a few dinners so that I wouldn't eat out all of the time. I try to eat healthy and give myself a couple meals a week so I can have fried food and not feel guilty about it. I love the local chicken place and they have a place on campus.

"So what did Coach say?" Joe asks.

"Nothing much. Just gave me some things to think about. I'm on clean up at team meals," I say, noticing how my chest tightens up. I open up the fridge and Adalee's face appears in my mind. It reminds me of when I blocked her in and how passion swelled in her chest and eyes.

"Ginger said Adalee was absolutely giddy this morning. Said she's never seen her like this, not even with Chaz."

"What do you mean *not* even with Chaz? Is he a better catch than me?" I wink at Joe. "Grab the napkins."

I reach in the bamboo cabinets, pulling out five plates. I only confirmed to Joe what Ginger already told him. Obviously not telling him that she did a little self-care herself on our video call.

He squeezes my shoulder. "It's going to be fun double dating and hanging out."

"It is." I can't remember being this happy since I was twelve years old and hit a home run in the Little League World Series.

Chapter Twenty-One

Adalee

GINGER DEMANDS WE GO TO THE MALL WHILE HAGAN and Joe are at practice. She's absolutely giddy that we'll be double dating all the time. Doubt creeps into my thoughts—are Hagan and I—a couple?

I spend all of my disposable income on a new outfit: a long sleeve ivory colored dress and a pair of black ankle booties. I take off the black clunky brace so I can try them on. Ginger finds me a pair of gold chandelier earrings in a different store which draws attention to my face.

I plop down in a round chrome chair with absolutely no padding while Ginger seeks out the perfect lipstick in Sephora. "Who knew shopping was exhausting? It's like we've been training for hours."

Three times, I tell her I love the color but three times, she puts it back in place. She's insistent on having lips that don't fight her hair color. After she finally decides on one, we check out and head to eat.

My legs ache from overuse which never happened until I suffered two injuries back to back. The high ankle sprain and the dreaded *falling for the transfer* ACL tear.

Umm. Where's my usual disdain for Hagan when I think about that night?

They're forgotten because his kisses are explosive. He makes my insides turn to mush. Last night was epic for me, and seeing the lust in his eyes spurred me across the finish line.

I hope he isn't turned off by it—and I really hope he doesn't think I'm just another girl trying to get into his pants. My cobb salad arrives, and I reach in my purse to see if Hagan has messaged me and realize my phone is missing. I check my pants and coat pocket. Empty. "Do you have my phone?"

"Oh, no. Do you think you left it in the dressing room?" Ginger asks.

Shrugging my shoulders, I ask, "Can you call the store for me and ask them to check? I can't walk anymore."

She calls and the operator transfers the call to the correct department. When no one answers, she switches her to lost and found. They take her name and number and promise to search the area and dressing rooms for my phone.

The food tastes so good I could eat two of these salads. I should have added grilled chicken for the extra protein but that was extra money I do not have now that I splurged on a new outfit.

"I still can't believe you let your guard down. Hagan is so fun to be around. Joe just clicked with him from the beginning. We need to plan our double dates." Ginger claps her hands four or five times then jumps out of her seat to hug me.

I lean my head into her side, and though I'm hopeful, Hagan hasn't defined our relationship. It's too early to be thinking of a future. "Slow down Ging. He didn't ask for my hand in marriage."

As soon as the word rolls off my tongue, images of Hagan with his arms around me on the beach flash in my brain. We're both wearing white gauzy material. His dark hair is perfectly messy and wears the sleeves of his shirt rolled up, showing off those amazing forearms.

She gets a text from Joe. Ginger covers her mouth while reading it then hands the phone to me.

"Hagan's been called into the Coach's office for fighting with Chaz. I'll call you later, Red."

"He's fighting over you, Addy Bug."

My whole face scrunches. Hagan shouldn't waste his energy on Chaz. Is Hagan having second thoughts about me? Maybe I'm the one not worth it.

When we get back to the apartment, I put away my new outfit and sit on the bed. I wonder if Hagan's tried to reach me, wishing I had my phone. Hagan can easily get a message to me through Joe and Ginger, but then again I could do the same.

One of us has to make a move. Hagan took all the risks in getting Logan to invite me to the ballgame. What can I do to prove I'm interested and not going to back off?

I doze off, and when I wake, most of the light from outside is now gone. The slats of my blinds showing shadows of tree branches. I put on my pajamas, deciding to sleep the night away. But first, I need to go to the kitchen for a bedtime snack and a glass of water.

As I open the door, I hear low rumblings and laughter coming from down the hall. Ginger and Joe are probably watching television. When I reach the living area, Hagan's sitting in the bean bag. His dimples are deep with his hands clasped behind his head as he laughs watching a comedy special.

"Addy, look who came to see you." Ginger's grin stretches from coast to coast.

Hagan slowly lowers his hands and scans my body, clearly thinking about last night. I feel exposed like I'm going through an infrared scanner at the airport. The smile drops from his perfectly formed lips as he licks them. His stare makes me feel like the most beautiful girl in the world.

I look down at myself and realize that my pajamas aren't sexy at all. No skimpy shorts and tank.

Nope. I have on fluffy, thick lounge pants that have dogs all over them and a long sleeve thermal tank and of course, I took off my bra. I spin on my feet to leave. "I'm just going to get dressed."

Hagan jumps over the chair between the bean bag and me. "No, I'll leave. Ginger said you were wiped." His hand grazes my arm and suddenly I feel the need to shed my clothes. "I love your pants."

He takes my fingers in his—not quite a hand hold—just fingertips. He leads me to the kitchen where he sits on the bar stool and pulls me into him.

I stretch my neck and raise my eyebrows. Is he serious? In the interest of keeping a level playing field, I say, "I like yours too."

His head drops looking at his jeans which are just jeans. Nothing special. Just blue jeans with a worn look. But he brings me between his legs, letting his arms skate around my waist. Hagan's touch lights me up. "I tried calling you. I was beginning to think you were ghosting me. Maybe our make out session didn't live up to your standards."

A laugh of disbelief escapes my throat. "My standards? You're the one with all the campus hotties."

"I've told you not to believe everything you hear. But yes, your standards." He nips at my nose. "I want to surpass every standard you have. I don't want there to be one reason why you won't go out with me, Adalee."

The tone of his voice is caring but authoritative at the same time. He's confident in what he wants and right now it's me. His hands splay across my back, holding me in place while taking my lips in his. It's a kiss that says, "Let's explore this."

Ginger's phone rings, breaking the spell. I forgot she and Joe were even here and that I'm sporting my fuzzy pjs.

"Hey, it's the department store. They found your phone. When do you want to pick it up?"

Before I can answer, Hagan says, "I'll take her to get it."

"No, it's late."

"Adalee it's eight thirty," Hagan says, grinning as he shakes his head.

Chapter Twenty-Two

Hagan

Monday morning hangovers are real. And no, I didn't drink last night, instead Adalee and I drove to the store to retrieve her phone. Then we went back to her apartment and watched a movie with Joe and Ginger.

I touched her the entire night. Either my hand was on her leg or holding her hand throughout the movie. Except when she dragged me into the kitchen to make popcorn. She drizzled chocolate over it, and tossed it, spreading it evenly throughout the bowl. Then she popped a piece into her mouth. I watched her chew, and that's the moment I fell for her.

Patiently waiting for her to swallow, I cupped her face with both hands, sealing our lips together. Her mouth was sweet and salty, smooth and warm from the hot chocolate. Our mouths moved like we had been kissing forever.

We were gone long enough that Ginger yelled, "What are you doing in there? We need food."

Adalee and I pulled apart with grins a mile wide pasted on our faces.

It was the best Sunday of my life—Sundays will forever be my favorite day.

So now, I'm hung over on love.

Concentration evades me as I shave, nicking my jaw. I roll up a tissue and apply pressure, but the cut keeps bleeding. Half the time I'm getting dressed, I don't remember pulling out my athletic pants or sweatshirt. I'm rooted in memories from yesterday.

Finally, I grab my backpack and hustle down the stairs. I tend to get anxious if I run late so I snag a protein bar from the drawer and a shake from the fridge. The Rover's windows are frosted over which is going to take a few minutes to defrost.

My phone buzzes inside my sweatshirt pocket. When I remove it, I see Adalee's name on the screen. Behind her name is black, which reminds me to take a photo of her. But should I make her my screensaver if we aren't officially a couple?

"Hey, gorgeous," I say and can almost feel the blush on her face by the way she stalls before answering.

"Hi, I can't be in class today. Can you take notes for me?"

My stomach sinks as I wonder if she isn't sure about dating me. If this is moving faster than she's comfortable. "I'm driving because I was running late. I'll swing by and pick you up."

"I have a doctor's appointment with the surgeon. He's doing more tests to make sure I'm ready to get the brace off. My dad doesn't...." Her voice trails off. There's definitely a story and sadness behind her words.

"I'll skip class and go with you."

She lets out a deep sigh. I know how much athletes hate talking about their injuries, much less sharing it firsthand with the doctor. I'm overstepping into a private part of her life, but damn I want to share it all with her. Then she asks, "Are you sure you wouldn't mind?"

There's a trace of vulnerability in her voice so I don't hesitate. "Be there in five."

Adalee's bouncing her knee. I place my hand on her thigh, hoping to have a calming effect.

The waiting room consists of blue uncomfortable chairs, bad lighting, and fake plants.

"They should have live plants here. The air wouldn't feel so stale," I say in earnest.

I'm rewarded with a hiccup of a laugh. "True. Maybe I could breathe better."

"Don't be scared. I've got you. Good news or bad."

It's been over two months since the night she fell, thinking about me. I have to admit it makes me grin—me being on her mind. It's hard to believe I first laid eyes on her that long ago. There was an underlying current between us, even then.

Good things come to those who wait. I say it's a combination of knowing when opportunity arises and taking advantage. When we were paired together for the engineering project, it was the beginning of us.

"Don't forget you're the reason I'm here."

"Aw, you love me." As soon as it comes out my mouth, I wish I could stuff it back inside. Adalee's doe eyes are not swooning, she looks like a deer in headlights.

Luckily, the nurse calls her name, and she looks to me, gesturing for me to follow. My heart swells. She wants me by her side to hear the news. To be her rock. But why isn't her family here? Archer, my parents and certainly Harper would be here with me. My other brother, Reggie, and sister, Sarah Jane, would be on the phone.

Even though I've fallen for this gorgeous woman, I haven't scratched the surface yet. We need to have long walks and talks.

The doctor comes into the room, takes off her brace and does a variety of tests. He's probably mid-forties and has an athletic build. As they talk, he tells her to be glad she didn't tear her ACL in his day. "I played basketball at Louisville when I tore mine, twenty years ago."

"We forgive you for wearing red," she retorts with a smile on her face. The doctor laughs at the rivalry between the two universities.

"Okay, Adalee, we're going to do an MRI. Your *friend* will have to go back to the waiting area."

I like how he stressed the word friend as if he can tell we're more. I stand while reaching for her hand. "I'll be here when you get out." She nods and I squeeze her hand twice.

An hour and a half later, the nurse says I can come back in. When the doctor gives us good news, that she can lose the brace except during extreme activity, Adalee wraps her arms around me in relief.

Us?

She suggests we go out for a celebratory lunch and surprises me with a Mediterranean restaurant. It's a little off campus but still close by. It's in a quaint little shopping center surrounded by smaller houses made of stone with well-manicured lawns. It reminds me of neighborhoods in the suburbs of Chicago.

She eases out of my Rover placing her weight on her other leg. I attempt to help, but she waves me off. I stand close, just in case.

The restaurant is an oasis inside with painted murals on three of the walls, a scene depicting the place where the sea and sand meet.

As the waitress hands us menus, Adalee says, "Do you trust me?"

I nod and she gives the waitress our order. "I like a woman who knows what she wants." I'm giving her my dimples because she's genuine and a little mysterious.

Her face reddens at my comment. "Did you contact your professors and let them know you were missing class."

"Yeah, I told them I was taking my girl... you...to the doctor. Our professor emailed back and said he understood and hopes you receive the *all clear*. I think he was worried about you being at the job site."

A mouthwatering aroma distracts me as the waiter lays a family style dish of chicken shawarma, falafel, and a cucumber tomato salad in front of us. In the center is hummus with naan bread on the side. Adalee makes little tacos with her bread, scooping up a little of each thing.

"My grandparents on my mom's side were born in Greece." Her obvious love for Mediterranean food is evident in the way she smiles at it before she takes a bite and hums afterward.

She doesn't say more about her parents. But we take turns talking about life. Not wanting to force anything, I just ask casual questions as they seem relevant. Her favorite vegetable is peppers. So a heated discussion ensues as to whether they are actually vegetables or if they're a fruit. We finally decide that it doesn't matter since they're healthy regardless.

We finish eating and on the way to her apartment, I'm surprised when she admits she loves baseball. "When I was little my parents would take me to Braves games. Ever since, baseball players are my Achilles heel. I wish they weren't."

My bubble bursts, choking down my disappointment. She continues. "I've always liked those tight white pants players wear. So, when Chaz asked me out, I was giddy. It wasn't because I was pining over him. I just couldn't believe someone like him wanted to go out with someone like me."

I cut in. "Someone like you? Do you *not* know how hot you are?" I flash her my right dimple because every time I do, she takes a short breath. It's the one time when I can see and hear the effect I have on her.

Adalee slaps my leg, and I take the opportunity to hold her hand. The conversation stalls. I'm not sure how much I want to hear about her dating Chaz. It makes me sick to my stomach to entertain any thoughts of her with another guy. Did they have sex? Did she ever pleasure herself with him on the phone? God, I'm making myself ill.

When we reach her door, we hear the boisterous laughs of Joe and Ginger. Before she opens the door, she turns to me and says, "Thanks for defending me against him. Just so you know, Chaz doesn't take up any room in my head or my heart."

I lean down and tilt her chin up. "I'll make sure to redeem baseball players in your eyes."

Chapter Twenty-Three

Adalee

THE TEAM CHEERS ME ON WHEN I RETURN TO THE gymnastics center—well, everyone except for Shannon. The doctor gave the trainer explicit instructions on what I can do this week. Since the doctor is also part of the university, he knows it's important for me to get back on the mat, but not at my expense. The fact he's had the same injury makes me feel like I'm in good hands.

No tumbling. No vaulting. But it feels good to have two bare legs on display. The trainer says I can do uneven bars as long as a coach is spotting me. "Adalee, only skills you've mastered until you get back into the swing of things. No pun intended."

"Yeah, right."

My coach says, "Let's go to the bars. I'll spot you but at least you can get in some practice," she says. "I know how much you love the bars."

Bars are my least favorite, but no one can wipe the cheesy grin off my face. I'm back on the mat.

I take that back. Shannon and I are paired together on the bars with Coach. I go through the list of strength conditioning exercises watching her perform flawlessly. I want to be happy for her, but something curls inside my gut.

When it's my turn, the coach lifts me at the waist to the low bar. Usually, I would springboard onto it, but we don't want any forces pushing on my knee. Working through a scaled down version of my bar routine feels good. An athlete is used to a daily routine, so when your schedule is thrown into chaos, it's discomforting, and you feel out of sorts. But at this moment, swinging up to the high bar, my mind calms and my body surges over the bar in complete control.

Control—that's what's been missing.

I cast to a handstand and hold it longer than I ever have. My arms begin to shake and I hear the coach say, "Giant." My legs, torso and head stay in a perfect line, fully extended, letting my own weight propel me three hundred sixty degrees. This time, I do a reverse grip on the bar and then let my body swing like a pendulum until my movement stalls, and I hang until the coach's hands support my weight and bring me to the ground.

"Can I go again?" I ask, as a smile spreads across my face.

Coach says, "Sure, let's put together a sequence that doesn't require your feet touching the bar for now."

I nod with excitement. Gymnastics keeps me centered, gives me a sense of purpose, and for the first time in months I feel like myself again. I've been a bear to live with since summer —first the high ankle sprain and then this ACL injury. There's a disconnect with not being able to keep my routine. Vault and Floor are my two favorite apparatuses, and not being able to practice what I excel at is depressing. But thoughts of Hagan have me flying high.

Shannon shouts, "Great job, Addy Bug." She's chastising me, but to the coaches it appears she's being supportive.

The coach talks about what she wants me to do, and I practice for a half-hour doing a simple sequence. Typically, people would call me a power gymnast. I like the pounding of my feet on the floor during a tumbling pass and the speed and force of the run toward the vault. The uneven bars are different. You have to be strong but graceful.

When I enter the locker room after practice, I overhear Shannon telling Darrah how she's been hooking up with Chaz since the beginning of the summer—which means, according to her timeline, he definitely cheated on me. "Chaz says Adalee stripped bare and tied a bow around herself for his birthday. But he said I rocked his world later that night. I'm better than her at everything."

Ginger fires back, "Get over yourself. Adalee rarely even talked about him. And if she bared herself for him like that, she would have told me. Adalee is the sensible one. She doesn't think of romantic interludes, except maybe with Hagan." The room quiets at the mention of his name.

"You should see them. They're absolutely adorable. I bet they win couple of the year at The Stallion Awards."

I want to see Shannon's face so I turn the corner in the middle of Shannon saying, "There's no way he would be with Adalee."

Opening my locker, I take out my phone.

Hagan: *You and Ginger come to my house after practice. Joe's with me.*

I hold up my phone and show Shannon whose name it is flashing across my screen. She tries to snatch the phone from my hand but I keep a firm grip. "You're such a li—" she starts, but then sees the message I'm holding in front of her.

"Come on Ging, we have two hotties waiting on us," I smirk as we leave Shannon standing with her mouth open.

Ginger asks, "Do we have time to shower first?"

"If you want, but I'm not sweaty." I give her the rundown on my bar work. She tells me what she added to her floor routine.

We run home and I freshen up while she takes a shower. She's done in record time because she bought a hair dryer that doubles as a straightener at the mall. Her auburn hair is beautiful, especially when it's straight.

The music blares from my Camry on this fall night. Ginger and I are singing Brett Young's song, "In Case You Didn't Know." I can't wait to see Hagan. We've seen each other every day either in class or at night after we've finished practice. We haven't gotten close to second base since the night we dry humped in his Rover. There's been no mention of me performing self-care in front of him. Honestly, I'm glad because it's embarrassing.

Hagan is waiting on the porch and hears us singing. As I walk up the sidewalk, his arms slide around to the small of my back, and he sings the rest of the song to me. Ginger walks past and mumbles something about getting a room.

He looks into my eyes and says, "Do you have plans?"

"Yeah, with you."

"No, I mean how far out do you have your life planned?" he asks.

I can see he's serious, his dimples aren't framing his face, but I don't know how to answer. His brows pinch when I don't respond.

"I may go to grad school next year, but it depends on money and if I keep my scholarship."

He shakes his head slightly then turns me around with his hand on the small of my back and walks me into the house. "Guys will be back down in a few minutes." His tone is strained but he laces his fingers through mine as I follow him up the steps to his room.

When he pushes through the door, he shuts it behind him and locks it. My belly twitches with nerves. Is he wanting to have sex? We haven't talked about it but lust swirls in his eyes.

He walks me backward into the bathroom door, our hands still intertwined. He's not pinning me in like he did against the fridge, but he's pushed his torso against me, and I feel his erection growing each second we stand staring. Breathing.

His soft, wet lips caress my neck like they are playing the faintest of songs. Notes dancing on my skin. A sensual shiver runs down my spine causing me to flinch. "Adalee, I want to know," he whispers. "How do I fit into all of your tomorrows?"

A tickle of my ear lobe with his teeth makes my core clench tightly. My body is on high alert. A squadron of firefighters couldn't put out the blaze out that Hagan has stoked.

"Tell me your mine," he rasps as he moves the neckline of my shirt. His mouth takes an elegant swan dive into the flesh right above my breast. His thumb swipes over my nipple through the cotton material. It feels so fugging good.

"Tell me you want to be mine and you want me to be yours."

He drops down to his knees and unbuttons my jeans. Peeling the opening back, he leans in and skims my skin with his mouth. Then he kisses lower and lower until he's dragging my jeans down to my ankles. He puckers his mouth against the slick material of my thong and pushes them down too.

Restless, raging with desire, my inexperience heightens the anxiousness inside me, so I pop my knuckles. He reaches up, grabbing my hand, "All you have to say is stop. Let me do this for you."

Well, who can say no to that?

He takes my feet out and tosses my underwear and jeans aside. I look down at him kissing my calves and being so tender as he kisses my knee with the surgery scar. His wavy brown hair falls on his forehead, and I reach down and run my fingers through it. He glances up, and I notice his dimples aren't showing. His hands squeeze my thighs before he sets his sights on my center.

His thumbs spread my throbbing flesh. "I can see that you want me, Adalee. You're soaking wet."

"Yes," is all that I can say. I've never been this far, and I'm not sure what to do. My mind is like traffic in Atlanta right now—too many traffic signals to obey. The answer is yes, I want to be his but English 101 sentence structure evades me.

He kisses my mound gently then stands back up. "Open your eyes." I try but I'm embarrassed. When I open them his eyes bore into me with such intensity that it's hard to look into them. The golden flecks are still there but the iris has darkened. "Be with me. Be mine and I'll blow your mind."

At this point, I'll say anything for him to get back into that position. But I am honest when I utter, "I'm yours." My skin hurts to touch. I'm aching for him and mumbling, "Please blow my mind."

Little chuckles flow from his mouth to mine. His body relaxes like he finally has an answer.

He mumbles into my mouth, "Can you be quiet?"

I nod. I mean I guess. How should I know? "I guess we'll find out."

His brow furrows for a moment like he's confused. Before descending, Hagan takes off my Stallions shirt and admires my push up bra, trimmed with satin. "You're perfect," he says, admiring my breasts. His hands roam over the bra but then he falls back to his knees.

I try to pay attention to what he's doing but my knees are weak and wobbly from all the attention. My body keeps sliding down the door. I'm seeking more friction against his face but I wiggle to stay upright. Hagan picks me up and carries me to his bed.

I must be dreaming. I'm in Hagan Chatham's bed. How did I go from hating him to here? I perk up—oh, that's why.

He worships me with every stroke of his tongue.

Slow. Torturous. Strokes.

Chapter Twenty-Four

Hagan

She's pretty in pink. Her swollen flesh glistens as she squirms seeking relief from my mouth. As Adalee's breaths become short, I know she's close. I tease her through her folds over and over before sucking her sensitive bud. She tastes like honey with a dash of salt. So sweet. I want to savor this and enjoy the moment but take her to a place so high she won't want to come down.

I slide my hands under her ass, squeezing and kneading the firm muscles. Everything about Adalee is flawless. As I jockey for the best position, she moans, "Don't quit, please."

My smile widens as I taunt her with my tongue and bear my face into her pelvic bone. She shrieks. Slow then fast. Hard then soft. Her muscles tighten.

"Don't fight it, babe. Come for me," I grunt as I circle her with my tongue, and she wraps her silky legs around my neck. I eat her like she's my last meal.

She's had a few mini O's but her body starts to shake. This time I'm not pulling back just so it lasts longer. My girl needs some relief. A few more strokes and she grips my head with her thighs and screams "Hagaaaaaan, I'm..."

It's so loud, my roommates surely can hear her, so I stick my finger in her mouth. "Suck my finger."

She clamps around it, moaning. "You're so... this is so..." She releases all over my face.

I jump up and take her head in my hands and kiss the fuck out of her. I love the way she moans, tasting herself on my lips and tongue. My boner is so hard it threatens to break out of jail. It wants more meals like that one.

Rolling to the side of her, I trace her stomach with my fingers. Just being with her and watching her fall apart by my tongue will be part of my morning ritual for endless amounts of showers. But now, seeing her in the small amount of light streaming through the window feels surreal. She spent so much time pushing me away and she's finally letting me in.

When she catches her breath, she turns her head away. "Hey. Hey, don't be self-conscious." I rotate her to face me. "You're everything I want, Adalee. I want to make you fall apart every damn day."

There are tears in her eyes, and she sucks her lips into her mouth. "What are you saying?"

"Just what I said. I want to be in a real relationship. I don't want to take the chance that someone else thinks you're available. I have flaws and it's possible that someone else could sweep you off your feet. Honestly, if that happened. I don't know what I would do."

She rolls over facing me and places her hands on my cheeks. "I've been lonely for so long, I don't know if I know how to be a good girlfriend. Chaz said I was—"

I kiss her to shut her up. "Chaz is an entitled rich kid with insecurities. He couldn't handle a strong woman like you. But I can. I know what you need—me."

"Is that so?" she asks, her eyes sparkling with that same mischief she granted me in the car that first night.

I shift my weight and roll her over on top of her almost naked body and I'm sure I have the world's largest grin on my face, nodding.

"What is it I need, Hagan?"

She's so sure of herself right now. She anticipates round two, and maybe we could go farther, but when I have her for the first time, there won't be people downstairs or dinner waiting. I'll have her all to myself. Possibly for days where she won't be able to walk. She clears her throat to get my attention.

"Food and water. You rushed over here, which I like by the way, but there's no way you had time to eat." I drop my head to hers, giving her a quick peck. "Let's take a quick shower so we can grab some grub."

Her almond-shaped eyes round into nearly perfect circles. It's not until then I realize I'm fully clothed and she hasn't seen me in the buff. There's a trace of uncertainty in her expression. The bob of her throat signals she's uncomfortable.

"Hey, you jump in the shower. I'll stay here until you're dressed. I'll go in and wash my face when you're done. Is that a good compromise?"

She nods as she pulls my full weight on her body. I need to shower so I can relieve my blue balls. They'll have to wait until she leaves which I hope is never. I hop off of her and grab a T-shirt from my drawer, then flip it to her. "I'm going to go down and warm up dinner."

"No. They'll know it's me in the shower and we've... done something."

"We're in college, everyone has sex."

Her brows pinch and her cute little lips corkscrew to the right. "Do they? So should I believe the rumors?"

I sit on the edge of the bed and pull the T-shirt overhead, and she sneaks her arms inside. "That came out wrong. Logan and Pearse always have someone coming down in a T-shirt. They won't think anything of it."

She bites her lip and says, "Have you had sex in this room and had a girl walk down in your shirt?"

Damn, she's blunt and it turns me on. I love having a woman that's not afraid of speaking her mind. I know she didn't at first because she was angry about tearing her ACL but now that we're together, I love it.

I pull her into my lap. "No and no. I haven't had sex since I came here, and if I'm honest, quite a while before that. But believe me, I'm a stallion."

She chuckles as we overlap our lips in short wet kisses. "Please don't go down there without me. I'll just rinse off."

"Okay."

After one more kiss she strolls into the bathroom in my shirt. I point to the towel rack and the shower gel. I have two types. The strong one I use when I'm sweaty from training, and stuff Harper gave me for our birthday. It's supposed to be unisex, but it smells like a sugar cookie. I can't wait for Adalee's smart ass remark about my shower gel.

I wash my face and brush my teeth before shutting the bathroom door. Plopping down in the chair, I lean back with my hands clasped behind my head and revel in the fact that I locked her down. She's mine. Adalee might not know it yet, but I plan on this relationship lasting forever.

Remembering my laptop is low on battery, I plug it in. When I raise my head, I see Adalee peeking through the crack in the door. This is the perfect time to play a prank. I stand with my back to the door and unzip my jeans, letting them fall to the floor. My tight boxers show every curve but then I decide to take it a step farther. My thumbs separate the fabric from my skin and I push them down to my knees, and I hear a gasp. Booming laughter erupts from my chest.

Quickly I pull them back up, along with my pants. "Come on out, peeping Tom."

The door creaks open and I drag her into my chest. The steam has made her hair curl at her hairline, framing her face.

"You dropped your drawers on purpose," she says with a smirk.

"Drawers? Do you mean pants? Underwear?" She's so stinkin' adorable one minute and lighting me on fire with her strong, feminine body the next.

"Pants. My mom always said, 'Pick your drawers off the floor.'"

I'm seriously trying to dial down my laughter, but she cocks her hip out and does that twist of her lips she always does. I want to sling her over my shoulder and drop both of our *drawers*. "This is going to be a blast," I beam, gesturing between us. "You and me."

She raises a manicured brow. Cupid just made the perfect shot to the heart, and at the end of his arrow is Adalee's smile that turns me inside out.

Her hand is in mine as we descend the steps—carefully so she doesn't re-injure herself. No one notices us at first. Ginger's sitting on Joe's lap, and they're thumb wrestling. Mac and one of the other freshman baseball players are playing video games.

Adalee lets out a puff of relief, but that's when we hear footfalls behind us. I turn as Logan says, "Little A, I *heard* you were here." His tone teasing.

My eyes narrow and he gives me a nod. Good he understands to keep his mouth shut.

To my surprise, Adalee advises, "You'll be seeing a lot more of me."

His focus shifts between Adalee and me, nodding his head. "I need to hear the whole story."

If Logan ruins this for me, I'm going to put Bengay in his jockstrap.

"Joe, did you warm up the chicken fajitas?" Joe shakes his head in the negative. I knock the cabinet door and ask Adalee to get out the plates. When I open the fridge, memories of me backing Adalee up against the stainless steel play on repeat. One of these days, I'm going to have sex in this kitchen with her.

I pull the veggies and chicken out that I already roasted and put them on a pan. Preheat the oven and stick them in.

It doesn't take long to warm up. I yell, "It's ready!"

No one moves and Adalee clears her throat and says, "Come and get it, last call." Everyone begins filtering into the room. She presses on her toes and whispers in my ear, "My granddad."

Adalee-isms. Life will never be dull.

My phone rings as I'm pulling out the heavy wooden chair, gesturing for Adalee to sit. I dig in my front pocket and realize it's my sister.

"Hey Hap. What's up?"

She's giggling and it reminds me of how she laughed when we were kids, before I was at Julia's side every spare minute. "I'm with Tackett and Talynn. We're at the playoff game, in the suite."

"Oh, damn, I forgot all about it."

Harper shouts, "What? Who is she? Hagan Chatham doesn't forget about baseball unless it's a girl." When I don't answer, her laughter slowly trails off. "Please tell me you're not back with Julia."

"No, of course not."

I'm not a glutton for punishment.

"Oh, is this the girl that's been busting your balls that Archer told me about?"

Okay, maybe I am a glutton.

Taking a long breath, I keep my voice low. "Hap, it's early."

This time I hear laughter erupt from others in the room with her. *Fucking Archer.* One thing about Archer and Megan is... they follow through. I asked them to get Tackett and Talynn to hang out with Hap for a week, and they made it happen. He wants to be a Kodiak so badly, but he has a two year contract with Atlanta.

Tackett takes the phone from Harper, and we talk baseball. But then I have to ask about my sis. "How is she?"

"She's good. Upbeat. She had one episode yesterday. Harper and Talynn have been playing Wordle. They're obsessed."

"Has she said anything about *him*? Tackett, is she waiting on me to ask her to move here?" I ask as I feel Superman's lasers beaming on me. I shift in my seat as Adalee's gaze peers through me.

"No. We're trying not to pressure her. You know, sometimes we have to go through shit. The game's starting. Talk soon. Don't worry and have fun with your new girl."

"Yeah, I will. Thanks. Go Kodiaks!"

He returns the sentiment and I hang up. Adalee's curious so I offer up. "That was my sister and our friend that plays for Atlanta. They're at the playoff game."

The room goes crazy because they are all in complete disbelief that we all forgot about the division championship game.

"Turn on the game."

"Where's the controller?"

All the guys take their plates and excuse themselves from the table, leaving the couples and Logan. He stays with us and asks, "So how's your twin doing?"

"Good."

Adalee's in the middle of a bite, stops and places her fajita on the blue ceramic plate. "You have a twin?"

Everyone at the table looks at each other and they say in unison, "Yes."

She looks embarrassed that everyone knew but her. But to be fair she just agreed to be my girlfriend an hour ago.

"Hap is short for Harper. The one I was talking to from three to five."

Relief washes over her as her shoulders relax but then she squirms. "So, do you want her to move here? Is she in college?"

"I'd love for her to be here, but I thought it was important for both of us to be individuals. I screwed up." I stretch my neck and kiss her on the cheek. "I'm sorry I led you to believe I was talking to another *girl.*"

She gives me a tight-lipped smile. "It's fine. It explains your neediness," she says then she stuffs her tortilla in her mouth like she's proud of herself.

Logan cries, "Whoa."

Joe pounds the table with his fist laughing, and Ginger gives Adalee a high-five. And even though they're laughing at my expense, it's the happiest I've ever been.

Chapter Twenty-Five

Adalee

THERE'S SO MUCH I DON'T KNOW ABOUT HAGAN. ONE thing I do know, is he knows how to turn a lady into a mumbling, moaning nymphomaniac.

Logan thrums his fingers on the table. "So, are you two together? That's a big step."

He looks at me, wearing Hagan's gray Stallions Baseball shirt. Heat creeps up my chest and into my neck. I knew what I was doing—my clothes were clean, but his shirt is soft and smells like him. After what happened in his room, I want him next to me, on me, all of the time. *He's mine.*

Hagan bails me out, saying, "I wore her down. She finally realized what a catch I am."

Logan and I burst out laughing and then Logan leans down. "He's got it bad for you, Little A. Don't hurt him. He's fragile."

The doorbell rings and in walks a raven haired girl, heading straight for Logan.

"Screw you, Mr. Heisman," Hagan says.

Logan just smiles as he places his hand on her back and they walk up the stairs, presumably to his room.

Joe and Ginger grab beers and we all sit down to watch the Chicago Kodiaks play the Arizona Cobras. The winner of this game will go to the World Championships. It's surreal watching the game with Hagan who knows nearly everyone on the team. But it's Mac who jumps out of the bean bag when his cousin, Patrick Callaghan, hits a home run in the third inning.

Joe gets up when the inning is over and glances over his shoulder. "Hagan, want a beer?"

"Nah, I'm good."

"Are you sure?"

He pulls me in closer with his arm around my shoulder. "Yep. I have everything I need."

If he's trying to get into my drawers, he's doing a good job. I might give it up before the night's over. How did I ever think this guy was an arrogant asshole? What I used to see as arrogance is charming. I love the way he looks at me.

We play Twister during commercial breaks. You would think Ginger and I would win because of our flexibility but we are at a height disadvantage. Joe's the shortest at five foot eleven. They can reach anywhere on the mat.

Mac's foot is under me. Ginger is at the other end, not currently entangled with the rest of us. I'm in a crab walk position, like you do in elementary school, and Hagan has one leg in between mine and one hand on the red circle beside my head.

He whispers to me, "Mine. You only spread your legs for me." The he skates his lips over my neck. I clench my legs together and fall. Hagan laughs then moves his leg.

"You're a cheater," I joke.

"Adalee, one thing you'll learn about me is that I never give up. And I didn't cheat. I used your weakness against you."

God I love that cocky attitude. It's a huge turn on. I wish the baseball game was over so we could get back to what was happening upstairs.

It's the bottom of the ninth. The Kodiaks are up by one run. Hagan and Mac lean forward on pins and needles. The Cobras have a man on first and second base with one out.

Hagan's mumbling, "If Cobras get a base hit, the game is tied."

"The pitcher should throw his nasty sinker ball," Joe says, giving his expert opinion. "Then the fast ball low and inside."

The batter digs in and misses the ball by a mile. On the next pitch, the batter swings. Shepherd dives for the ball, sidearms it to Callaghan at second, letting it fly to first for the double play.

Everyone jumps up. "We won!" Hagan shouts.

We watch the Kodiak's dynamic duo do what Hagan says is their trademark handshake. They've practiced it a lot because it's not a short simple fist bump or two. It's long and it's a show.

Hagan says, "Come on, Mac. Let's show everyone how it's done." They get up and perform the handshake with style. Joe feels left out and they try to teach him. Ginger and I look on in horror. Joe has zero rhythm. The other baseball player, I think his name is Zane, is filming it all.

During the celebration, Logan and his raven girl come down. He walks her to the door and she leaves. Is it really that simple? If it's that easy, why haven't I done it? And if it makes both people happy, even momentarily, who am I to judge? Heck, I'm more judgy about myself. I've never truly wanted to have sex until now.

"Kodiaks win?" Logan asks.

"Yep. Look there's my family," Hagan says as he points to the television.

I recognized Archer and Megan. But there's a whole slew of them. Then I see the girl in the picture on his desk—his twin sister. Now I see it. I touch the television, "Is that your sister?"

"Yeah, that's Hap."

"Damn." Logan states. I don't think he meant for words to come escape his throat, but they did.

Hagan's mood changes instantly. "She's off limits."

Logan's voice cracks when he says, "Take it easy. She doesn't even live here."

Hagan's face reddens. "Doesn't matter. I'm telling you now. She's. Off. Limits."

Hagan is protective of his sister. Maybe that's a twin bond. How often does he talk to her? I remember him acting uneasy in the car when he took her call.

Logan playfully punches him in the arm, and they jostle around a bit. But for as big as Hagan is, Logan is four inches taller and thicker. It takes a few moments but Hagan's smile slides back on, and it makes me weak in the knees.

We go into the kitchen to get some pop and that's when Hagan asks, "Will you spend the night with me?"

If I look like a person in surgery when they shine that bright light in your eyes and tell you to count backward from ten, and you only get to eight before you're out, I wouldn't be surprised.

I want to but I don't. I'm scared and I'm not ready to have the *I've never had sex* conversation.

But then his lips caress mine. My core tightens and I can't think of a single reason not to stay with Hagan.

"Just stay." His golden brown eyes hypnotize me as he touches me lightly. I feel my back hit the fridge. Oh God. My heart bangs against my rib cage. And I melt into his touch. Sink into his arms.

"Okay."

Chapter Twenty-Six

Hagan

Fear flashes in her eyes before she relaxes. Neither of us know what to expect, so I keep kissing her until Joe and Ginger interrupt us. "Hey, we're leaving. I'm staying at the home run house with Joe tonight. Do you want us to drop you off on our way?"

I look at her hoping she doesn't change her mind. "No. Umm. I'm staying here tonight."

Ginger, who has absolutely no filter, says, "Well hot damn, Addy Bug." She pulls Adalee into a hug and drags her into the other room. Ginger's jumping up and down like she won the grand prize at a carnival.

"Okay, Joe, let's go. You two have fun."

With a little nod, they leave. Zane leaves. Mac takes a call from his girl in Texas. And Logan, the most focused fucker in the world, turns on game film.

We slip upstairs undetected. I realize I left my phone downstairs, and when I walk into the living room, Logan has my phone in his hand.

"Hey, your sister texted a bunch of pictures, "he says as he throws the phone.

"Thanks."

When I get back to my room, I show the pictures to Adalee. She keeps shying away from me, but I scoot closer, pointing out each family member, and of course, the most well-known Kodiaks and their families.

"Wow. You have a large family. Is it suffocating?"

Even though I had a sweet treat in mind for dessert, the downturn of her lips and the gentle blinks of her lids, leads me to believe that she's lonely. But I answer honestly. "It can be. But when one of us is carrying a burden, all of us help bear the load." I remove the phone from her hand, setting it aside. "You know how we are taught to disperse the weight in engineering to support the load?"

She nods.

"Well, that's what my family does for each other. It's what I can do for you. What I want to do for you. If you'll let me."

A few errant tears glide over her cheeks falling into her lap. Adalee's lips flutter against each other, making small popping sounds. Because I'm from a big family that loves hard, I know what she needs right now isn't talking—she needs to be held.

At first, I slide my arm around her waist and pull her close to me, but the tears start falling faster. With a slight twist of my body, I lift her up and place her on my lap. She snuggles her face into the slope of my shoulder.

My hands trail over her back, reassuring her that I'm here and I'm never fucking leaving. She may not understand yet, but I mean ever. Nothing can keep me from loving this girl. With every somber sob, I squeeze her tighter, and soon, her embrace tightens around me too.

Thinking through my experiences with Harper's anxiety, I don't speak until she releases me from the hug. I wipe away the residue from the tears and press my lips against hers. It's not sexual or wanting—it's comfort.

"What made you so sad?"

She shrugs and I see the uncertainty in her eyes. Instead of pressing her, I stand and pull my shirt over my head. "Let's get in bed. It's late and we both have early mornings."

Despite her sorrow, her face lights up as she inspects my abs. I'm sure she's seen lots of guys with six packs before. She's a gymnast, and although those guys are smaller in stature, they're ripped. Chaz flashes through my mind. She's been with Chaz...ugh. How could he say Adalee isn't worth it? She's worth every risk in the world.

Once her gaze meets mine, I wrap my fingers around her wrists and bring her hands to my skin. The cutest little gasp escapes her mouth as her hands skate up, stopping on my pecs. Then her hands fall, hitting my forearms as she backs away.

Now it's my turn to watch her nimble fingers push through the button on her jeans. They're skinny jeans so she shimmies them down. They get stuck at the ankle and she reaches for me to steady herself. Instead, I bend down and tug her feet from the jeans.

Despite wanting nothing more than to feast on her body, my intuition says I need to nourish her mind and feed her heart. My fingers graze her calves and thighs as I stand, linking our hands together. I pull back the edge of the gray and navy striped comforter, motioning for her to get in.

When we're both settled and our bodies face each other, I tuck her hair behind her ear, staring into her eyes. Her lips move like she's speaking but words aren't coming out. I wait for a minute before I say, "I'll help you carry the load; I promise."

Her hand floats over my cheek. "There's so much. I don't know where to begin."

"Start with now. Am I the cause? The last thing I want is to make you sad or upset."

The inhale of her ragged breath leaves me discouraged before she squeaks out, "No, you're unexpected and caring. My mom died when I was eleven." She focuses on my hair, fiddling with the waves. "My dad... just didn't know what to do with me or for me."

I angle her head toward mine, hoping she'll continue to open up. If one of my parents died, one of my older brothers or sisters would have stepped up. Adalee's told me she was an only child during one of our bantering sessions, which now I believe was just foreplay.

"He kept me in gymnastics so he wouldn't have to deal with me. I resemble my mom, and I think it hurt him to look at me, especially as I got older. Our conversations are superfluous, so we don't know each other like I think a parent should know their child."

This explains why she kept pushing me away. She doesn't trust men to support her in good times and bad. "Have you tried talking to him and telling him how you feel?"

"Not really." My heart cracks open, hearing the sadness in her tone. "It just hurts, you know."

The problem is that I don't know. I can't even imagine how the death of a parents stings. And talking about anyone's problems in my family has never been an issue. My family faces obstacles head on. We talk about them—together. When Archer was taking Xanax and combining it with drinking to numb the pain of his girlfriend cutting off their engagement and marrying another man for no apparent reason, my dad confronted him. I was young but I remember their hushed conversation in the kitchen while I was in the den playing video games.

Archer kissed his wife at my sister's wedding, and he didn't even remember her. It was bad. Dad told him he wasn't taking over the Triple A team, the Sarasota Sharks, until he got his act together. But it wasn't just words; my parents had a standing dinner with him once a week. They always picked a night where I had baseball practice and Harper would tag along with me.

"Adalee, you need to tell him how you feel. Maybe he doesn't realize or maybe he needs someone to tell him that he can be better. He needs to be better."

A simple tight-lipped smile graces her face. "I know." She pauses. "Will you just hold me?"

"Of course. Turn over."

She rolls over and I pull her back into my chest. With her head tucked under my chin, I can't resist kissing her cheek. "But you need to unburden yourself. Maybe not tonight, but no matter what's going on, I promise, I'll be here to listen."

As I tighten my hold around her waist, she whispers, "Thank you."

Chapter Twenty-Seven

Adalee

FINDING TIME WITH HAGAN IS NEXT TO IMPOSSIBLE because our schedules don't mesh up. When I'm going into the weight room, he's coming out. When he has practice, I don't, and vice versa. So I've worked with the coach while he's at practice, mostly bar and foam pit work for now.

I never thought I would thank God for our engineering class, but it's the only day I've seen him for any length of time. He picked me up and drove us to the job site both days and then comes over for an hour to work on the research phase of our project. We've come up with options but now we have to do a deep dive and to be super impressive, we want to turn it from theory to reality. Hagan has access to engineers that work for the Kodiaks so he has sent them several questions.

When Hagan asked me about my future—our future—I was speechless. He thinks far in advance like every good architect or engineer should. But there is so much to do when you're an engineering major.

After completing a degree in engineering, you still have to go through four years of what's akin to an apprenticeship. Then, you have to take an exam before you are a true *professional* in the eyes of the workforce.

Hagan and I both came into college as juniors with the exception of a couple of classes. I consider myself a junior because it's my third year in college but technically, we're seniors.

I pout as he turns to leave and he leans against the door, stroking my hair. "I'm sorry babe. I wish I could stay, but I have to serve my punishment."

Hagan has to do clean up duty at the team dinner, which ended up being moved from breakfast because the coach had a community service PSA to film. Hagan wouldn't be cleaning up at all if it wasn't for Chaz. I'm sure he was taunting Hagan, but Hagan doesn't talk about him. He told me on the phone, "I have you and that's all that matters."

"Can you come back after clean up duty?" I ask, jutting my bottom lip out. "Maybe stay the night here?"

"I'll try. I have a shit-ton to do."

Then he grabs my face to kiss me. It lasts so long, our temperatures rise. I can feel his erection against my abdomen, and I press into him needing friction. I never needed any of this before. Now these feelings surface the instant I'm in his vicinity.

When we part, he hits the door with an open palm. "Damn. I wish I didn't have to go."

He's buried in two papers. His mind is just as amazing as his body. Or at least what I've seen. I giggle thinking about it. "What?" he asks.

"Nothing."

"Tell me." He starts poking me. Breathing on me. Teasing me.

Biting my lip, I say, "I was thinking about how defined your body is." And just like that, he fires off a cocky grin that's panty melting material.

He tilts his head ever so slightly, like he's dancing to a sensual song as he eliminates the centimeters between us. "What do you do when you think about my body?" His gravelly voice sends hot tingles shooting through my veins.

Playing the vixen, I say, "Come back over and find out."

"Be careful Adalee, you might need an extinguisher to put out the raging flames inside me."

Laughing, I jump up and wrap my legs around his waist. We bang into the siding. "It's been five days since we slept in the same bed, and I want to do that again."

"Me too, babe. I'm going to get these papers done tonight so we have the whole weekend together. Okay?"

"Okay."

Three more kisses and he's gone.

It's hard to believe he's mine. But I wasn't joking, I miss him —the feel of his arms around me and his phantom kisses on my neck. I miss his dimples and the way he combs his fingers through his thick wavy hair.

Ginger comes home from Joe's because he's at the team dinner too. We're both happy at the same time which makes our friendship even stronger. We're best friends and our guys are best friends. They both have a ton of friends, but I would say Joe and Logan are Hagan's besties.

Joe's the partier and always has some funny story to tell. They share the connection of the baseball team and now they date roommates. I love saying that I'm dating Hagan Chatham.

There's been no more sexting in our late night calls and texts. I think he's giving me space to tell him more about my family life. But, I haven't gone there. The pain seems to come back stronger when I think about it or talk about it.

But now I know his favorite color is green. When I asked why, he said because he grew up helping the groundskeepers at Kodiak field. He loves how the blades of grass glisten on a sunny day and how mowing it in different directions makes patterns.

His sister, Harper, is anxious about being separated from him and he feels guilty for transferring. She told him to go and actually encouraged him, but that doesn't take away his sense of responsibility for her.

The one thing I was shocked about is that he attended boarding school. My face hung long and eyes wide when he told me. I can't believe a family that is so close would send their children off to school. He assured me it was within an hour drive, and they only went for three years. "Babe, we were never lonely. Someone from our family was with us every weekend. They definitely ruined many parties," he said, chuckling.

Ginger turns on our Alexa and plays music while we dance around with spoons in our hands. Singing like we're two of the Spice Girls. We twirl each other until she gets dizzy and falls into the chair. I lay down on the floor beside her until the giggling stops.

"Ging?"

"Yeah?"

I sigh. I've never told Ginger that I'm a virgin, but she may have come to that conclusion on her own. "I want to have sex with Hagan."

"Of course, you do. Who doesn't? Well, except me. Joe and I are one hundred percent exclusive." She cackles. "Wait, you haven't been together that long even though you've danced around each other since the end of summer."

Breathing in deep, I grab the collar of my shirt, preparing to spill my guts. "I've never been with a guy. Hagan has no idea. He went down on me at his house, and I didn't know what to do. Where to put my hands. Where to look?"

She turns on her side on the kitchen floor and says, "First, you and Chaz never?"

I shake my head. "We did some *second base stuff*, as he put it. He wanted to check off boxes, he didn't actually want me."

She curls her lips. "Yeah, Chaz is an asshole. I told you that. If I didn't want Joe so bad and to tag along to a few games with you, I would have made you break it off with him."

"Gee, thanks."

"Anyway, once Hagan went *downtown*, I'm sure intuition took over, right?" She waits for me to respond. When I don't, she continues. "Addy Bug, everything I've seen and heard about Hagan is that he's going to do what you feel comfortable with. He's a good guy, and there aren't that many of them. Just let him know what feels good and you'll both be happy."

She leans up and circles her arms around her knees. Her red straight hair is frizzy from practice. "I'm spending the night at Joe's, so you and Hagan can have some privacy to talk about having sex or just having sex. Now let's make some dinner so we both have energy to please our men."

I smack her in the arm. "Thanks Ging. I'm so glad you and Joe are in love and happy. I hope Hagan and I can get to that point because I've never had all these sexual feelings before. He brings out the naughty in me."

"It's fun being a naughty good girl. When you do something they don't expect, they get a high you can never imagine."

We cook some chicken and put it over a salad, and I make grilled cheese sandwiches. We watch Friends re-runs for an hour before she showers and heads to the baseball house to shack up with Joe.

I primp a little by putting on some eyeliner and mascara. I flat iron my hair in case Hagan comes by and brush on a little peach lip gloss to attract him to my lips. God, I'm so enamored with him already. My feelings began the first night I saw him. Unfortunately, it was also the night I tore my ACL.

It wasn't his fault, but I have so much riding on my scholarship that I was upset, displacing my feelings. I'll give him credit. He's persistent and the most patient guy I've ever known.

I'm sitting alone in my room with my textbook open in front of me. I'm trying to focus on the words on the page, but my mind keeps wandering to Hagan and how I want to take the next step. So, when the doorbell rings, I hop off my bed, check my face in the dresser mirror, and run my fingers through my hair. Then, I fly down the hall to the front door. Excitement fills every corner of my body. Tonight's the night.

I swing the door open. "Yay, you...came."

"Hey sweetie, we need to talk."

The man in front of me doesn't attempt to hug me after not seeing me for months. My dad, who lives in Alabama, stands in the doorway. I feel like the robot from *Lost in Space.* "This does not compute." My feet are locked in place, unwilling to make a move toward him. He's never been here except for my freshman year.

"What are you doing here? And at nine at night? Why didn't you tell me you were coming? What if I wasn't here?" Questions keep rolling of my tongue until my dad takes a step toward me and gives me a hug like you give a great uncle twice removed at a family reunion.

That's when I noticed a woman behind him. She's pretty, blonde, and definitely younger than my dad.

My dad frowns. "Adalee, please let us in. It's chilly out here."

I step aside as my stomach tumbles. He wouldn't be here if something major hadn't happened. My dad walks by and the blonde points her gaze to the floor as she enters. "Have a seat, Dad and...?"

"Adalee, this is my wife, Paula," he states in a flat tone.

I cock a brow. What? She extends her hand and I stare at it in disbelief. I'm afraid if I shake her hand, I might break it. Not any of this is her fault but I'm raging mad and might need restraining order against my dad.

"Did you say *wife*?" My focus travels up to the ceiling, down to the floor, and scans the entire room before my eyes meet my dad's.

He inhales and on the exhale, he says, "Yes, but—"

Bile travels up my throat as I interrupt, "You got married and didn't invite me to your wedding? You never told me you were dating. I guess that goes right along with how you never talked about Mom. Never told me things she did. Never reminded me of how much she loved me. She would say good riddance to you if she knew how you've treated me for the past decade."

"Honey, it all happened so fast and you had surgery so..."

"Oh, no. Don't blame my surgery *for you* not telling me about your marriage. You didn't even bother to attend or talk to the doctor about. Mom would be ashamed of the person you are. I do know that. And Paula, good luck. Because if he acted like he was father of the year, or a father at all, he lied!" I scream just as I hear knocking on the front door.

"Adalee, are you okay?" It's Erika from upstairs. Ever since Hagan brought her home and she stayed here, she's been a wonderful neighbor and a friend. Erika admitted that she knew Shannon was having sex with Chaz while he and I were dating, and she didn't want to get involved.

I run to the door and step out, closing the door behind me. "My dad showed up out of nowhere. Married."

She gasps and her hands fly over her nose. "I'm sorry. If you need to talk, I'm home tonight."

"Thanks, I better get back inside."

Erika tips her head, hugging me before walking up the stairs.

I needed those minutes to calm down but I'm still mad as... fuck. Yep, I'm mad as fuck. I don't know if that even makes sense. Internally I say the word a hundred times until I start laughing. I go back inside and face my traitorous father.

My dad claps his hands, glancing at me. "Adalee, I'm sorry I didn't tell you, but we decided spur of the moment." He rubs his lips together, tucking them inside his mouth before continuing. "I'm moving to Florida. I wanted to deliver the news in person."

"Why Florida?"

My dad shifts his body position like he's uncomfortable. Paula chimes in, "Because I have twins. They're eight and I share custody with their dad. So, your dad is transferring to a bank branch in Florida where we can be a family."

I nearly choke on my own tongue. But with my lids ready to spill over, I suck it in. "Congratulations. I hope he's better to your kids than he has been to his own. How did you even meet?"

"At a banking conference. Honey, I'm sorry." His voice is thick with what sounds like regret, but part of me thinks it's a show for Paula.

"Too little too late, Dad," I choke out. "Now, I have to study, so please leave."

They both stand as I stay locked in place. He bends down in front of me. "I hope you'll forgive me one day. I was lost."

My dad touches my hair like he used to when he and Mom would tuck me in at night. That touch—I miss it. I miss my mom and the family we used to be.

"Evidently you found your way. My anger has nothing to do with Paula—it's all directed at you. Now please leave. Text me with your new address. I do want to know where you are in case of an emergency. If my leg falls off, you might want to know."

I don't need him. I don't.

Chapter Twenty-Eight

Hagan

WHY DOES ADALEE ALWAYS REV MY ENGINE WHEN SHE knows I have to leave? Her voice drips with sex appeal. *Come back over and you'll find out.* As soon as I'm finished with the team dinner I call. I can write my papers after I skim her skin with my lips and make her scream my name.

No answer.

Again, no answer.

Again, no answer.

Where is she? Driving straight to her house, my Rover comes to a screeching halt as I jump out of the car. My gut tells me something is wrong. Did she fall in shower and hit her head? Did someone break in? Did she go for a run and not take her phone because that shit isn't safe at ten in the evening.

I ring the doorbell, wait two seconds and knock on the door, then five seconds later I'm shouting, "Adalee. Adalee, open up."

Erika bounces down the steps. "She left."

"For where?"

"I don't know. Her dad came here unexpectedly, and they got into a heated discussion. I saw him leave, and then a little while later I heard the door slam and saw her running."

"She's not supposed to be running yet. Fuck." I remove my hat and rake my fingers through my hair. "Which way did she go?"

Erika points to the left. "Thanks." I run and hop in my vehicle, going through streets of the apartment housing. I go by the baseball house. Ginger and Joe haven't seen her. They try to call and still no answer. Then it occurs to me that she might come to me. We haven't been dating long but she did tell me her mom died and her dad wasn't going to win any awards for parenting.

Shit.

When I pull up at my house, she's sitting on my front porch with her arms wrapped around her knees. I can't get out of the car fast enough. She stands as she sees me coming and runs into my arms. "Fuck, babe. I've been so worried. I called you a hundred times and then you weren't home or at the baseball house. And why didn't you go inside?"

Her nose is against my shoulder, wetting my shirt with tears. "Nobody answered."

"Oh, yeah. They're gone because they have an away game at LSU Saturday. I forgot they were scheduled to leave earlier tonight. Come on, let's go inside. I'll make you feel better," I move my brows in quick succession in an attempt to lighten the mood.

Instead of getting a smartass remark like *you wish* or *in your dreams*, she says, "Okay. So, we have the house to ourselves?" The breathy tone in her voice leaves no doubt that she wants to have sex.

We break our embrace as she peers at me with her almond shaped eyes. "Yeah," is all I can say. I want her skin to stick to mine and feel how our bodies respond to each other, but not until she tells me what happened tonight. I want our first time together to be because she wants it so bad she can't wait any longer. Not because she's upset at her father.

Scrambling for my keys, I unlock the door. "You need a door hanger." Adalee attempts a joke at least I hope it was a joke—guys don't have door decorations.

My brain can't think of anything to say, so I hold her hand and sit down on the couch bringing her with me. I angle toward her. The air inside is thick and smothering, reminding me of practice on a hot August day. "Erika said your dad came by. What happened?"

She sniffs. "I don't want to talk about it." She reaches for my face, clearly wanting to kiss me. "Please just have sex with me. You said you would make me feel better."

"No, babe. Not until you confide in me. I promised you I'd be here for you. And as much as I want fuck you into tomorrow, we're not doing anything until you tell me."

Her eyes widened. Her face trembles and teeth make the sound when you're cold or crying. The floodgates behind her lids open and she sobs. I pull her into me. I don't even understand what happened but my eyes blur with tears too. Damn. When my girl hurts, it hurts me too.

I do everything I know. What I've seen my brothers do—rock her gently, hold her tight, and stroke her hair. This is heartbreaking. When her sobs slow and a normal breathing pattern returns, I whisper, "Why did he come here?"

She sucks up her tears while laying on my shoulder. "He...he...got remarried and didn't bother to tell me until he showed up tonight."

Fucking bastard.

"I'm so sorry." I hold her tighter. Does her father not have one ounce of human decency? It's one thing to be full of grief and withdraw from the world but to deliberately get married and not tell your daughter is an asshole move.

She shrinks out of the hug, using her hands as windshield wipers for her tears. "He hasn't come to a single gymnastics meet in college and only a handful of times since my mom died. All I wanted was for him to love me like he used to."

"Oh, babe." I kiss her hands.

"We're supposed to be dating, having fun, but I drop all my problems on you."

"I'm yours and I want to help you realize your worth." I almost tell her he's not worth her sorrow...but it's her dad. This is so foreign to me. My parents text me daily. Sarah Jane and Reggie reach out at least once a week. Archer calls every couple of days, and Harper messages me around twenty times per day.

It seems Adalee raised herself and she did a damn good job. She doesn't curse or drink. She's so fucking intelligent and a *Division I* college athlete.

She climbs onto my lap. "He's moving to Florida with Paula. She has eight year old twins. He's going to be a real father to them. He wants me to forgive him, but how can I?"

She's been holding so much of her family life in that I'm just seeing the effect it's had on her. But it explains her distrust of men. The pads of my fingers make circles on her back. I don't know what to say.

"I have a stepsister and stepbrother. They're just like you and Harper."

She cries and again buries her head in my neck. "We'll get through this together. Don't feel bad because you're angry. It's okay to be upset and hurt."

"My dad hasn't been here since freshman orientation. He didn't feel the need to come for my surgery, but he's so filled with happiness that he felt now was the time." Her voice seeps with sarcasm. "Correction, he came because he feels guilty."

Right now, I want her to let her feelings out. I'm trying not to judge him outwardly, although he should be glad I wasn't at the apartment when he showed up.

Since she brought up her surgery, I realize that the way she's sitting on me, all of the pressure is on her bent knee. As I lift my hip so I can unfurl her leg, she resists. "Not going anywhere, I just want you to straighten your leg."

She sniffs again and raises it with me, but instead of kicking it out straight, it wraps around my back. Her weight shifts and she sinks onto my groin.

"How did I mistake you for one of the bad guys?" she asks as she comes nose to nose with me. "You're the best person I've ever met." She throws my royal blue Stallions hat on the floor.

Damn it feels good hearing that from her. Our faces move from left to right and it serves to dry her tears. But then she starts moving her hips. It's okay as long as it makes her feel better. We can make out. Then her head drops to mine, peppering me with wanting kisses.

Adalee always surprises me. She leans back and strips off her shirt, throwing it onto the floor.

The hot pink-lacey bra keeps her breasts a secret. I can't believe I've seen everything but her breasts. "You want to do the honors?" she purrs.

"Fuck, Adalee. I don't want to do this when you're vulnerable. I do—just not when you might regret it."

This time she rolls her hip so that her breast push into my face. "I've wanted this for a long time. Ask Ginger, I told her I wanted you."

"You're sure?"

Watching her chest rise and fall, there's no doubt she wants this. "I had it all planned out. I just thought we'd be at my apartment. Why do you think I'm wearing this *come fugg me bra*?"

A small chuckle filters out her mouth. But none of this is funny. I'm so hungry for her, I'm afraid. She keeps maneuvering herself to where I can feel the rising temperature of her on my groin. I reach between us and her yoga pants are soaked. I rub circles against the black smooth material. Her breathing is labored as her head falls back.

Struggling to stay in control, my voice shatters into a thousand wavelengths. "Take it off."

"My pants?"

"All of it. I can't wait another minute to be inside you," I say in an admittedly demanding tone. It's pent up frustration from her torturing me for months. I knew. Damn, I knew she was special. She stands and strips in front of me. When she begins to unclasp her bra, I stop her. "Wait, I want to do that."

"Stand up, transfer."

I might shoot my load from her aggressiveness. I love that she feels comfortable with me and I do as I'm told. She pushes my sweatpants down. "What is it about guys in gray sweatpants?" She licks her lips and rubs her palm over the bulge in my tight boxers. "I like these."

"I'm all about performance."

With a twinkle on her eyes, she responds, "We'll see about that."

She rakes her hands under my shirt until it's gathered at my neck. I take it the rest of the way off. We're in the middle of my living room naked with the exception of her bra. My head swivels to make sure the front door is locked then I lift her by the waist and she snaps her legs around me as I lower us back onto the couch.

My fingers crawl up her back, finding the clasp to the pink penis teaser. The clasp is small for big hands but as I pinch, it pops and falls between us. My hands roam up and down her sides. She's muscular everywhere, yet as feminine as a woman can be. I push her back so her tits are in my face. They're small but fit her body and my mouth perfectly. I nip on the rosy buds. I take a peek at her and she's watching me suck her tits. "It's hot—you watching me."

She has three supple areas, her lips, her breasts and her vagina. The rest of her is pure muscle covered with silky skin.

"Hagan?" It comes out breathy.

She glides along my dick soaked with her juices. It's like an adult slip-n-slide. Jesus, she's sexy. "Damn, I want you so much."

"Now, can we do it now?" she asks or more like demands.

I pull my mouth from her breast, replacing it with one hand. Rubbing the smooth mound with the tight little peak. She squirms wanting more but she watches me fist myself and give it a couple of strokes.

I'm getting ready to nudge into her entrance when she says, "Give me more than one chance."

"Babe, your chances are endless."

She leans forward kissing me while mumbling into my mouth, "Good. Because you're the only person I ever want to have me."

My brain is like scrambled eggs. I must have misheard. Or maybe she *meant from this day forward.*

She takes control because I lost conscious thought. Her hand is over mine and she raises and then lowers herself on me but only a little of me. She's so tight and the head isn't even all the way in.

"Hagan, you know how I said I had something to tell you the other night?"

'Yeah." I do but all I can think about is getting all of the way inside her. She moves and we're in an inch or two. She moves a little more and more until our skin meets.

Desire pools in her eyes and I almost come by the sound of her voice pleading, "Help me."

I guess she's never been on top. Or maybe never had sex sitting up. I squeeze her hips, helping lift her up and down. I mutter, "You're so tight. Just keep rolling like you were before. Your body will adjust."

Once we establish a rhythm, we move flawlessly, like a well-oiled machine. I catch her bottom lip and tug on it with my teeth. Her tight walls clamp down as her forehead creases, and she takes short, ragged breaths. The feeling of her warm silken muscles squeezing me shoots painful pleasure up my spine.

No, I can't come yet. I've never come this early. Think about something else. What can I think about? Shit. She's all that's on my mind.

"Hagan. Oh please, I... I don't know what to do."

I can barely speak and when I do, it comes out hoarse and an octave lower than normal. "You're beautiful babe. I can't hang on."

She moves faster and faster and her core clenches around me. "I'm sorry...I've... I've never done this."

I steady her movements to a slow boil. We're still moving but I'm processing what she just said. The intensity in her eyes burns like someone poured gasoline on me and lit a match.

"Hagan. Hagan, I need to go faster."

"Give me a minute." Admittedly, I'm shocked. I knew she was a rare find but I need confirmation. My hand squeezes the dip in her waist. "Adalee, are you... a...a...."

She closes her lids and when they peel open, her body shakes. "Yes. I'm a virgin."

Admittedly, I'm shocked. I didn't know there were any virgins left in college. I grip my girlfriend tight. I thought I knew what love was, but it was nothing like this. The intensity. The ache. It's different with Adalee.

My eyes fill with emotion. I swear tears better not come out. She'll think I'm a pussy.

We're keeping a steady rhythm as I peer into the windows to her secrets and desires.

"I just didn't want you to treat me with kid gloves." Then she asks, "Are you mad?"

I shake my head. Everything in me wants to beat my chest like Tarzan, my Jane. "No, I'm fucking honored you chose me."

Chapter Twenty-Nine

Adalee

"We chose each other. It just took me a while to trust you wouldn't hurt me," I confess.

Hagan's caramel eyes sparkle and the smirk on his face disappears as he turns serious. "Never. I'm a loyal fuck. Trust me, Adalee. I'm all-in."

Hot lava unfurls in my core as he kisses me passionately, moving our bodies like a rowing machine. Then changing it up where he lifts me up and down, smacking our bodies together. His mouth stays attached to a part of me at all times. My chest in his face and there's no room between us. I climb so high to a place I've never been before. I've given myself plenty of orgasms, but those were sparklers, these are fireworks so large and bright, they're blinding.

The strength of his hands holds me in place as he pumps against me. I fall on his shoulder as my arousal coats him and his legs. But he's not done. He squeezes my chest against him and a visceral growl rumbles from deep in his chest. He lifts me up off his shaft and proceeds to fist himself as he comes all over his stomach.

Mesmerized by his glistening hard torso, I say, "That's the sexiest thing I've ever seen." I run my hands through it and smear it on his chest, playing with it like it's finger paint. "I can't believe you're mine."

His hands caress my skin. They're everywhere as he lets me come to terms with losing my virginity. "Believe it, but your first time should have been in bed and romantic." His eyes shoot downward.

I want to run my fingers through his hair but now they have sticky cum on them. Instead, I tilt his chin up. "No. my first time was with someone that cares about me. It wasn't planned out which helped my nerves. It just happened and it was A-MAZ-ING. Plus, you told me you would give me a second chance."

He stands up, carrying me, but then throws me over his shoulder and smacks my butt. "I love your hard ass. It's fucking sexy. I think we need to shower. You made a mess."

I can't see his face, but his backside is smiling up at me with the dimples in his lower back and his full butt cheeks. "Me, you're the one who..."

He takes the stairs two at a time, holding me like I'm a towel strewn over his shoulder. I'm not heavy but I'm a hundred five pounds of muscle. My abdomen bounces against his shoulder causing me to giggle.

When we reach his room, he opens the bathroom door, strolls in, and turns the water on. I look in the mirror at my long brown hair hanging to his knees. But more intriguing is the outline of his shoulder, back and butt. He's not obsessed with working out, yet his body is a live sculpture.

Hagan slides me down the hard planes of his chest as he opens the glass shower door. I was in here once before but alone. Suddenly, I feel self-conscious. As if he senses it, he pulls me close once again. The water beats hard against his back, shielding me.

The clear orbs sit in his thick hair, and I can't believe I'm the person that this man wants. I'm fairly flat in the boob department. I have zero experience in the sexual department so I'm not going to blow his mind.

"Don't," he rasps while barely moving his head from left to right.

I swallow as I look into his translucent golden brown eyes. "What?"

"Don't second guess that you're everything I want." He rasps, "Because that's exactly what you are—everything."

He reaches out, his hand brushing softly against my cheek. His heat radiates through my skin, and I shiver in anticipation. He looks deep into my eyes, and I see truth in his gaze.

Expectation builds in my spine as he devotes all of his energy to my mouth. It's soft but hungry. I walk into him, making him step back so the shower rains down on us. Tiny orbs turning into streams creaking and trailing down our bodies.

This is beyond anything I've dreamed. Sure, I've read about it, but Ginger told me that she and Joe took a shower, and it wasn't all it's cracked up to be. She said they couldn't find the right angle and it wasn't slippery enough. The water hindered him from staying hard.

Maybe we're just going to kiss. God, please tell me what to do.

Nope. There is nothing right about asking God to help you have sex.

Speaking of hard, his length shoots up into my stomach.

Arousal licks through my core. Is it possible to have another orgasm that close together? I close my eyes, smelling baked cookies. "Here," he says as squirts shower gel on my hand then swirls some in his own. It builds as he places my hand on his smooth as silk shaft, and surrounding my hand with his, he assists in the firmness of the grip.

It's so intimate, and even though I've touched Chaz, nothing came of it. He wasn't interested in teaching me. If it didn't happen immediately, he made an excuse. I always thought it was his fault but now I realize it was me. I wasn't interested and didn't want to make him feel good. It felt like an obligation.

"I love the way your hand feels wrapped around me," he whispers as he moves the wet strands of hair from my face, laying my head on his chest.

With Hagan, every moment is treasured. He gives me confidence even though I'm clueless. It makes me want to please him, so I drag my other hand over the dips and ridges of his torso. I want him to feel worshipped, so I drop down to my knees. But Hagan stops me. "No, not in the shower. It's not good for your knee."

He squeezes every heart string I have that he's thinking about me. "But..."

"No," he says as he's lifting me back up with one hand while I keep the pace stroking him. "Adalee, when you take me in your mouth, it's not going to be easy. I'm going to pump into those sweet peach lips and touch the back of your throat. You're going to sit on the edge of bed where you can't blow your knee out. Then I'm going to come all over your chest."

I just had an orgasm as his filthy words blanketed my skin. Hagan emits masculinity. His browned chest with perfectly defined muscles is buttery smooth. How can he look like the Adonis of men when I probably look like a drowned rat? Yet he makes me believe I'm the most beautiful girl in the world.

While I'm thinking of him, his hand floats down my back, skating over my butt cheeks. When he inserts his finger, the angle hits a spot I didn't know existed. All my thoughts go to wanting and pleasing. "I want to give you what you're giving me," I beg.

"You are. We're going to hit this climax together."

I'm panting and my arm is tired. This is not an exercise that I've ever done with success. I need to change hands, but I'm distracted by how he makes me soar to a place unknown. But finally, I slide my arm around his back and take over with my left hand. Of course, this hand isn't as coordinated so he guides me until I hit my rhythm.

I back him up against the wall, so the water slaps against my back. He tips his chin up, with his raspberry lips parted. He's trying to hold off. His muscles in his jaw and upper body flex and my inner walls tense. Everything is ready to explode. We're in total synchronicity. It's almost painful, like when my grandmother used the pressure cooker and one day the top rattled until it blew off, leaving vegetable soup splattered all over the kitchen.

And that's when blinding flashes of light overtake my senses —except for the faint smell of sugar cookies. A liberating grunt bursts from the depths of his chest. Then his body goes slack, except for his arms which travel up the small of my back and sandwiches us together. He's the peanut butter and I'm the jelly. Sticky and sweet.

When we're breathing regularly again, we dance back into the shower stream. As I stare at Hagan's mouth, I read my name on his lips but it's soundless. Maybe I'm in sexual delirium. Then he remarks, "We're really fucking good together."

I'm not delirious, I'm in heaven.

The sound of shampoo squirting breaks my gaze from his juicy, wet lips. He bends to give me a plump kiss, blowing a raspberry on my cheek.

"How are you a sex expert one minute and a little boy in a candy store the next?"

"Part of my charming boy next door routine," he cackles.

"So when you're talking dirty, that's charming?" I ask with a smirk.

He massages my scalp then stretches my hair washing the ends. The whole time my arms are around his waist, relishing the post sexual euphoria. "You can't fool me anymore, Adalee. Dirty talk turns you on, doesn't it?"

It does...more than I care to admit. But I play coy. "It wasn't *that* dirty."

He scoffs as he rinses my hair then whispers the dirtiest oration in my ear—definitely not meant for public consumption. When he feels my nail dig into his skin and my body seize, he laughs.

"Okay, okay. Point taken. I like it and I can't wait to do it."

He rewards me with the deepest dimples of the night.

He balls up my hair and lays it against the top of my head. "You'll be a beautiful old woman."

Why did I fight this?

Chapter Thirty

Hagan

Cuddled in bed, Adalee wears one of my tanks that I use for weightlifting. I rain kisses all over her neck as I absorb her body into mine. Then she lets out the sweetest hum. Julia seems insignificant now. Not unimportant, but a stepping stone to someone deeper. When I first laid eyes on the brunette laying in my bed, there was a spark, as I watched her move around the party. We saw each other and even she couldn't deny that I crept into her brain the same way she did mine, especially since she tore her ACL thinking of me.

She falls asleep with me stroking her hair. As I'm about to doze off, I remember that I have two papers to write. They're due on Monday. With my goal to graduate summa cum laude, I sneak out of the bed, leaving the warmth of my girl.

Exhausted, I drag my backpack downstairs, so I won't disturb sleeping beauty. I make some hot tea to wake me up while I read over my engineering notes from a different class.

Double majoring while playing division one baseball can be particularly challenging given the time demands of being a collegiate athlete.

Time constraints have me finding creative ways to do the research for my papers. During dinner, I research the topics to learn, bookmark them on my phone. When I'm running or training, I pop ear buds in and listen to the information rather than reading. It took time to get used to listening instead of reading because it's a different skill set. One of Dad's players offered that nugget of advice because he played college before going to the majors. Did I mention he's the current MVP?

Luckily, I've already done the research for this one and my outline is ready. All I need to do is put it into words. There's only six weeks of the semester left. If I can knock at least one of these out tonight. I can do the other one on Sunday. I love having Adalee in my life, so I'll figure it out.

It's four a.m. when I slip back into bed beside her. She shivers when I raise the covers and the cool air hits her bare legs. It's that time of year when it's between needing air or heat. I scoot closer and the next thing I know, I'm the one waking up to an empty bed with light shining through the slatted blinds.

It's Friday and we have class at the job site today. At least I don't need to pick her up.

I love having her here with me and smelling my favorite food filtering through the house is icing on the cake. Bacon on anything makes it better but since spending the summer with

Tackett, I only partake once a month or so. I deserve a reward for a job well done—on the couch, in the shower and on my paper.

I pull on my plaid lounge pants Not bothering with a shirt, I gallop down the steps. I stop dead in my tracks. She's changed into my practice T-shirt that has my number on it. Thirteen in large block letters takes up her back. But the hem lies right below the curves of her ass. Damn.

"Making yourself at home, huh?" My arms snake around her waist. I move her hair off her shoulder so I can kiss her neck.

"Umm, well I worked up an appetite. You do realize that I did all the work last night?"

"I guided you, keeping you on the tracks. You may have run off the road you were wanting to go so fast." She quiets and I turn her around. "Are you okay? About us?"

She stills before facing me and giving me a chaste kiss. "Yeah. I'm glad I did what I did."

I chuckle. "Me too."

Her forehead creases and her eyes crinkle. "You were right. I needed to tell my dad how I felt and I did."

"Oh."

"You horn dog. I wasn't talking about us."

Who says horndog? Probably her great aunt Gertie.

Adalee-isms.

I pretend I knew. I grab some paper plates because we don't have time to do dishes. I tell her that I finished one of my papers. "Oh I forgot. You have two. When did you do it?"

"You were knocked out so since I was wide awake thinking about you and...us...I wanted to complete one of them so we would have more time together this weekend." Her eyes crinkle when she receives a compliment. "But we've got class this morning, so I'll drive."

After we finish eating, we return to my bedroom to get dressed. She pulls her yoga pants up and keeps on my jersey with my name across the shoulders. Chatham. Adalee Chatham. I like the way it sounds.

"Can I wear it to class? I mean, Ginger wears Joe's sometimes."

What? Why am I bat over fucking balls for this girl? My girl. I basically told her last night without saying the words. But I used words like *forever* and *everything I need.*

Julia never wore my jersey or practice shirts. She bought a shirt and had my name heat pressed on it so it would fit her perfectly. But this is different—this my shirt—that I wear. "You know if you wear my jersey, it means you're mine for life. It's an unwritten rule."

Her grin falters and disappears. "For life is a long time. No one's ever loved me forever."

And I make a promise to myself to love Adalee until death separates us.

Chapter Thirty-One

Adalee

Our project is running smoothly. Turns out Hagan and I are perfect business partners. His strengths are my weaknesses and vice-versa. The professor and the project coordinator ask us to take a leadership role. We will be the liaisons between the students and the company's point person. All we have to do is keep a list of questions the students ask and put them into a spreadsheet by categories like mechanical, electrical, or structural engineering so the company can easily funnel them to the correct person.

We'll receive up to five extra points on our assignment. And with Hagan's goals, it could be the most important five points of his college career. It could mean the difference in a 3.8 or a 4.0. He's crazy over his grades. I can't believe he went down and wrote a paper after we had sex and then shower *stuff*. I'm waiting in the car while he runs it into his professor's office, even though it's not due until Monday.

Last night was amazing. I'm falling hard for him, which is scary—a beautiful thunderstorm of emotions. Then I remember my father is married to someone with twins and he's happy. Why couldn't he be happy with me?

Hagan's running toward me with his phone next to his ear. His parents must have the genetic code of God himself—he's perfect. His hair bounces as he slows his pace, and I can see his eyes reflecting the autumn sunlight from here. When he swings the driver's side door open, his dimples hit me like tropical force winds. They simply take my breath away.

I love him. Is that possible? Already?

He slams it shut. "Let's go pack you a weekend bag." He stretches across the console pecking my cheek. "We're going to Chicago."

"What? When?"

"Now. We're finished with classes. We're going to watch the Chicago Kodiaks win game three of the World Championships," he says as he reverses out of the parking space. "The first two games were in Texas. Now they come to us."

I love how he says us, like he's on the team. He's excited, talking non-stop. "You'll meet Harper, too." He and Harper were probably the cutest two toddlers on the planet.

Clapping my hands quickly in succession, I respond. "Okay, I'll go. Are we driving?" On one hand, it's exciting to go away with Hagan, but on the other, it's nerve-racking to know I'll be meeting his family.

He pats my leg. "Dad has a private jet waiting for us at the airport."

"Do you think your family will like me?" I ask.

We snag a spot right in front of my door. And when we come together on the sidewalk, he reaches for my hands. "Of course. Archer and Megan already do. Megan loves your spirit and that you made me work for your time and attention. But we both knew you were hot for me." His head sways back and forth as a grin takes over his face.

I love that he's not just one thing.

Not just cocky.

Not just sweet.

Not just intelligent.

Not just sexy.

Not just playful.

He's everything.

His hands slide under my backpack, giving me a lip disintegrating kiss. *What did I do right to deserve this man?*

My gymnastics bag serves as a suitcase since I don't have one. I throw clothes into the bag. Hagan looks in my underwear drawer and says, "Can we take these?" They're thongs with leopard print. Then he twirls green lacey ones on his finger. "But these may be good luck. The Kodiaks are green. Definitely taking these."

"Because baseball players are superstitious?" I ask.

He chuckles and when he throws his head back his hair swooshes. "No, because I have plans."

He stalks toward me.

"You do? Big plans?" I ask, twitching my brows.

His golden brown eyes dance when he says, "The biggest... you've seen it."

"I have."

And we kiss for the next five minutes. We make a pit stop at his house. I stay in the car calling Ginger while he packs. I told her that Hagan and I had sex and how wonderful I feel. I didn't have time to fill her in on my dad coming over. There'll be plenty of time when I get back.

She's so excited when I tell her how understanding he'd been when I said I'm a virgin. Then she asks, "So was it soft and slow or fast and hard?"

Cackling, I answer, "Well, I was going so fast he didn't want me to come off the tracks. He slowed us down. Don't tell anyone."

"I would never. But Joe already knows. Hagan texted him saying, and I quote, 'She's my lifetime girl.'"

I'm shocked, but every nerve in my body tells me it's true. At first I thought it was because I've never been in love, but it's more than that. The connection between us has been there since before we spoke even one meaningful word. I had to find my way to give him the code to unlock the padlock on my heart.

Soon, we're on the tarmac waiting for the flight to take off. The thrill of flying in a private plane circumvents my heebie-jeebies. How experienced are the pilots? We're sitting in cushy seats, listening to a beautiful, leggy flight attendant tell us all the ways to escape the plane. Does everyone want to be reminded of how we could die? Not me.

After take-off, she brings out snacks and offers beer and wine. Hagan says, "Just water, please."

There's a private part of the cabin with a couch that turns into a bed. "I'm tired, wanna take a nap? We have family dinner as soon as we arrive."

Following him back, I sit on the couch while he shuts the curtains separating the two cabins. He unfolds the bed, grabs some pillows and blankets from the overhead bins. He lays down and pats the glove leather bed. He pulls me in close, kissing my neck, nibbling my ear. He whispers, "We can check *mile high club* off the list."

My brows shoot up. "What?" Yesterday I was a virgin, and now I'm contemplating sex on a plane. My world has finally turned right side up. Someone wants me.

"Last night I made a list of all the places we're going to have sex in our life." His voice is confident and strong like he's one hundred percent positive of his feelings for me. He rolls me over, facing him. No smile or dimples ,just the most serious expression I've ever seen on him. He pushes a strand of hair behind my ear. He does it over and over. "I don't want to scare you, but I never want this to end."

My breath catches in my throat.

Is he trying to tell me he loves me?

No one has told me they love me in so long. I get cards for my birthday and Christmas from my grandfather on my mom's side. When my grandma died, he moved to Alaska. At first, it was just to be alone and come to terms with losing his daughter and his wife a year apart, but he made a life there, and I've only seen him one time when he came back to Alabama to sell their house.

Tears well in my eyes.

"It's okay if you don't feel the same way...yet," he says, his voice low and gentle. "I'm here for you, whether it's today or months from now." He leans forward and captures my lips in a passionate kiss. I can feel all of my fears melting away as I surrender to his embrace.

His hands travel up and down my body, exploring and caressing as he whispers sweet sensual words in my ear. Finally, I pull away, breathless and aroused. "Make love to me," I mumble.

Maybe it's the altitude or the hum of the plane, but my heart feels like it may combust at any moment. The way this man loves me is beyond my wildest dreams. He strokes every inch of my body with his hands and peppers my skin with spine tingling, toe curling kisses before he hovers over me and his hair falls forward.

"I love running my fingers through your hair. I love your dimples." I can see in his eyes that he wants me to say those words first, so I feel in control. "But it was your laugh that struck my heart like lightning."

There's some light fondling and warming me up, even though I could light the Olympic flame without a torch right now. Hagan's eyes never move from mine. When I need to close them because I'm so close, he commands, "Eyes on me. I want to see every emotion in your eyes when you come."

Tiny explosions go off inside me. "That's it. God, I love that I can make you come just by talking."

"It's...it's perfect. I love seeing your eyes too." I wrap my legs around his back, hoping he'll like it.

He holds himself with one arm and he caresses from my knee to my hip as he inserts himself into my wet, hot center. He's making love to me. This angle is deeper, and I feel excitement building in the deepest vault of my core. My nails dig as I tug him closer, but he's anchored in place.

"We're almost there, babe. Damn, you're beautiful all the time but when you're flushed... damn, I'm a lucky guy."

Our eyes widen and then he pinches them closed but strains to open them back up.

I rasp, "I'm the lucky one. I.. I.." He moves faster and my words become a jumbled mess. They mimic my emotions, my muscles.

We lay in each other's arms. My smile mirrors his—wide and sated.

When we dress and return to the main cabin, Hagan pulls out a notebook, flips to a page and hands it to me. I peruse the list and cover my mouth on some of them. "You made a list."

"I did, but this isn't about checking off boxes, it's about enjoying each other in every situation." Then, he leans over, pencil in hand, and marks a line through 'Airplane.'"

I love this man. Now I need to tell him, but the flight attendant comes over the intercom and says, "Please fasten your seatbelts. We'll be touching down in twenty minutes."

Chapter Thirty-Two

Hagan

WE DESCEND THE STAIRS TO A WAITING BLACK SUV when our driver peeks around the vehicle. "Hagan." Willy greets us with hugs.

"Mr. Willy, it's good to see you."

He smacks my back twice, glances at Adalee and says, "Keeping out of trouble?"

Adalee blushes as I take the overnight bag from her. "Yep. She's making sure of it. This is my girlfriend, Adalee."

Willy puts his arm around her, "You tell me if he doesn't treat ya right. I know all his secrets."

"I don't have any secrets. You're thinking about Archer and probably Harper."

She clams up as he opens the hatch and I pack our bags. We slide into the back seat, holding hands. Her palms are sweaty and she's quieter than usual. I pump her hand once and she glances away. "What's wrong?"

She shrugs. "I guess I didn't realize you're so rich. That wasn't the team plane—it's too small. You're so normal." Then she stretches her neck to my ear. "And you have a driver. Who has a driver other than billionaires?"

Kissing the smooth skin on the back of her hand, I say, "My dad's a billionaire, not me." She offers me a sheepish grin.

As we ride to the northern suburbs of Chicago, she looks out the window, taking in the sights. I love her innocence. She traveled for gymnastics, but it was smaller SEC cities like Columbus and Baton Rouge, not major U.S. cities.

When we come to a stop in front of my family home, Willy opens the door for Adalee. He pats her on the back. "Have a good time. I've been with them twenty years. They're good people." Adalee gives him a polite smile.

Willy usually drops off at the back entrance, but I guess my mom gave instructions to use the front door since the whole family is coming. I drag Adalee up the steps. "Aren't you forgetting our bags?" she asks.

I freeze. "Oh, umm Willy will grab them."

Her peach lips turn upside down as she rubs them together. "I'm not comfortable with that. We don't have much. We're at least carrying our backpacks."

"Willy, you heard the woman. I'll take the bags."

He laughs. "Alrighty, you can carry them inside, but this is my job and I'll take them to the room your mother prepared. She won't forgive me if you go to your rooms before the pajama party."

Adalee gives me a quizzical glance and mouths, "Pajama party?"

There's no sense in me explaining, she'll have to experience it for herself. So, I keep it simple, "Welcome to the Chatham's."

As soon as I open the door, I'm attacked by my sister, Sarah Jane. Wow, she's excited to see me. It's been a few months since I've seen her. She flew into Lexington in August to see me before going to a marketing meeting in Cincinnati.

"You must be Adalee. You two are the cutest couple ever. Aren't they, Lorenzo?" Sarah Jane asks as her husband walks up behind her, pulling her into his embrace. It's possible he's restraining her.

"Yeah, adorable. Now give them some air. We don't want to scare her off." Lorenzo winks at Adalee.

Admittedly, Adalee appears frozen with the exception of her eyes darting around the grand foyer. She sticks out her hand and Sarah Jane grabs her hand, yanking her into a hug.

Adalee squeaks out, "Pleasure to meet you."

Sarah Jane hauls her into the living room where everyone in the room lights up but Harper. She hates Julia and even though Archer has given his thumbs up, she's hesitant. Her anxiety can get the best of her. She may not be the only one —Adalee's popping her knuckles.

I look between them and walk straight to Harper. My family knows that Harper and I come first for each other. Sarah Jane broke the chain. Harper stands and I open my arms and she jumps out of the navy blue club chair. She's in my arms and she whispers, "Thanks for coming home. I need you."

When I think of home, there's barely a memory without her. Holding her, I can feel the tension in her muscles ease. She probably worried that something would happen to the plane or we would have a wreck.

"I'm here. We're going to fix whatever it is. I promise," I say where no one can hear.

"Harper, give us all a chance to hug your brother," Mom says.

Hap slinks out of my arms. I kiss her on the cheek. "I love you, Hap."

It takes ten minutes to introduce Adalee to everyone. And I give an excessive amount of love to my family. At first, Adalee seems out of place until Megan comes up and takes her into the kitchen. I don't want her out of my sight even though I know my family will love her. But Harper grabs my arm and says, "Don't."

We go into the sunroom and talk. She tells me Tackett and Talynn will be in the suite tomorrow for the game.

"Is she pregnant? That would be Tackett's luck that he would get the girl pregnant that he lost his V card to." I chuckle but Harper's not amused, and neither is my girl-friend who has rounded the corner.

Adalee clears her throat. Shit. I probably have some explaining to do since I'm making light of someone losing their virginity. "Umm, your mom said for you to take me to my room and for me to change. There's a surprise waiting for us. Why would your mom have a surprise... for us?"

Harper snickers. "You haven't told her?"

"Stop, no."

I smack Harper's arm, lacing my fingers with Adalee's. "Come on, let's all go up."

When we reach the bedroom, mom told Willy to put *our* stuff in *my* room. I'm stunned. We're twenty-one but I didn't think my mom would stand for that. Adalee trails her fingers over my dresser, looking at all my pictures. An entire wall is filled with my baseball portraits and action shots. But the dresser is filled with family pictures. Sarah Jane is an amateur photographer but good enough to be a professional. She never poses us because she likes to show the moment—whether it be happy or serious.

She picks up a picture of Harper and I that was taken in high school. Then one of all of us. I wish I knew what she was thinking but she seems in deep thought. I sweep her off her feet to lighten the mood. "Don't worry, Little A."

"Oh God, do not call me that. I hate when Logan calls me that."

I grin. "I know. Every time he says it, I can see you cringe."

She pretends to make her body shiver. "So, is your mom expecting me to have a formal gown for dinner? Is that what she meant by *for me to change?*" Adalee's voice has a twinge of annoyance in it.

Harper swings on the door jam. "Open and find out." Harper points to the box on the bed and wiggles her eyebrows at me.

Adalee blows out a breath before running her finger between the box to open it. She lays the top to the green box on the side as she gently unfolds the tissue paper. She pulls out pajama pants and immediately looks perplexed. They're pajamas. I don't know why she's looking at them so intently. Then I realize she's looking at the back, and I'm looking at the front.

Her eyes pool. Harper's eyes deadpan on me like *what the hell?* Why is she tearing up? I motion for Hap to leave. That's when it hits me like a ninety-eight mile per hour fast-ball. Mom always puts The Chatham Family on the back with the number of the year we were brought into the family, so Adalee's says 23 on it.

"Come here." I draw her to me, and she clutches the pajamas into her chest. She sits on my lap and cries into my shoulder.

She stammers, "I... I don't understand."

Since I talk to my parents all the time, I've told them how much I care about Adalee. I didn't think twice about asking her to come with me to my hometown—it was as if it was already written in stone. My family is full of strong women and the men who love them, so even though mine and

Adalee's relationship is only a few weeks old, I know she belongs here with me. With *us*.

"Because my mom understands me. I never brought Julia to a pajama party night with the family."

I immediately want to take back my words, fearing it would make Adalee sad that her mom isn't here to confide in or lean on. She looks at me with those almond eyes that are wet with tears. A deep V emerges between her brows. "Pajama party night?"

I explain that we will all be wearing pajamas to dinner, then it's game time and we'll finish with a movie in the theatre room.

Her brows shoot up as I wipe away a tear. "Theatre room?"

"Yeah, now let's get you out of those and into these."

Chapter Thirty-Three

Adalee

A non-existent family—that's what I've always had. Emotions rolled deep in my soul when I opened the pajamas, and I cried. Part of me wants to get to know his family and the other wants to retreat to a safe place—alone, where I feel safest. Or go to the gym to work out. Instead, Hagan dragged his hands up my sides, removing his jersey from my body. He kissed his way up to my lips. He's the first person to ease my pain.

He moves to part two of how he gets "ready" for pajama party night. Inserting his thumbs between the fabric and skin, he pushes down my pants. His breath warms my center as I step out. He kisses the scar from my knee surgery. I feel an ache that wants to be satisfied. I must push him closer because he lets out a short breathy laugh and stands.

"They're expecting us downstairs. I wish they weren't..." he says, as Hagan holds the pajama top in front of me. I only saw the back. "Adalee, think about what you have and not about what you didn't have."

I nod as I read the front of the pajama shirt. "World Champion Family" with the Chicago skyline in the shape of a heart. Underneath it says, "Win or Lose." It's cheesy but add in the number on the back and it's adorable. And they gave me a set. I still don't understand why.

We finish dressing then go into Harper's room. They share a Jack and Jill bathroom. But Hagan says they rarely enter each other's rooms that way anymore. He said Harper would sneak into his room a lot when they first got their own rooms.

They take me on a tour and Harper talks to me more than she was earlier. Their house is beautiful, full of photos—they're everywhere. It doesn't jive with boarding schools and private planes. People with this much money are supposed to be snobbish and pretentious, and they don't seem to fit that category at all.

Reggie, his brother who owns his own restaurants, peeks into the living room, calling out, "Dinner's ready!"

We call it supper in the south—unless someone asks you on a date. His nephews and nieces clap. Reggie's children look to be about eight to ten years old. And Sarah Jane's are toddlers.

The kitchen table is set for sixteen. They also have a dining room, but I guess it's too formal for pajamas. The long walnut farmhouse style table has benches on both sides with two cushioned chairs on the ends. The table is adorned with flower arrangements, which are also in the Chicago Kodiak colors.

Hagan says, "Adalee, tell them what your grandfather said when dinner was ready."

My face reddens, not wanting undue attention, especially in this atmosphere. It makes me wonder if Hagan is making fun of how I grew up. Luckily I'm saved by Reggie plopping down a platter of barbeque brisket. He looks at me and says, "Everything is better in the south."

Then his wife semi-shouts from the other end of the table. "Damn right, except for all of you, of course, and the Kodiaks."

This is the most relaxed bunch of people that I've ever been around. Archer and Megan ask me questions they already know the answers to and make me feel at home.

The meal Reggie prepared is not on mine and Hagan's athletic diet, but Hagan is digging in, so I guess this is one of those treats he was talking about. Corn on the cob, potato wedges, baked beans, roasted Brussel sprouts, and macaroni and cheese round out the meal. I can't remember the last time I had homemade mac-n-cheese. I've never had Brussel sprouts with barbecue but it's the first side to be demolished.

Conversation is easy. Hagan's hand drifts up my leg while under the table. It's a good thing I have on pajamas. Everyone takes their plates to the sink, rinses, and loads them into the dishwasher—including Hagan's dad. I'm in the twilight zone because a billionaire is like the rest of us.

Mrs. Chatham calls us all into the living room. "Chatham's unite for pajama party night." She holds a tray of drinks in her hand that looks like shots of vodka or tequila. All of the adults reach for a drink, except me. I look at Hagan and he sets the shot in his hand back on the tray.

"We don't drink," Hagan explains. "But hold on." He leaves and returns quickly with a flavored water spritzer.

Mrs. Chatham, Christina, says, "Since when?"

Hagan doesn't balk, not even for a second. "Since I met her." Which isn't exactly true. He's had a beer or two but never more. "If she doesn't drink, neither do I." His mom looks like she's going to explode with joy and pride, and I don't blame her. She raised a fantastic son—and it looks like three times over, his brothers included.

We start out with Pictionary, not the new version but old school style with the big dry erase board in the center. We divide into teams by alphabet so Hagan, Harper, and I are on the same team. Hagan has his arm around me while Harper draws. She squiggles a black line, horizontally across the surface, and Hagan yells, "Creek!" in two seconds. I shout "Snake" right after.

Harper points at Hagan, and he jumps up and I watch them clap hands and dance around as they say, "It's good to be a twin. Take that." Pure joy is plastered across their faces. The love and happiness in their eyes is overwhelming in the best way.

The Hagan/Harper combo proves unbeatable, but when he isn't drawing or celebrating, he's kissing my cheek or rubbing my back.

When it's my turn to draw, the word is *storm*. It takes time to sketch, as I'm detailed. Mr. Chatham rapidly shouts random words in succession. Then Hagan says, "Dad, give her a chance." His dad continues but finally says the word. I do a standing back tuck in the middle of the living room. Both teams cheer as I take a bow. His dad, George, rushes over, hip bumping me as we attempt to dance like Hagan and Harper.

"Take that," he says, grinning from ear to ear.

Hagan pushes to his feet, pulling me into his arms, "She's mine. Babe, you need to be careful on the knee. I want to cheer my girl on at her gymnastics meets." Then he puckers up, giving me a chaste kiss.

The other team consisting of Megan, Sarah Jane, Lorenzo, Reggie and Opal, all make it known that they want to come to my meets, too.

I've never had this kind of support from my small family. Emotions get the best of me and I can't hold it in. "Excuse me." I quickly walk into the nearest bathroom, hoping they don't notice, I'm getting ready to break.

There's a knock on the door and I fully expect it to be Hagan but it's his mom. "Adalee."

I splash water on my face, drying it with the fingertip towel before opening the door. Mrs. Chatham's arms swing wide, embracing me. "I know we're too much. We're not good at restraining our feelings."

"You have a wonderful family. My dad pays for my stuff, but I can't remember the last time he came to a gymnastics meet. Encouragement is something I haven't had from my family in a decade. This family is perfect."

She scoffs, throwing her head back. "That couldn't be further from the truth. But we love each other fiercely."

Mrs. Chatham insists I call her Christina and asks me to help in the kitchen before we continue playing games. She made cookies decorated with the movies we're going to act out. She places the cookies bottom side up onto the tray. I saw one and she tapped my hand. "No cheating. Since you've seen it, let's eat this one."

She breaks it half, handing me half. My mom would love Mrs. Chatham. If *Parenting* magazine was doing an article on how to raise successful, competitive, loving children, she should be on the cover.

"Adalee. I've never heard Hagan any happier than he is right now. There's a musical quality to his voice like he's singing your name all the time."

I blush, embarrassed. This type of openness is new to me. "He's a great guy. If I would have talked to him that first night, I may not have torn my ACL. Maybe he would have given me a ride home," I say as I carry in one of the aluminum baking sheets filled with green and yellow Oreo balls.

She ducks into one of the cabinets, coming out with a ceramic tray that says *game night* on it. We begin to organize sweets on the dish as we talk.

"Now that you're together, you need to let him help carry your burdens. Don't make him guess. He told Archer and Harper that your mom passed away. I'm sorry." The click of a camera shuttering catches my attention and I notice Sarah Jane is taking pics. "Megan lost both her parents when she was nine. Hagan will listen but if you want someone that has been through something similar, Megan is strong like you are. I think my boys are attracted to strong women."

Wow, having the matriarch of this family call me strong has me reeling with confidence. I've never considered myself strong, at least not internally. I just like to portray it on the outside. But it's true. I am strong.

Chapter Thirty-Four

Hagan

After Harper and I run upstairs to check on our nieces and nephews, we have a heart to heart in the nursery. She lets loose of what she's been holding in. I knew something was gnawing in her gut because something was wrong with mine. When she's emptied her thoughts I ask, "So?"

The one person I need on my side is Harper and she knows it. We rock in the two gliders, our voices a trace above a whisper.

She says, "I like her more now. The back flip thing really sealed the deal."

More?

I raise one brow, questioning her.

"You're my twin. I want you to be happy," she says as she bites her lip which is my sister's tell that she's struggling to be honest. Hap is a tough cookie. She didn't like Julia, and maybe it was because Julia took my attention away from her, but Adalee isn't taking anything away from Harper. We don't go to the same school. and I talk to her every day, definitely more than when I was with Julia.

Frustrated, I push off the chair and look at her over my shoulder. "Is anyone ever going to be good enough?"

"Come on, of course. But how are you two going to make a relationship work once both of your seasons start?" she asks.

I've thought about the same thing. Our seasons are at the same time. We'll be traveling to the different SEC schools as well as out of conference. I sigh. "Hap, we'll work it out. She's the most genuine person I know."

"Okay. I like her. It just took so long for you to get back to being *you* after Julia. You were great at acting like you weren't in pain with others. Do you know how many times I had to tell Tackett you weren't interested in Talynn, and that you were just trying to survive a breakup? I don't want you to be heartbroken again."

"I know. My feelings hit hard and quick."

She stands and wraps her arms around my waist and asks, "Do you love her?" I nod. "Have you told her?"

"Not using those three words, but I do. I've known for a long time. Something inside me knew she'd be the last woman I would ever kiss."

My sister springs into my arms. "Am I the first person you've told?"

"Yeah."

"You need to tell her. You should have told her before me."

"I'm waiting for the perfect time. Let's go before mom sends Megan after us." We laugh, noting that Megan's a perfectionist, never late. It's no wonder she fits in nicely.

Everyone draws numbers to select the teams. Number one is Mom's team, and number two is Dad's. And that's exactly how it is in our family. What Mom says is the final word. Sometimes, my parents will come to conclusions together, but my dad always says, "I married your mother not only because I love her, but I also trust her with my heart and my children."

Harper and Adalee end up on Dad's team and I end up on Mom's. Although Mom is sitting the guessing out because she baked the cookies.

I watch Adalee interact with Hap, Dad, Megan, and Lorenzo, working with them flawlessly. Sometimes I'm not even concentrating on what my team is acting out. Instead, I'm looking at my future—the future of my family.

When one of us brings a person into this family, it affects us all. The dynamics shift with each new member. Of course, Megan had known the family since she and Sarah Jane were in college together. But still, Sarah Jane had to find her new normal with her brother marrying her friend. I hope Harper and Adalee can be as close as Megan and Sarah Jane.

Adalee bounces on her toes as Harper guesses *The Old Man & the Sea* correctly.

"So easy," I say laughing. It's hilarious because Adalee walked like an old man then pointed to her eye. Harper's room is filled with books of all genres. She loves to read so it's no wonder she guessed it so easily.

Adalee makes a comeback. "Oh yeah. I'll pull another cookie, and if you get it right before your twin, I'll give you ten dollars and drive to class next week."

I stalk toward her, "I always win, Adalee. And we're going to raise the stakes."

She pops her hip, folding her arms across her chest. Then she cocks her head. "I don't have more than ten dollars to spare."

The air crackles between us and a rare hush blankets the room. I move in, touching her arm then her hair. I cup her jaws with both hands. "If Hap guesses correctly first, I'll give you fifty dollars, and I'll do your dishes every day. But If I win, you have to kiss me. Right here in front of my family."

Hap leaps off the floor. "Take the deal, Adalee."

"Deal." Adalee sticks out her hand for me to shake.

I slip my hand into hers, caressing her palm with one finger. An almost hidden smile twitches on her lips. If I was her, I'd want to lose just so we could kiss, but I know better. We're collegiate athletes and competitiveness courses through our veins. "Deal."

She draws a cookie then my girlfriend runs around the living room. Damn, I love this side of her—a happy little spark plug. The women root for Harper and the men for me.

Suddenly, Adalee stops and walks slowly down the center of the room. She glances to the left and right when Hap shouts, "Runaway Bride."

"Yes. Yes." Adalee shouts as they hug, bouncing around. The room is roaring with laughter. Yep, at my expense. I'm fifty dollars down with more dish duty in my future.

Hap squeezes her tightly and yaps, "We're keeping you. Even if you break up, I'm keeping you." She holds her pinky up and Adalee follows. "Soul sisters."

My best friend and twin sister just chose my girlfriend over me. I don't know whether to be happy or sad. Hap has never chosen someone over me. On the other hand, I want Hap to love Adalee as much as I do.

Archer puts his hand on my shoulder. "You did good. She fits us perfectly."

He's right. She does. This is a glimpse of how I want my life to be.

The rest of the night my sister and my girlfriend are inseparable. One thing is clear—I'm going to need to find my sister a boyfriend.

Chapter Thirty-Five

Adalee

It's a *suite* life. The university suite has nothing on this VIP room at Kodiak Stadium. Most of the family went earlier than us because Hagan had to work on his paper. He hopes to be celebrating tonight so he wanted to finish it and not have it hanging over his head.

There's more than family in the suite. Megan introduces me to her sister, Talynn, and her boyfriend, Tackett, who plays for Atlanta. They explain that they all know each other from the Sarasota Sharks so everything starts making sense.

There are wives and girlfriends standing in front of the glass, looking out on the field. I assume they are player wives because they're wearing jerseys with names and numbers. Callaghan #15 and Shepherd #23. Megan gestures for Talynn and me to follow.

"Hey girls," Megan shrieks. "It's been so long. Every time I've been in town, you ladies have been at away games."

They all exchange hugs then Megan introduces me. "This is Hagan's girlfriend, Adalee."

"I'm Avery and I'm obviously ready to pop. Please tell me you are in nursing in case I go into labor."

I chuckle, popping my knuckles. "Sorry, engineering. Congratulations."

Avery gently slaps Talynn on the back. "Well, Talynn you're the winner. A massage therapist is close enough."

Megan looks at the woman standing next to her. "And this is my best friend, Kenni. She works in marketing for the Kodiaks."

I notice Kenni is counting her fingers thumb to pinky before she greets me. "Hi, I don't know Hagan well, but we went to the same college for a couple of years." She leans in and whispers, "I dated a guy on the baseball team." She steps back. "Wils told me Hagan transferred to Kentucky. Is that how you met?"

I knew she looked familiar; Kenni and Wilson Shepherds' love story has been all over the sports channels. They're building trauma centers completely funded through their charity.

Out of the corner of my eye, I see Hagan's within earshot, so I raise my voice a little louder and say, "Yeah, he tore my ACL."

He comes up behind me, skimming his arms around my waist. "Tell the whole truth." I can't see his face, but he must flash his dimples because I watch everyone's face soften and give the look of *aww*. "Tell them how you couldn't quit thinking about me. You were dreaming of me while walking across campus at night. You know that's not safe."

The pregnant woman, Avery, asks, "Were you thinking about having sex with him?" Kenni smacks her arm while everyone else laughs. Evidently, Avery has no filter, reminding me of Ginger.

When things quiet, I say, "I was thinking about his laugh. I hadn't met him yet, but his laugh choked me. It's so...."

Hagan kisses me on the cheek. "She loves me." I feel my face redden. "But she made me work for it."

My face warms. Neither of us have said those three little words but Hagan isn't shy about hinting at the fact and letting me warm up to acknowledging my feelings out loud.

The announcer comes over the speaker and asks us to stand for the national anthem. I hear Megan say, "I can't believe Archer and I married on home plate at the beginning of the season."

Avery and Megan put their arms around Kenni, both squeezing her shoulder. "You're up next."

"I'm only twenty-three. Even though we've loved each other forever, we have more work to do on the trauma centers and Kodiak Kove before we get married. Megan, we have a plot of land waiting on you and Archer."

Hagan gives me the rundown on the land the star Kodiaks bought. They're constructing a neighborhood called Kodiak Kove. It's intended for all the best friends and their families so the wives and children have a support system while the men are playing away. Wilson and Kenni, along with Patrick and Avery, are building houses for their parents too. They're saving a few plots of Archer and Megan and a couple of their other best friends. They want their children to grow up together.

Then Hagan drags me away. He's weaving me in and out of fans walking the Kodiak Koncourse. We finally end up in an empty room filled with cables and electrical wires. Hagan has the look in his eye like he's the bear and I'm the honey pot.

This is the look he had this morning when he asked for a study bonus. I sat on the edge of the bed, exactly like he explained to me. It was the sexiest moment of my life. He stood naked in front of me with one roped forearm hanging to his side—the other guiding my head. Occasionally, he would stop, pulling out running over my lips while rasping dirty thoughts. "You want this salty goodness on your skin or in your mouth?" Since my mouth was full, he answered for me. "Let's go with... skin. My good girl loves it dirty."

He gave me a pearl necklace. It was hot watching his face morph from pleasure to tight to relaxed with that easy going smile, then we showered together since his family was gone.

Hagan backs me up against the concrete block wall. Kissing me for several minutes. Each motion digs into my mouth deeper. His hands work fast, ridding me of my pants. He stares at the sheer black lace thong then rips them off. Two days ago, I was a virgin and now I'm having sex in a closet at a major league baseball game.

He never fumbles around. It's smooth like he's practiced a thousand times. I stiffen and he recognizes the change in my body language. "What's wrong?" His words glide across my skin.

I swallow, "How many times have you done this?"

"In here? None."

His lips travel over the inside of my thigh but then he rises and takes my shirt with him. "God, I'm so happy I transferred."

I suck in a deep breath feeling the heat between my legs. "I mean..."

He stops dead in his tracks. Even in this dimly lit electrical closet, I can see the glaze covering his irises. Why am I asking what he's done before me? Does it matter?

"Adalee, you know I've had sex before you but that's in the past. You're my future. And now that I've had you, no one else but you will do."

My shoulders rise and fall in deep, lengthy motions. My breath hitches. "I don't want to disappoint you."

"Never." He takes his shirt off and pushes his jeans down his muscular legs, stepping out. I feel his erection against my stomach. He lifts me up. "Wrap your flexible body around me."

I snap my legs around his waist. He focuses on my eyes. "I love you, Adalee."

We gaze into each other's eyes until he feels I'm not saying it back. He tenderly takes my lips into his and mumbles, "Don't say it until you're ready. Just promise me if you know I'm not the one for you, you'll have mercy on me and tell me soon."

"You're the only person I've ever wanted," I say, pulling back so he can see *my* truth in my eyes. "Now, please do everything you wanted when you dragged me into this closet."

His gaze sparkles with a mixture of lust and happiness. My hands trail his carved arms as he leans me against the wall with one arm holding me up. He inserts with his other. We start out to a low, slow drumbeat. It's incredible the way he can hold me up and move us both in perfect symmetry.

My back scrapes against the wall but it intensifies my pleasure. He whispers that he loves me over and over. And I feel how much he loves me through the connectivity of our bodies. This is not sex. It's something purer. He's right—it's love.

My muscles tighten around him so hard, it's possible I could be breaking his hip bones. "Yes, yes. Hag.. Hag... Hagan, please."

"Please what? You want me to make you come?"

"Yes, I'm so close." But what does he do? He slows down. "Do you want me to beg? Please."

He repositions himself so that he slides his fingers between my folds, circling my nub with fiery fingertips. "Is this what you want?"

I pant. "Both, I want both."

He begins moving in and out slow while he makes circles, pressing in harder and faster. "Yeeeeessss."

When he feels my body constrict around him, he let's go. His juices inside me. Neither of us say a word while we come down. Finally, he pulls out then slides me down his body. "I'm sorry. I shouldn't have done that. You just felt so damn good."

He hangs his head as I press on my toes. "I've been on the pill for years to help me regulate. I'm sure we're fine."

He parts his lips, taking mine one more time before looking for something to clean us up. He finds a scratchy blue towel in the corner. I furl my lips, shaking my head, emphatically —no.

He shrugs me off. "We have to Adalee."

I grab my torn underwear from the floor, wiping my legs and center, fold them and wipe off his body parts. "There's no telling how long that blue rag has been here. It could have raccoon pee on it."

He belly laughs, the sound that made me fall for him. Literally and figuratively.

"I really do love you." He claims once again as we dress.

When we get back to the suite, Harper asks, "Where have you two been? Patrick hit a home run."

"Just showing her around." Hagan grins and turns to shield my face.

"Did you show her your favorite hiding spot?" Harper asks and he jerks her into a hug and rubs his knuckles against her head, causing static to build.

"You know, when you get a boyfriend, I'm going to know everything too." He winks and she hugs him tighter.

I wonder if my dad's step-twins are this close.

The Kodiaks end up winning the game, and they're set to play tomorrow. If they win, then they are back to back champions. The players start filtering in, receiving congratulatory hugs from the Chatham's, and of course, their wives and girlfriends.

We congregate around the wall of televisions watching the ending of the Kentucky versus LSU game. Patrick sets Avery on his lap, wanting to watch his cousin, Mac Callaghan in this big game that will determine who's number one football team in the nation.

Harper, Hagan, and I sit on the green leather tufted couch with big, rolled arms. Logan throws an interception with seven minutes left in the game and Kentucky's down by three. He comes over to the sideline and throws his helmet. I've never seen him lose control as a friend or on the field. Mac walks over, patting him on the back and the camera zooms in on them. They exchange words. I'm not a lip reader but it appeared that Logan said, "Where the fuck were you?" Mac points down to his feet but turns with his back to the camera as his arms flail.

Patrick and Avery aren't the only ones watching intently, Archer is too. Logan told me, if he decides to go pro after the season, that he wants Archer to be his agent.

Suddenly, Harper yells, "Yes!" The defense caused a fumble. Logan and Mac put their helmets back on, jogging back onto the field. Logan taps Mac's helmet, and the previous play is forgotten. They're on the same team and roommates.

They march down the field and score on a forty-eight yard pass from Logan to Mac and win the game. The sideline reporter interviews both of the star players. Harper leans over to me and says, "Is he this sexy all the time? Umm, the sweat, the longish, matted hair he pushes behind his ear...and everything about him!"

I slowly turn to face her, and by the expression on her face, she's not kidding. "No. He's annoying as fugg, all cocky like everyone wants him," I whisper, knowing Hagan would go all alpha brother.

Harper bumps my shoulder. "Well, I'm sure every woman does." Then she snickers.

Every girl on campus wants him and some have gotten lucky.

Archer says, "We're linking them up on satellite. Mac wants to talk to Patrick." We wait so Patrick and Hagan can talk to Mac, but when the satellite link comes on, it's Mac and Logan.

Mac jumps up and down in excitement. "Did ya'll see my boy? A perfect spiral for a touchdown. He's going number one in the draft."

Like a proud papa, Patrick says, "We did but you had to catch it and you flew down the sideline. Congratulations, now go celebrate with your friends."

Logan envelops Mac. His sandy blond hair drips with sweat.

Hagan says, "It got ugly for a minute, but you pulled it off. Congrats roomies."

Logan winks and swipes his hair from his face. "I think everyone should come to the SEC championship game. Goodluck tomorrow. Win this on your home field." Then he pauses. "Hey Callaghan, thanks for sending your cousin here to play with me and for bringing Hagan along. I couldn't ask for better roommates and friends."

Harper digs her fingers into my arms, mumbling, "And humble. He's fucking humble."

He's a good guy but humble isn't the exact description I would give.

Hagan pulls me into him, kissing me on the cheek. "And thank you for making me go to the party. And for asking her to pick you up. I never thanked you for that."

"What are best friends for?" Logan responds. Hagan smiles and I can't tear my gaze from his profile. He's the perfect combination of sexy athlete and boy next door.

"Safe trip guys. We'll see you Sunday night."

For some reason, I feel like I have a family that I've made on my own. A family of friends and Hagan's family. I can't wait to tell Hagan that I feel the same way he does, but I want to do something special.

Chapter Thirty-Six

Hagan

It's getting cold on the job site. Adalee and I are here twice as much now that we took on a leadership role. Our project analysis is due the week after Thanksgiving to give the company and the professors time to look them over. If you come up with the option that they've already decided on then it will be an automatic eighty percent. But eighty percent doesn't help you graduate with ropes and summa cum laude. The other twenty percent is in your cost analysis.

Joe rides home with us today because we're going on a double date tonight with our girls. We stayed the night at their apartment a few times over the past couple of weeks. We cook together. Well, Joe and I cook, and the ladies bake us cookies and brownies that we have to work off and neither of us mind our exercise routines—at all.

Tonight, we're taking them to an upscale Italian place downtown. It's a surprise for Ginger's birthday before the Thanksgiving weekend.

When we get to the apartment, Adalee and I take a nap. We've fallen into a routine where we nap together before we have practice. Luckily, both of us have a few days off, so we can sleep until it's time to dress for dinner. I love her soft purrs as she sleeps. We start off spooning, but she always rolls onto her stomach and hikes her leg up over my waist.

Nudging her awake, my voice rumbles from my chest as I say, "Babe, I have something I want to try."

"Okay..."

"We shouldn't waste your flexibility. You may not always be this bendable." I flash her my dimples, which she says is comparable to a toddler giggling—irresistible.

It takes her a few minutes but then she's game. It's another reason I love her so much. She's willing to experiment to find out what both of us want and enjoy.

She hasn't said she loves me, but she does. Adalee expresses it to me every day, just not in words. She's found a family in mine. Harper calls or texts her almost every day. And when I ask her what they talk about she just laughs and says, "Wouldn't you like to know? Some things are between girls."

The sex with Adalee feels different than it has before. I can't say it's a position or an angle because that's not it at all. We're just two middle pieces of a puzzle that found their way to each other. We're not a corner or an edge, we're everything in the center that makes the picture complete.

Joe and I sit in the living room and wait for the girls to come out. They nearly take our breath when they appear in dresses, earrings, and their makeup. They're stunning. Our mouths hang open because we're just *that* speechless. Ginger and Adalee blush as they walk toward us.

I slide my arms around Adalee's waist. "I don't think I'm good enough for you, Adalee Summers." She has on black strappy heels that show off her legs and an ivory sweater dress that hugs her curves and contrasts with her chestnut brown hair.

"I bought this when Ginger and I went to the mall. You're fairly handsome yourself."

I raise an eyebrow. "Fairly?" She keeps telling me that my eyebrows betray my emotions. Those little muscle movements giveaway my thoughts, and as much as I try to not use them, it's in my DNA. I wear my feelings on my sleeve for her, and I don't care if everyone knows how much I love her.

After dinner, Joe and Ginger have one glass of wine, and then we head to the dance floor in the other room. It's all classical music, and Adalee loves it. I love learning new things about her, but classical music doesn't jive with her favorite candy, Blow Pops. Although it may be why she's a natural. We slow dance next to Joe and Ginger, and I'm loving every moment of it.

There are only a few others on the dance floor when Joe drops down on one knee. Ginger gasps, and so does Adalee.

"Red, I know we've only been together six months, but I know I love you and want you with me for the rest of my life. Will you marry me?" He flips the top of the box open.

Ginger's hands fly over her face. This is not an act; she had no idea this was coming. She's crying. Adalee's tearing up.

"Yes. I love you Joe."

They're on their knees kissing and hugging. I have to admit, I'm a little jealous. I was hoping Adalee would vocalize her feelings, but if she said she loved me now, I know it would be forced.

Love is patient.

We dance the night away until we drop Joe and Ginger at a nearby hotel to celebrate by themselves. Adalee and I talk about our best friend's engagement on the way to her apartment. How will this work? "Will they get married and kick me out of the apartment?" she asks, as she corkscrews her mouth.

"I think Joe wanted to show her how strongly he feels about her. We graduate in a year and a half. Technically, Joe or I could be drafted this year."

"What? You could leave?" Her voice is thin and scratchy laced with anxiety.

I know that tone anywhere. This is how Hap felt when I left. She put on a brave face but I knew it was going to be difficult for her. If I was drafted, I wouldn't take the offer. I can't leave Adalee.

"Yeah, but that's not what I want. I'm not sure I want to play professionally. If it doesn't happen it won't kill me." I need to figure it out though. I have an extra year of eligibility so technically I don't have to decide anything now but it's in the forefront of my mind. Because when I do propose to Adalee one day, I want to have a plan. In my family, we make plans, lists, and goals.

"Oh." That's all she says. It's a perfect opportunity for her to tell me she loves me. Damn, maybe she isn't feeling it the same way I am.

We go inside and change into our sweats. We have everything packed to leave for Chicago early in the morning.

We make notes about our project outline—hoping to finish it while we're in Chicago for Thanksgiving. I asked Adalee if she wanted to go to Florida to see her dad, telling her I would go with her, but she refused. I can't imagine not seeing my parents on Thanksgiving.

Her dad *did* invite her, but it would be a seventeen hour drive each way, and he didn't give her money for a plane ticket. When I offered to pay for the plane ticket, she said, "Money isn't the reason."

He moved to Florida right after he came here and told Adalee that he remarried. Her childhood home is on the market. Her dad said he would give her half of the profit. He's trying to make amends, but he doesn't realize it isn't money that Adalee needs—it's love.

"No pajamas?" Adalee asks my mom.

She chuckles as she uses the hand mixer to mash the potatoes. "No. That's reserved for when the entire family is here. Reggie and his family alternate Thanksgiving between her family and ours. But everyone else will be here shortly."

"Thanks for having me."

She turns off the mixer and taps the silver prongs against the edge of the bowl. "You don't have to be with Hagan to come here. You can call me, or George, for that matter, whenever you need anything."

"Call me about what?" Hagan's dad asks as he comes in with a copper hammered bucket of ice that matches their cabinetry.

After he sets the bucket on the island, he saunters over, kissing Mom on the cheek. "Just telling Adalee we're here if she needs us."

"Hagan, how about you and Adalee show me your outline while we wait for your mother to finish basting the bird?"

Adalee retrieves her backpack from the bedroom, and we meet in the sunroom. Dad smiles as Adalee's face lights up as she shares our engineering project. Dad makes some suggestions. Then to my surprise, repeats what Archer told me months ago at the football game. "Son, you're gifted. When it's time and you're ready, I want you to be the visionary for the new construction of Kodiak Stadium."

My dad was never a professional baseball player, and I think part of him doesn't want that life for me. Maybe he thinks I'm not suited for it. Archer was suited for it but got hurt. Me, I would be happy with a nine to five job if I was able to see my wife and kids every day. But I love baseball, and I'm fucking talented, so who knows?

I'm in awe. My dad is a loving man but he's also fiercely competitive. "Thanks Dad. I'm not sure what the future holds." I'm majoring in architecture with a minor in engineering, so I'm leaning toward using my degrees. It would be a monumental accomplishment if I could leave a lasting legacy on Kodiak Stadium.

"And Adalee, I'll extend you a job offer the day you graduate. I've never seen a woman's face sparkle over concrete studs and electrical placements."

I wink at Adalee and clear my throat. "Oh, she loves electrical. She's been trying to decide where to put the electrical closet." Her face turns a dark shade of red and her eyes narrow.

We go upstairs to put our stuff away, changing out of the sweats we wore on the plane and into casual but nice clothes. Most of the time my mom doesn't care, but on Thanksgiving, we must look nice. No hats allowed, which means I had to shower and tame my waves.

When I walk out of the bathroom, Adalee walks straight into my arms. "I'm sorry. I wanted this to be special, but I can't hold it in any longer."

"Are you pregnant?"

"What? No. I wanted to do something special for you, but we've been so busy and I... I... love you, Hagan Chatham."

She gives me a fleeting glance before looking down. I tilt her chin and her gaze follows. "You love me?" She nods. "Like *really* love me?" This time as she nods, a scant smile appears. "Don't be scared of loving me."

Adalee lays her hands on my chest and says, "Hagan, please don't hurt me."

I cup her cheeks as my thumbs skim over her cheekbones to her lips. "Babe, loving me is the safest thing you will ever do." She presses onto her toes, and we kiss until our lips are swollen and Hap bursts in. I whisper, "I love you," before releasing her.

"Okay, okay love birds. Dinner's ready." Hap grabs Adalee's hand, dragging her down the hall.

Our family has a tradition, like most families, to say what we're thankful for, and my mom says," I'm thankful the Lord brought Adalee into Hagan's life and into ours."

I watch as Adalee's lip trembles and a blurry beautiful film covers her eyes. It's not her turn but she speaks anyway. "I'm thankful for all of you. You've given me the best present parents could possibly give—your son. Hagan's an incredible person, and I'm lucky he loves me. I didn't make it easy on him. He told me he loved me weeks ago when we were here. He didn't expect it back and gave me time to come to terms with someone loving me. Today, I told Hagan I love him, too."

A stray tear falls over her cheek. I squeeze her hand, letting her know she doesn't have to do this. Her eyes drop to mine as she spills her heartaches. "I haven't sat at a Thanksgiving table for years. My dad and I went through the motions of having turkey and dressing, but it was a normal dinner with no fanfare. We never said we were grateful for anything because we weren't. We dealt with losing my mom separately. Now, if anything ever happened... I have a family that will help me cope."

My siblings and I are lucky to have wonderful parents, and I had never thought about it until I met Adalee." I tug her under my arm as each member of my family says, "We love you. We're here."

Then I kiss her cheek and say how thankful I am for her, my family, for Mac suggesting I transfer, and for my new best friends, Joe and Logan.

When my family is settling down to watch some football, I sneak away and make a call.

Chapter Thirty-Seven

Adalee

"Hurry up, Hagan." You promised to take me to Navy Pier. We have one day left so he can show me the city. There's so much to do here, and I want to walk the Magnificent Mile and do all the touristy stuff.

It's been the best weekend. Thursday was Thanksgiving, then yesterday, we worked on our project a bit before heading to Sarah Jane's house with Archer, Megan, and Harper.

"Don't rush me, woman," Hagan jokes as he places his ball cap on his head. The edges of his hair curl underneath.

I spring onto his back. "I swear, you take longer than me to get ready."

Hagan takes me everywhere I want to go. We eat all the things we shouldn't—like cotton candy, big pretzels with mustard, and soda. But my favorite is sitting in the Ferris wheel, closed in but looking out over the Chicago skyline.

All I can think about is how small we are in this world. And how in just two months, my whole world has shifted. My life revolves around the man holding my hand and would be meaningless without him.

This would have been the quintessential time to tell Hagan how I feel but I couldn't hold it in. But I want this to be special, so I squeeze his hand and look into his liquid browns and say, "Hagan, thank you. I don't know what I would do without you."

He pulls me onto his lap. "Same. It's a good thing we don't have to worry about that. Love you long time."

"Love you long time." He's been mumbling that to me for weeks now, and I finally say it back. I'm sure of our relationship, and every word spoken between us makes me fall deeper in love.

It's Sunday morning and we have to fly home on the team plane. The party is over. There's no mile high anything because we work on our project non-stop because it's due this week. We have everything we need; we just have to put it all together and type it up.

Hagan says he has a surprise for me tonight, and I can't wait because he has the best surprises.

———

HE TAKES ME HOME BECAUSE HE SAYS HE NEEDS TO GET the surprise ready. I hope it's not like Joe's surprise. I need to take baby steps. Ginger left with Joe for Thanksgiving. He wanted her to meet his family and show off her diamond ring. I hope she comes home soon because I want to hear all about his family and how she feels now that she's had time for her engagement to sink in.

I also want to tell her about Hagan and me. She'll be just as happy for me as I am for her. I text her to see how far they are, but she doesn't respond.

My phone buzzes against my dresser. "You ready?" Hagan asks.

"Yeah, I took a nap. I hope casual is okay," I say, walking out, locking the door behind me.

Hagan hangs up and walks around opening the door for me. "Have you heard from Joe or Ginger? I texted him and he hasn't texted me back."

"They're probably at his house having... you know."

"Sex. Yeah I know what that is."

Yes you do.

He leans over and kisses me. "You know, I'm fifteen minutes early so we have time to... you know." He laughs as he runs his hand up my thigh.

The warmth of his hand feels so good, but I want the surprise. "I really do love you."

"I'll never tire of hearing those words from you." He peppers me with kisses before setting out for the adventure he has planned.

We wind through campus and there's a traffic jam at the main intersection of campus. We can't see what's happening. Hagan's antsy, tapping his fingers against the steering wheel. He keeps looking at his watch.

We move inches in ten minutes. It's rare to see Hagan upset. I saw it two times before we were together, and it was only at me. Both football games before the night I finally admitted my feelings for him. But he isn't concealing his anxiousness which makes me start popping my knuckles.

I touch his arm and slide my palm into his, hoping it calms us both. We round a corner seeing flashing red and blue lights. Sirens blare as I make out a fire truck. "I bet it's a wreck."

"Yeah but we're stuck. We're going to be late."

I slide my hand out of his hand and rub his thigh, getting dangerously close to the ridge that's starting to swell in his pants. He places my hand on the bulge in his jeans. I love how a simple touch affects him. I laugh and say, "This is probably why there's a wreck. Horny couples that can't wait until they get home."

He chuckles. "I'll keep it in my pants, but I love it anytime you touch me."

As the distance between us and the wreck disappears, two ambulances pull away with their lights on and a third is sliding a person in. We only see feet. The cop directs us in the other direction. We finally get to The Jugger Joint, and we're forty-five minutes late.

Hagan approaches the hostess stand, "Reservations for Chatham. Sorry we're late. There was a big wreck."

"No problem. We're slow on Sunday nights." She smiles showing us into a private room. The table is decorated with a *Happy Thanksgiving* flower arrangement on the table. I didn't notice if the tables on my way in had the same decorations.

The waiter asks, "Can I get you drinks while you wait for the rest of the party?"

Hagan narrows his gaze at the waiter, but replies, "Two Pellegrino's please."

"Who's joining us?" I ask.

"You'll have to wait and see."

We talk about our seasons starting soon and what we can do to make sure we have time together. Discipline is the key. Study while the other one is on away trips or at practice. Fifteen minutes pass and Hagan looks at his phone and puts it back down in frustration only to pick it back up and text someone.

"Maybe whoever is meeting us is caught in the same traffic." I reach for his hand. It's probably Joe and Ginger or Logan and Mac meeting us for Friendsgiving. Hagan's fidgety and it's out of left field.

A few minutes later, my phone rings. "It's Ginger," I say excitedly.

"Hey, where are you?" I ask.

There's a long pause, then she stammers, "Joe and I are at the hospital. It's bad, Addy Bug. He was bleeding." Her words become cries.

University hospital?"

Hagan's lips ask who.

"Yeah."

"We're on our way."

I hang up. "Joe and Ginger are in the hospital. Let's go."

He doesn't hesitate, we're in the car and at the hospital in a matter of minutes. Hagan runs in, holding my hand all the way from the emergency parking lot. "Joe Danke's room please."

"I'm sorry sir, he's in testing. You'll have to wait."

I interrupt, leaning forward on the counter. "Ginger Bell's room?"

She taps her fingers on the keyboard and looks up. "Three twenty nine. Only two people at a time."

We're flying down the hall. We hit the button that opens the doors into the emergency room corridor, and it opens like we're opening King Tuts tomb; it's so slow.

We look to the left and right, figuring out which way to go. When we come to her room, we stop, composing ourselves before walking in. We need to be calm, because on the phone, Ginger was agitated and distraught.

Hagan turns the knob, and I walk in before him. Ginger sees us and starts bawling. I'm holding her and Hagan's holding me. There's blood in her hair. It's a deep almost blue, hue. "Are you okay?" I ask. "I mean is anything broken?"

"I don't think so. I may have a concussion. But Joe, he was bleeding and wasn't talking. I yelled and yelled for him, but he didn't respond. Please Hagan find out what happened to him. I'm supposed to marry him when we graduate next year."

I sit on the bed, running my fingers through her hair hoping it will calm her down. Then I pull her into my chest. "He'll be okay. Whatever it is, you know Joe will put up a fight. He loves you. He's going to fugging fight to be with you. No, you know what, he's going to fucking fight for you."

That draws a vacant smile. "Thanks, Addy Bug."

Hagan says, "What happened?"

"All I remember is Joe saying, 'Shit! That car isn't stopping!' Joe tried to swerve but the car hit us, and we hit a pole. I don't remember if it was a streetlight or an electricity poll. God, please let him be okay."

"Do you know if Joe's parents have been called? Or coach?" Hagan asks. She shakes her head, no. "Okay, I'll call Coach."

Hagan excuses himself as he calls the baseball coach. Ginger and I stay silent until she finally says, "One minute we're discussing wedding dates and the next minute we're in the hospital. It can't be God's plan for us not to be together. It can't."

"Let's say a prayer." She nods. "Please give Joe the strength to heal his body. Give the doctors the knowledge to heal him. And most of all, please tell Joe we love him, and we want to dance at his wedding next year."

Then, Ginger and I sob together.

Chapter Thirty-Eight

Hagan

Coach said he'll handle everything. I wander the halls searching for Joe. No one is keeping me from seeing him. I look at the dry erase boards beside the room numbers, searching.

Danke... Danke... Danke...Summers... What Summers?

And that's when my world crashes. Adalee's dad was late to dinner. Fuck, no. It can't be. But Summers isn't a common last name. My mind is on a loop.

"Sir, this is Hagan Chatham, Adalee's boyfriend. She wants to be part of your life. While at Thanksgiving with my family she talked about not having a real Thanksgiving since her mom passed away. I want to give her Thanksgiving with you. We'll be back in Kentucky on Sunday. I've arranged for a private flight to bring you and take you home and a hotel for the night. Please say yes. Please say you'll do this for your daughter."

"Yes, I want that too. Send me the details. Thank you."

No, no, no. As I slide down the hospital wall, anger and guilt fill my body like never before. I had a weird feeling in the car when we saw the wreck ahead of us. I didn't recognize the cars, so I pushed the feeling down. What have I done? What has Mr. Summers done?

A nurse comes by and tells me I need to wait in the lobby or go into the room. That's when I see Joe being wheeled into a room. I follow along behind the rolling bed. The transport nurse asks who I am.

"His best friend. His parents live out of town. Please let me stay. His fiancée is in another room." My eyes swell with tears. "Please."

"Check in with the nurse station. I'm sure they'll be okay with it for now."

"Ma'am, is he in a coma?"

"No, we sedated him to prevent further injury," she answers. "The doctors will know more when they see the test results."

I nod. When she finished hooking him to ten machines. She looks at me and says, "You're a good friend."

No, I'm not. I'm the cause of all of this. Why couldn't I mind my own business?

Me: *I'm in the room with Joe. He's sedated.*

Adalee: *Is he okay?*

. . .

Me: *No. I don't think so.*

Adalee: *Talk to him. I've always heard people can hear you even when they are sedated or in a coma.*

Me: *And tell him this is all my fault?*

Adalee: *What?*

Me: *Nothing. The nurse is coming in. Talk later.*

I lie. It's the first and only time I've lied to her. This keeps getting worse.

Adalee: *Okay. Love you.*

I don't respond. Worse.

I have to make sure that it's her dad up the hall. If Adalee finds out before I tell her, the damage I've caused may be irreversible. My body aches, my stomach shakes, and bile creeps into my throat as I walk into his room.

He's asleep. A laceration extends across his forehead. A different nurse comes in asking if I'm family. I explain the situation and how I put three people in the hospital without being there. She pats my hand. "It's not your fault." She's lying.

"Can you tell me if he'll be okay?" I ask.

"Yes, he'll be severely bruised, but he doesn't have any obvious breaks. They'll take him for testing in a few minutes to make sure."

So, I sit. I'm hoping he'll wake up because I need to know what happened. I stay in there until they take him, but he never wakes. They unhook him and he doesn't move.

I end up back in Joe's room. I know I need to tell Adalee about her dad. I need to tell her this is my fault. And Ginger...

Will they forgive me?

I talk softly to Joe, telling him how I asked Adalee's dad here to surprise her. How sorry I fucking am. I didn't mean for any of this to happen. I was just trying to reconnect my girl and her dad.

I look at my phone and Adalee's texted me twenty times. It's midnight when the doctor comes in. "Is he going to be okay?"

The doctor asks, "And you are?"

"His brother."

The doctor squirrels his mouth to one side. "We'll do everything we can. Are your parents around?"

"No sir. We go to school here, but they're on their way."

"Your brother has a brain bleed which will require surgery. He hands me a card. Not being cocky but I'm the best neurosurgeon in the state. If he has a chance, it's with my hands."

For some reason, his cockiness in this time of need puts a smile on my face. It's how I am when I'm playing baseball—confident and self-assured. Those are good traits for a doctor.

"But you'll have to leave for a while. When your parents get here make sure the nurse calls me."

I put my hands on my knees and nod. "I love you, Joe. I'm sorry." The doctor's brow furrows. He probably thinks I was driving.

When I reach the waiting room, I'm stunned to see Archer walking toward me and surrounding me with his arms. I think I hear the word sorry. God, I hate that word. We throw it like a baseball around the diamond. What's he sorry for? I'm the only one who should be sorry. I am and I can't live with myself.

"Where's Adalee?"

I shrug and my voice comes out rough. "Ginger's room, I guess."

He steps back, placing both hands on my shoulders. "Look at me."

But I can't, it's like looking into a mirror. And I feel like I've aged enough tonight to be him. Now I know how Mr. Summers felt when his wife died. Grief is an albatross around your neck. I'm just like her dad. I can't deal with this.

His voice becomes firmer. "Joe needs you to be strong." Archer takes me outside. "What's going on?"

I walk around the small courtyard, searching for the words to explain. "Adalee's dad is in the hospital too," I say as Archer's eyebrows rise. "I called him and set up Thanksgiving tonight with Adalee. He didn't show and then Ginger called Adalee. I walked down the hall looking for Joe and saw a door with *Summers* on it. All of this is my fault. I need to go. I can't be here."

"Does Adalee know?" he asks as pulls me back into his chest. "It'll work out. But you have to tell Adalee. Text her now and tell her to meet you out here. Then I'll take you home."

I take out my phone and text her, asking her to meet. A few minutes pass, and I see my soon-to-be ex-girlfriend exiting the automatic doors. Archer slaps my shoulder. "Be honest, that's all you can do." Suddenly, she steps into our orbit, and my stomach crashes. My brother gives me a head nod before saying, "Adalee, thanks for calling me. Luckily I was in Cincinnati for a meeting tomorrow."

She nods as Archer goes inside. I sense her frustration as she crosses her arms over her chest.

"Why haven't you answered my texts?"

I run my fingers through my hair, but when she tries to do the same, I jerk away. Something is lodged in my throat, keeping me from speaking.

Shame. Guilt.

"Hagan, I know you're worried. We all are."

I snap. "He has a brain bleed. So yeah, I'm worried."

She takes a step back, gasping as one hand flies to cover her mouth. "Ginger doesn't know. Does his family know?"

I shake my head. "I pretended to be his brother." I hand her the doctor's card. "When they get here, tell them to call this number right away."

"What do you mean? You're not leaving," she says, seeing the grimace on my face. "Why?"

"Because you won't want me here when you find out what I've done."

She places her hands on my chest, and her palms burn through my clothes. I love this woman so much, but I know this is the last time she'll touch me. I shut my eyes, breathing in the sensation of her final touch. Gently, I wrap my fingers around her wrists and come clean. "I invited your dad here for Thanksgiving dinner. I was irritated that he was later than we were. But he's here. He caused the accident that put our best friend in a fight for his life. It's all my fault."

Nothing can stop the waterfall of tears on my cheeks. At first, her head turns in confusion, then her hands squirm away from my hold, and I know it's over. How can one decision to help the person you love change the whole trajectory of your life?

Chapter Thirty-Nine

Adalee

"How long have you known my dad was here in this fucking hospital? Tell me." I push my hands against his chest. For someone that doesn't curse, I'm throwing around the F-bomb a lot tonight. "Is he hurt too? Will he be okay?"

He wipes his tears, but they keep coming. Seeing Hagan cry is gut wrenching, but I'm not sure I can take it tonight. He finally chokes out, "I sat with him for an hour. They took him for tests but based on his bloodwork, they don't think it's anything major. I've been in Joe's room the rest of the night."

"And you thought it was fine to leave me in the dark about my dad?"

He mumbles, "I'm sorry."

About what? Lying? Meddling? Omitting?

He stutters, "I... I was trying to... fuck."

His beautiful face is taut with remorse. His jaws tremor and as much as I want to hold him and tell him that Joe, Ginger, and my dad will be okay...I can't. If Joe dies, Ginger will never forgive me or him.

"How am I going to tell Ginger that my dad put her fiancé in the hospital?" I tuck my lips over my teeth while attempting to keep my composure.

He reaches for my hand, but I turn away. "I'll tell her. It's my fault."

"No, it's my family, I'll do it."

He tries to pull me into a hug with sorry on an endless repeat. "I love you, Adalee."

"So that's why you waited four hours to give me a heads up that my dad is hurt enough to be in the hospital? In this hospital. The accident isn't your fault but if you love me, you should have told me immediately. That's love? You promised..."

His phone pings and buzzes a hundred times, and mine hasn't rung once. "Answer your phone, Hagan." His friends, his family. I was wrong, they're not mine. They're his but they are only mine as long as I'm in his life. My dad is mine.

He peeks at the screen. "You're more important. I know I don't deserve another chance but..."

His voice trails off as his teammates converge on us. Mac hugs him but Hagan shies away. Just like that Hagan slinks away with my heart. "Hagan, wait."

Then Mac and Chaz hug me. "I'm sorry, but whatever you or Ginger need, I'm here." I watch Hagan glance back over his shoulder and sees me in Chaz's arms. Since Hagan and I became a couple, Chaz has finally backed off the immature name calling and setting off Hagan. I have a feeling the change is because he has a new girlfriend himself.

Archer comes running out, chasing Hagan. I mumble loudly, "Take care of him."

I update the baseball players on what I know, minus the brain bleed. Because his parents and Ginger should hear that news first. I rub my fingers over the doctor's card.

When I reach my dad's room, the floodgates open, and I can't quit crying.

"Sweetie don't cry. I'm fine. How are the people in the other car?" he asks. This makes me feel better that it's the first question he asked. I explain that the people in the other vehicle are mine and Hagan's best friends. I don't tell him much about Joe because I'm not supposed to know, except they moved him into critical care.

When I asked him what caused the wreck, he was honest. Now I know what to tell Ginger.

"Dad, I can't believe you came. For me."

He winces as he changes positions and his body scrapes across the scratchy sheets. "Well, your boyfriend is convincing." He is. Hagan will wear you down until you submit to his charms. "Is he with you?"

"He left."

My dad's brow furrows into one wavy line. "Huh. He didn't seem the type to roll over. He seems like the kind of guy that would figure out how to solve problems."

I nod. My dad nailed him. But this is grief and if anyone knows how difficult it can be, it's me. I hold his hand. "Dad, he knew you were here for hours. He sat with Joe until midnight without telling me you were here. What if?"

"Adalee, I'm by no means an authority on relationships. Obviously, I let us grow apart. Grief can consume you. I'm sorry but I promise I'll be the best dad from this day forward. Can you forgive me?"

Nodding, I lay on his chest. "Dad, Hagan's the best person in the world, and I just made him feel like this was all his fault."

"If it's anyone's to blame, it's me. He wants you to be happy. All he wanted was to help us repair our relationship. Nothing was his fault," he says as he strokes my head.

I lay on his chest until I hear him snoring, and then I sneak out. By the time I get to Ginger's room, her parents are in there, so I head to the waiting room.

Me: *None of this is your fault. Please call me.*

No response. No bouncing dots. Nothing.

The baseball players have left—or at least they aren't in this waiting room. But I see a man that looks like an older version of Joe walking through the corridor. "Mr. Danke, I'm Ginger's roommate." And then I blurt out, "And my dad is the one who hit them."

His eyes widen but stay soft. I watch his throat bob before he speaks. "Adalee, they talked about you and Hagan all weekend. Thanks for being here. But go home and get some sleep. They're both sleeping. Come back in the morning. Tell Hagan thanks for getting us here so fast."

Did he hear me? Hagan?

"Okay, I'll be back early. Oh, Mr. Danke. Hagan asked me to give this to you." I hand him the card, and he takes it from my hands, reading it as he walks down the hall.

Before I leave, I peek through Ginger's door, and her parents are asleep on the couch and Ginger's snoozing. It doesn't surprise me because earlier the doctor said they would give her something to sleep.

I walk out and then realize that Hagan drove here. I don't know the code to start his car. It's the middle of the night, and I don't want to call a car service.

Me: *Can you give me the code to your car so I can drive it home?*

Hagan: *Archer will pick you up. Please don't drive home.*

Me: *Okay, none of this is your fault.*

No response.

THE NEXT MORNING, I TEXT HAGAN, STILL NO response. Maybe he's at the hospital. I drive over there and go straight to Ginger's room to admit what my father did to her and Joe. I take a huge breath before I open her door.

"Addy Bug."

My stomach is empty, not having eaten since Sunday morning, but whatever is in there threatens to come up. I choke it down. "Hey. How are you feeling?"

She looks to her parents. They nod.

"Better today. They said Joe is doing well too. He's having new tests done this morning. His dad said they have the top neurosurgeon on this side of the Mississippi." Ginger grins. Her effervescent personality percolates.

"What's his name?"

"Dr. Newcastle. He's from the Cleveland Clinic."

I smile, even though I know that's not the name that was on the card that I handed to Mr. Danke. "I need to tell you something. My dad was the person that ran into you and Joe."

Her mom says, "Honey, we know. It was on the news, and your father came in and told us the whole story."

I've always been strong on the outside but Mrs. Chatham made me believe I was strong on the inside too, but I'm not. My eyes dart around the room. "Ging, do you hate me? Hagan? We're so sorry." I fall apart when I should be comforting her.

"Come here. It was an accident, and you're my bestie on and off the mat." I can't believe the compassion coming from her.

She hugs me. "Joe will pull through, and we'll go back to double dating and letting the guys cook for us."

She's putting on a brave face. Maybe Hagan was wrong about Joe's condition. But why would a doctor lie to him and give him his card?

"Has Hagan been here this morning?" I ask, knowing how pitiful I sound.

"No and Joe isn't allowed visitors except for his parents. Evidently, Hagan lied to them telling him he was Joe's brother." She smiles. "Hagan and Joe hit it off immediately. They'll be best friends for life." Ginger exudes positivity. She knew she would have Joe one day. All those games we attended last year, she never gave up. And she got her man.

"They're letting me out today. Do you think you could stay at Hagan's while my parents are here for a few days?" she asks.

I tuck my lips and lie. "Umm, sure. I'll figure it out." I can't tell her we haven't spoken since last night. The same kind of lie Hagan did to me. A lie of omission. "Listen, I've gotta go see my dad. Thanks for not hating me."

If Joe doesn't make it, she'll change her mind about Hagan and me. She won't want to be around either of us.

My dad's been discharged so I take him to the hotel where he was supposed to stay the night. Hagan set him up with a suite. He said he would stay until he knows Joe pulls through. Whatever Hagan said to him worked. Why didn't I talk to Dad about our grief and what I needed from him?

I ask if I can stay with him while Ginger's parents are at my apartment and he agrees. Hopefully, it's just a day or two.

"Dad, I need to run to class, then I'm going to the apartment to get some clothes." He waves me out.

I have my dad back. He still loves me, and I owe it all to Hagan. Before I go get my man, I run to each of Hagan's classes, hoping to see him, but I really didn't expect him to be there. I give both of his professor's information on what happened. Tomorrow is our engineering class and our project is due on Thursday.

I'm on my way to Hagan's when I get a text.

Harper: *I'm at your apartment. What's your ETA?*

Me: *Five. You're here? I was on my way to Hagan's.*

HARPER: COME HERE FIRST.

Me: *K.*

She meets me on the sidewalk. "Is there a park nearby with swings?"

"Yeah but it's cold."

All she says is, "Perfect."

I drive us to Forest Park. It sits on the edge of campus next to the employee day care center. They have their own fenced in park but this one is across the street. Each pathway is lined with Oak trees. We walk until the swings come into view. I grab the chains covered in some sort of rubber material.

She does the same. "These are fancy."

A small breath escapes my chest. We swing—legs out—legs in.

Finally, she says, "I've never seen him like this. He won't even talk to me. It fucking hurts. I'm his twin." She pauses. "He's not talking to Archer either."

"Didn't Archer have a meeting in Cincinnati? And when did you get here?" I ask.

"Got here around five this morning. Archer cancelled his meeting. The whole family will descend on this sweet little town by six p.m."

"Why?"

"One, because Hagan doesn't just *think* this is his fault. He *believes* it with one hundred percent certainty." She pulls back as her legs soar into the sky. "Has he told you that I have anxiety?"

I tuck my legs in as the swing goes backward and then pull, letting the momentum fling me into the light blue sky. "He's mentioned it but hasn't given me specifics."

Swinging is really freeing.

"Well, him not speaking to me is giving me fucking anxiety. I can't tell him because it will put more pressure on him, and he'll believe my anxiety is his fault too."

She stops her swing and starts twisting the chains. I slow down, dragging the tips of my chucks in the dirt. "Harper, I pushed him away when he needed me most. I should have comforted him. Joe is one of his best friends."

Harper lets the swing unwind, her balayage hair swaying in the wind. "God this is fun. Why do people think swinging is for kids? It's therapeutic." She pauses. "Do you love him like you told us at Thanksgiving?"

"Yes."

"Do *you* believe the accident was his fault?"

"Of course not. But he kept my dad's involvement and his condition from me for hours. I'm not blaming him for the accident but him not being honest with me is heartbreaking. He's the one person I thought I could depend on."

"Come on, Adalee. He was surprising you with your father's visit. Most people would put that surprise into the PRO column, not the CON."

She's right. "Harper? Are you here for Hagan?"

She twists her seat letting go again. "I'm here because I love him, and I love you by extension. It's hard to explain—the twin thing. Last night, I had an abdominal cramp so bad I ended up on the floor. There was no rhyme or reason for it. I hadn't had anything greasy or any unusual food. It was around seven thirty. This morning I saw on the news that's when the ambulance arrived at the hospital. That must be when Hagan found out. I feel what he feels."

Hagan said we were forty-five minutes late at seven fifteen, and it wasn't much later when Ginger called. "What time did you call him?"

"I shrugged it off for an hour trying desperately to just sit up in a chair. I called for five straight hours with no answer. He always answers me, and I was afraid that he had died. He always answers me, Adalee. Always." I nod because I know it to be true with the only exception being during our sexy times. "Anyway, I called Archer, and he was on his way to the hospital. He called me once he talked with Hagan. Then, he said to get on the first flight here. I felt bad being relieved that it wasn't Hagan in the hospital, but when he explained, I knew I had to be here for both of you."

My phone rings and I slip it from my back pocket.

"How ya holding up?"

"Logan, thank God. How's Hagan?"

He takes a sharp breath that I hear through the phone. "He just ordered everyone out of the house. He said he'd leave if they didn't. I told him it was my fucking house and I'm staying. He slammed the door to his room. I think everyone needs to give him some time. He'll be better once he hears that Joe's going to have surgery."

I guess I'll be staying with my dad. I would have rather stayed with Hagan. "Archer said his family is renting out the penthouse floor of the new boutique hotel downtown, beside the job site you two are working on. Archer wants you with them and your dad is welcome too."

"Me?" Why am I surprised? They've treated me like part of their family from the moment we met. It's calming and comforting, knowing I have people fighting for me. And for mine and Hagan's relationship.

"Yeah, he said he was texting you."

"Logan, if Hagan will listen, will you tell him I love him? He isn't returning my texts or calls."

"Sure will, Little A. Umm is Harper with you? Archer said she left mad. I want to make sure she's okay." He clears his throat. "For Archer and Hagan."

"Yeah, we're together." All I can think of is how Hagan has made every person in my life more meaningful.

Logan went from an annoying friend to the matchmaker behind the scenes to the only male other than Hagan that I can talk with about my personal life.

Joe went from someone Ginger was hooking up with—to an animated decoration in our apartment—to a friend.

And Hagan's family is not just worried about him, but me too. Harper and Archer are here with me.

"Good. I'll keep you updated. Don't hesitate to call if anyone needs me."

Chapter Forty

Hagan

NEVER IN A MILLION YEARS DID I EXPECT TO BREAK MY own heart. The events I put into motion have shattered my world. How can I ever look anyone in the eye or expect them to love me? When Adalee stared at me with disappointment in her eyes, I felt the crack getting wider. And Joe might die. Ginger and my teammates will never forgive me. I've lost Adalee, my friends and baseball.

I threw my phone out the window. The calls. The texts hoping I'm okay. Do they not understand that Joe is the one fighting for his life? Why are they wasting their time on me, the guy that put him there?

I demanded everyone leave the house and leave me alone. Logan told me to fuck off. That did make me chuckle inside. We all pay rent, so I have no right asking anyone that lives here to leave. But Pearse was gone anyway, and Mac said he was going to stay with a friend for a night or two.

Laying on my bed, I throw a rubber baseball against the wall. Thump and it's back my hand. Thump and it comes back to me again. Over and over until it's dark outside. It's peaceful without a phone. Without all the *sorry* texts.

There's a knock on my door. "Stay out."

The asshole doesn't listen and comes in anyway. He leans his six-foot-five body against the door jamb, barely fucking fitting under it. "Do you need a dictionary on what the words *stay out* mean?" I snap. I start throwing the ball again.

"Your coach called. Joe's tests came back as a positive candidate for surgery. The surgery is scheduled for Wednesday." Logan's voice holds a genuine concerned tone.

"Thanks."

He turns to leave but instead says, "I talked to Little A."

"Moving in already. That was fast."

He hits the wall with his palm. "Wow. I did everything you asked to help you snag the girl of your dreams. Don't let her go. And by the way, she asked me to tell you that she loves you. She's staying at The Waterford with your family."

"Why isn't she at her apartment?"

"Do you care? Cause if you do, here's your phone. Call and ask her." He throws my phone onto my bed. "I'm here to talk if you need someone other than your family or Adalee." He knocks the wall twice and leaves.

I haven't slept since Sunday. We woke up at six a.m. to head home from Chicago. It's close to midnight on Monday night, so at least thirty six hours. I've thought about everything Logan said but I can't bring myself to look at my phone. I saw forty nine notifications before I threw it out the window.

Family. I love my family but I'm angry and ashamed. I shouldn't have meddled in Adalee's family life. I'm no better than her dad. I can't face her.

By three a.m., I'm still not asleep so I pull on my sweats and sweatshirt and run to the baseball complex. It wasn't my intention, but something guided me here. I jump the fence and go into the dugout. I sit on the back instead of the seat because Joe and I always sit this way.

The sun begins to rise on what looks like a clear day. The blaze of pinks and reds light the morning sky. It gives me an idea about our project. I walk around until I end up at Ginger and Adalee's apartment. I know she's not there. I'm not ready to talk anyway so I meander around, going through all of the actions that occurred because I called her dad, before heading back to my house. It's eight a.m. and Logan's in the kitchen.

"Where you been?"

"Couldn't sleep. Took a run." I start running up the stairs.

He follows me up. "Listen. I'm your fucking friend. You're probably my best friend that just wants to be my friend because of me, not because I'm the QB." He hands me a bottle of water enhanced with vitamins and a bagel. "When's the last time you ate?"

Shrugging it off, I say, "Sunday in Chicago."

"It's Tuesday."

I shake my head. I know what fucking day it is. He touches my shoulder and I jerk. "Eat, drink and sleep. When you wake up, we're talking about all of this."

As he walks out I ask in a tone so quiet, it's almost an inner thought. "Have you heard from Adalee again?"

He drops his head. "Are you accusing me of something? Because..."

I cut him off. "No, is she okay?"

"She called at six a.m. wanting you to know that she and her dad stayed with your family last night. Nobody blames you."

I choke back tears. "I blame me, Logan. Why is it so hard to comprehend for everyone? My friend might die because I brought her dad here."

Two guys standing in silence because neither of us know what to say. We haven't been through any of this. I know he's trying to help when he finally says, "Get some rest. I have class but I'll lock the door so only roomies can get in."

He shuts my door behind him. I set the water and the bagel on my nightstand. I look at the drawer where Adalee pulled out my T-shirt and slipped it over her head. It was the first night I saw her body. I thought I was dreaming. Now I'm in a nightmare of an escape room, and I can't find my way out.

I take a drink of water and a bite of the bagel and lay back down. I need to call my professors and coach, but I don't have the heart to explain to my professors. And if Coach gets mad because I'm not at practice, I don't care. I throw the baseball until I miss it and am too tired to get off the bed to retrieve it. I down the bottle of water and leave the bagel. My lids feel heavy.

When I wake, it's dark. My eyes strive to adjust. I slept and I have to admit I feel a little better. Still like a piece of shit but I can function. When I stride into the bathroom, my face looks worse than I thought. I hate my reflection, so I take out my shaver that I use on my face. Instead of running it over my jaw and chin, I run it through my hair. Huge chunks of hair fall into the sink. Stroke after stroke, I cry. I end up on the floor sobbing.

Logan finds me on the floor with my back against the wall. He rests his backside on the counter with his arms folded over his waist. "Did someone shave a black Goldendoodle?"

I laugh and snot falls from my nose. He hands me some toilet paper. I clean myself then clutch my head with my elbows on my knees. The tears fall continuously. "Let it out," Logan says as he somehow manages to sit beside me in the confined space.

A little later, he pulls out an envelope and hands it to me. It's from Adalee. Her handwriting is impeccable. She insists on writing everything because she can't read my chicken scratch. I always tell her that's why computers were invented so everyone could read.

"What time is it?"

"Almost six in the morning. Wednesday. I've had to turn your entire family away three times in the past eighteen hours. I hope they don't hate me after this. Your twin is a handful. *'He's my brother, he wants me here yada, yada.'* But she's hot."

"We've had this discussion. She's off limits."

"She's too angry for me anyway. You know I like 'em agreeable, and I don't want to see them all the time."

I laugh and it feels good. "Logan, thanks. But you wouldn't ever see her."

"Umm, she has a different plan. But she's crazy man. If you don't call Adalee, please call Harper because she scares me, she loves you so much." He starts to walk away.

I grab the hem of his shirt and he stops. "Don't hate her. Hap and I feel each other's pain...literally. This isn't fair to her. She had her tonsils out in sixth grade while I was at school. In math class I started screaming from the pain. My parents told me that was the exact time when Hap woke up screaming in the recovery room because it hurt so bad."

His large hand strokes my back a few times. "I'll keep that in mind when I kick your ass for having to run interference for you. Read the letter and call your family. I need some sleep."

He walks out. I brush my teeth staring at my newly bald head, saying to myself, "I'm with you Joe." I lay back down in bed and turn on my reading lamp, tearing open the envelope.

Hagan,

I know you don't want to hear I'm sorry but I am. I don't blame you. We both made mistakes. You should have told me about my dad, and I shouldn't have gotten so mad. You made sure he was out of the woods because you are kind and caring.

You're an amazing, thoughtful, and generous person. You flew arguably the best neurosurgeon in the world here to perform Joe's surgery. You flew in Joe and Ginger's parents, all without telling a soul. That's what you were doing when you were sitting in Joe's room pretending to be his brother.

I do have one question, and I need to see your face when you answer it. I need your answer before Joe comes out of surgery. I need your answer to be based on your feelings for me, not on the outcome of the accident.

Up until now, your life has been close to perfect. I know pain and anguish. Hagan, this is how it looks, but you don't have to go through it alone like I did. Your parents are here. Every one of your siblings is here. Megan is here. Tackett and Talynn said they will be here in five hours, just call. Do you know what I would have given for this support? Don't waste it.

You said two things to me that I'll never forget.

"Don't be scared of loving me. Loving me is the safest thing you'll ever do." Right now, you're scaring me. The thought of you giving up on us is torture. I'm not sure if I can survive another heartbreak.

The other is when you said, "You know if you wear my jersey, it means you're mine for life. It's an unwritten rule."

I responded, "Life is a long time. No one's loved me forever."

So, the question I need you to answer is—are you the man that's going to love me for life?

Because your pain is safe with me.

Love you for life,

Adalee

I find my phone and read every message from Adalee, my family, and my friends. I shower, call Coach, and ask him to give me a few days to get my head on straight. He supports me fully. I run downstairs and ask Logan, "Do you know when Joe's surgery is?" He couldn't have slept more than a couple of hours but now he's watching game film while eating breakfast.

"Your mom said she thought it was starting at seven thirty this morning. But I'm not sure."

I grab the bagel out of his hand and a bottle of water off the table and run out the door.

Me: *Hap, is Adalee still there?*

Hap: *Nope. Where are you?*

Me: TRYING TO FIND HER.

Hap: *She went to class and was going to wait with Ginger at the hospital. Why?*

Me: BECAUSE I FUCKING LOVE HER.

Hap: *It's a Pretty Woman moment.*

. . .

Me: *WHAT?*

Hap: *Never mind, go get your girl.*

Me: *HAVE EVERYONE AT MY HOUSE AT FOUR.*

Hap: *Okay. This feels right.*

Me: *It is right.*

I park as close as I can to her classes, knowing I may be late. I run to her lecture hall but she's nowhere to be seen. So, I get in my car, driving straight to the hospital. I pray that I'm not late and Joe's surgery isn't over. I'm against the clock but I work best under pressure. By some miracle there's a guy valeting at the hospital entrance. I race to the elevator. Floor 2...floor 3...floor 4. The doors open.

Chapter Forty-One

Adalee

That's the thing about wishes—they're like dandelions blowing in the wind. I've wished for days that Hagan would talk to someone, hoping it would be me. So, I went by Hagan's late last night and dropped off a letter. Logan said he would give the note to Hagan, but he didn't want to wake him because it was the first time Hagan had slept since we returned from Chicago.

It's the first and only time I've seen Logan look defeated. "I wish I had good news. We have had a few short conversations but nothing that tells me he's ready to see anyone."

"Has he talked about the accident or me?" I asked.

"I told him that you and I talked. He accused me of moving in on you but when I told him you were staying with his family, he was irritated. Other than that, I informed him Joe's surgery was scheduled." He paused. "He did say thanks.

Little A, Hagan's in there somewhere but you have to tell his family to back off—he's processing. He knows you're all here for him. Harper and I have had it out a few times already. She thinks because she's his twin that it trumps everything. I'm just doing what he asked. I promise if he doesn't come out of it soon, I'll let everyone in."

I nodded in understanding because I thought being his girl-friend trumped everything too. I assumed he would confide in me and that I would hold him until he was ready to talk.

"Adalee, he loves you. He blames himself. It doesn't matter whether it's true or not."

I responded, "I know. I just wish I could take back what I said that night. I know he loves me and is trying to protect me."

Grabbing a tissue from my pocket, my fingers land on a hard round object. I pull it out and it's a mint that Hagan stuck in my jacket when we were at Navy Pier. I remove the wrapper and roll it around my mouth as I come back to reality.

I lean my head on Ginger's shoulder while waiting for Joe's surgery to conclude. I explained why Hagan wasn't here and what was going on between Hagan and everybody. She keeps patting my leg—comforting me—even though her fiancé is in surgery.

If I'm quiet, I can hear Hagan calling my name. It sounds a hundred miles away, echoing like he's in a tunnel. I must be dreaming. I shake my head and wipe my eyes, but I still hear it. Ginger nudges me with her shoulder.

Suddenly, Hagan stands towering over me with my name on repeat. "Please, Adalee, say I'm not too late."

My eyes travel from his athletic pants up his chest to his face. There are zero dimples and his hair is gone. He has black circles under his eyes, and his face is thinner. He crouches down, with uncertainty in his gaze. He hesitates to touch me.

As I stand up, he does also. Bursting into tears, with an almost silent, broken voice, I ask, "Are you okay? Oh my God. Are you okay?"

My stomach churns at how he's been beating himself up and the part I played in causing him to spiral. I touch his sunken cheeks and he leans into one of my palms. It's his way of communicating that he needs me and my touch.

He tips his head, reassuring me as he blankets my body with his arms. His tone is gentle, but he speaks fast like he needs to spit this out or I won't give him another chance.

"Logan gave me your letter. I'm sorry. God, I'm sorry."

"I don't need an apology. I need your strength and your love." My hands stay firmly in place because I can't let him go.

He peers into my soul with his caramel brown eyes. "I'm going to love you for life. No...even longer. I'm loving you forever because even when I die, I won't stop loving you." His hands run up and down my back. "Longer than life, Adalee."

I slide my arms around his neck, jumping up and surrounding his waist with my legs. It's his favorite position whether we're having sex or playing around. While I cry into his shoulder, he keeps saying, "Tell me. Tell me." They're tears of relief that no matter what happens in our life, we're facing it together.

I whisper, "You're just in time. I love you, Hagan Chatham."

Even though all eyes are on us, and we hear mini claps in the background, Hagan brushes his lips across mine. "I love you. I'm so sorry I put you through this." Another kiss and one of his tear's creeks over his top lip and onto mine.

Our reunion is cut short as the double steel doors open and two doctors walk out. I slide down Hagan's chest with my feet, now on the floor. Hagan grips me around the waist, resting his chin on my head. His hold tightens when doctors pull their mask down almost simultaneously. Then they grab their hats, wad them up and throw them in the trash. The tension in Hagan's body returns.

Mr. and Mrs. Danke rise, and I see the fear in their rigid stance. Joe's father steadies his wife, placing his arm around her shoulder. The baseball players are holding hands in solidarity.

It's taking forever for the doctors to walk thirty feet. The elevators open behind us. Hagan's chin comes off my head, and we both look over. In walks my dad, Hagan's entire family, and all three of Hagan's roommates. Hagan squeezes me and I feel him relax, a little.

But it's Ginger who darts to the doctors. "How did he do? He's strong. Is he awake?" she asks, peppering them with questions. They smile and I feel the whole room expel a breath.

Who knew a simple smile could say so much.

Hagan presses his lips against my hair, and utters, "He made it." I nod letting him know I hear him.

The doctors ask the Danke's if they want to talk somewhere private and they shake their heads. "All of us love him so whatever you say, we need to hear it at the same time," Joe's mom responds.

I notice one of the lab coats says, "Dr. Henry Newcastle." He's from Cleveland Clinic.

Dr. Newcastle is the first to speak. "Joe is in recovery. He's still asleep. We want his brain to rest after surgery, so he'll be out for a while."

Ginger says, "But he's going to be okay?"

The other doctor says, "I'm Dr. Wilcox. He's young and you're right, he's strong and has a thick skull." This brings some much needed levity. "Based on his age, his overall health, and no pre-existing conditions, we expect he'll have a full recovery. But it will take time, so please don't pressure him.

"I also want to thank Dr. Newcastle for flying in and performing this surgery with me." He pauses, scanning the waiting room. "The first night one of you said Joe was your brother, and I knew then I needed to get a second set of eyes and hands on the patient. The man smiled but it hit me that asking for help to save a young man is worth it. Thanks to the Chatham's for contacting the best neurosurgeon in the country and bringing Dr. Newcastle here. It was a pleasure assisting you, Doc."

I lean my head backward and look up at my life—Hagan. I see a tiny dip in his cheeks.

"You're the best."

"It wasn't me." His voice waivers like he's questioning it too.

Joe and Ginger's parents receive instructions from the doctors, and everyone hugs each other, including Hagan and Chaz. Chaz whispers something in his ear and Hagan smiles.

Hagan hugs his family and my dad. But it's Harper he takes into his arms and holds in an embrace for five minutes or more. They're talking into each other's ear, but I can't make it out.

Logan says, "Alright, there's food at the house, and every-one's invited."

Hagan breaks the embrace, and Harper snaps, "I'll quit hugging him when I'm done." Hagan grabs her one more time and sways her from side to side as he tells his twin, "I love you, Hap."

Minutes later, we walk into Hagan's house and Logan reveals a smorgasbord. I've never seen so much food, not even at the Chatham's Thanksgiving dinner. Hagan hugs his mom. "Thanks for getting this delivered. I'm sorry I caused so much trouble."

"Oh honey, this is what families are for. You always take care of the rest of us. Making sure we know we're loved. What college guy talks to his mom two or three times a week?"

Logan almost chokes on a chicken finger. "Umm. Yeah roomie, that's not normal." But Hagan doesn't care, he hugs his mom again.

He clears his throat, garnering the room's attention. "These have been the worst four days of my life. Logan was my lifeline and I'll never forget it. I was so ashamed of causing this accident that I didn't want to see the disappointment in your eyes."

His siblings chime in at the same time, "But it wasn't your fault."

He nods. "I know and it wasn't Mr. Summers' fault either. He was just trying to reach the restaurant and damn Siri kept telling him to turn left but the street's one way on campus. It was an accident. One of my best friends could have died, and I felt responsible. I'm sorry that I pulled you away from your kids." He looks at his family. "Now, which one of you called Dr. Newcastle?"

Reggie, the quietest of the Chatham's, raises his hand. "He has a vacation home in Charleston. We're friends. When Archer filled me in, I called Doc right away and set up the consultation with the hospital and Dr. Wilcox."

Hagan rushes him so hard that the sound of their chests smashing together sounds like an MMA fight. "Thank you." Emotions are raw and we're all somewhere on the spectrum of tears. Some bawling and some with a film blurring their eyes.

We're sitting on the couch eating when Hagan springs to his feet. "I have to go." We look at him like he's crazy. "I haven't called a single professor. I had a paper due, and Adalee, we haven't finished our project."

I reach for his hand as he walks away. "Hagan, I did it all." He turns with his brows pointed down. Again, I whisper, "I turned in your paper. I spoke to all your professors. Logan gave me your laptop, so I had all the work we did while in Chicago."

"All of it?" He caresses my face with his large hands, and I've never felt more cherished.

"Yeah. I know this guy. He transferred here and told me once that he plans to graduate summa cum laude. I couldn't let him shatter his dreams." He looks at me like he's staring at a sunrise. "This is when you kiss me."

The laughter rumbles and Hagan blinds me with his panty-dropping smile. Yes, I did succumb to the dimples.

"Are you sure because we haven't kissed in days? You may not be able to handle me." He twitches his eyebrows and yep, the panties would be on the floor if there wasn't a room full of people.

His mouth takes mine. Long and slow. "Love you long time." Another kiss.

Logan says, "Okay. That's enough. Take it to your room."

Harper says, "Are you a neanderthal? Can't you see they're having a moment?"

Logan smiles, walking back into the kitchen and Harper follows him. I can hear them bickering from here.

Sarah Jane says, "Go on. You're an adult. Plus, I have a surprise for both of you in Hagan's room." Hagan looks at me, and I don't know if we ever want to try and surprise each other again.

"Thanks everyone. We'll meet tomorrow after class and go check on Joe." He looks at my dad. "Mr. Summers, thank you for staying with Adalee. I can't wait to be part of your family one day. And I can't wait to meet the twins."

The entire room chatters, and I hear someone say, "Twins. Aww."

"Goodnight. Hagan and I need to talk through what happened alone. But all of you are amazing, and I couldn't have made it through the past four days without you. I'm honored that you came and helped me through this time." I hug them all making sure they know how I feel.

Hagan pushes the door open slowly and his room has been transformed in a way. Above his bed is a large picture of us. I'm sitting on his lap during pajama night. His hands are around my waist. My eyes are squinted looking up at him. He's looking down at me with his dimple framing the side of his face.

I truly didn't think I had any liquid left in my body, but tears climb up and spill over my lids. "It's us." He strokes my hair.

But that's not all. There are pictures with everyone in Hagan's family. I'm in a few of them. But all are recent, either at Thanksgiving or when the Kodiaks played in the World Championships.

"They love you. I'll never be able to repay my family and your dad for taking care of you when I couldn't." He tears up but he holds them back. "I don't know if I can forgive myself for not being there for you and Joe." His thumbs wipe away my tears.

"The nurse said when Joe talked on Tuesday, he asked if he had dreamed of you being there with him. She laughed and told him about how you wouldn't leave and how you lied and said you were his brother."

We laugh and a snot bubble blows from my nose. He takes the hem of his shirt and wipes it away. Now that's love.

"He knew you were there sitting with him that night. He knows you love him." My voice cracks. "You know how we distribute the weight to carry the load? I'll help you carry the load." I use his words, hoping he understands that I'll always be there to help him.

Hagan and I spend the night talking through our feelings about the wreck. Well not the entire night, Hagan is fantastic at multi-tasking. I think we were asleep by nine, which must a college student record. But we wake up at five a.m. and drive to the job site.

We sit on the floor with puffy jackets because it's December, and the wind is whipping. He pulls me onto his lap. My back is pressed against his chest and all feels right in the world as we watch the sunrise.

"I want to build our house where we wake up seeing sunrises like this. The pinks and purples streaking the sky."

I lean back and looking into his gorgeous caramel brown eyes that are free of guilt. "I'd live in a shack with you if we woke up to this."

He tightens his grip then flips me around so I'm straddling him. "I love you so damn much." He sighs. "Do you think Joe's going to recover?"

"I do. He may not be able to play this year, though."

Hagan stills, probably not expecting me to say the truth. He traces my hairline. "We were talking one day about him taking care of Ginger when she was sick. He said, *'If taking care of her is the last thing I do on earth, it will be a life that was worth living.'* I know now if he passed away, he would have been happy. The rest of us would have been devastated but...thankfully, we don't have to cross that bridge."

We soak in the sunrise and the feel of being in each other's arms, when I ask, "Why did you shave your hair off?"

He takes a deep breath, and it looks like smoke coming out of his mouth. "When the doctor explained about the brain bleed, I came home and looked it up on the internet. I did it in solidarity with Joe. If his head was going to be shaved, so was mine. But I did it to punish myself—my hair is my best asset."

"Really, I thought your best asset was…"

"Babe, that asset is reserved for you—for longer than life."

Epilogue

Hagan

THE GYMNASTICS CENTER IS FILLED TO CAPACITY. TEAM Adalee is out in full force. Every single one of my family members and their children are here. Mr. and Mrs. Summers are here with her twins and Megan is fawning all over them. I'll be surprised if she makes it a year without being pregnant. But it's Harper that takes them under her wing.

Mr. Summers has been present in Adalee's life, even from Florida. He calls her almost every day, asking her about school and how her skills are progressing. If he doesn't understand, he asks her to send a video.

In some ways, Mr. Summers knocking on Adalee's door that night was the best thing that could have happened. It made her open up to me on an emotional level and the sexual part defies physics too. Sometimes we'll be lying in bed, and she will do a handstand over top of me. She's so strong that she can bend her elbows far enough to kiss me before she presses back up.

When the gymnasts are introduced. I look down at Adalee with her hair in four braids then pulled into a bun and her royal blue leotard has rhinestones in the shape of a stallion. She shifts her weight from left to right as she stares at something or nothing. This is how many athletes get into the zone. Our minds zero in on a spot on the wall or an empty space and let our inner thoughts speak.

I can do this. I'm a winner. Perfection.

Sometimes, I'm amazed that Adalee is my girl and that she stayed with me. But damn, I'm glad she did.

Joe sits beside me with his noise cancelling headphones. Adalee was right, he isn't playing this season yet. He's on the injured list for the time being. He's living with Ginger and Adalee because the home run house is too noisy. He's still having headaches, but the doctors insist his recovery is on schedule.

The meet begins and Ginger is first on the vault, which is Adalee's favorite apparatus. For now, she isn't competing on the vault. Adalee's goal is to perform her new vault by the end of season.

"You've got this, Red!" Joe shouts.

I watch my girl popping her knuckles as her gaze drills in on Ginger. She's talking to herself. Ginger takes off running and pounds into the springboard and flies into the air. She twists one or two times, it's hard to tell from here. The vault is on the other side of the gymnasium. Then she hits the landing. Our section goes crazy. After hugging the coach, the next person she embraces is Adalee.

Adalee performs her floor exercise flawlessly. It's a watered down version but she's happy with it for now. The doctor, trainer, and her dad want her to come back slowly. She's graduating in May in only three years. My girlfriend has a brilliant mind and a beautiful body. Her dad told her if she wants to stay for her fourth year and start on her master's degree, then he will continue to pay for her apartment.

Adalee doesn't have much time before her bar routine. The coach talks to her, and I see Adalee take a deep breath then lift one hand, indicating she's ready. I'm holding my breath each time she releases the bar. What if she falls? What if she tears her ACL again? Then I blow out a breath because if she does, I know our love is strong enough and we'll handle it together.

I don't know what the skill is called but the crowd gasps as she crosses her hands on the bar and swings two times around before releasing and doing a double layout. Her feet hit the ground at the same time and the smile on her face is as wide as it is beautiful. The crowd goes nuts. The judges give her a 9.94. Her teammates, even Shannon, circle her in jubilation which means the Kentucky Stallions Gymnastics Team win the meet.

We race down to the mat when it's over, and Joe and I take our girls in our arms and swing them around.

"Babe, you did it!"

"Yep. And it's all your fault," she says smiling, and if I look confused, I am.

Ginger chimes in, "Get with it, Transfer. If she wasn't thinking about you, she wouldn't have torn her ACL. "

Adalee says, "I'll take it from here, Ging." She leans her head back to get a better look at me. "If I didn't tear my ACL, I wouldn't have been competing on bars. I used to hate the uneven bars, but I learned being graceful doesn't mean you're not strong."

She stops, pressing up on her toes to kiss me. My family surrounds her, hanging on every word.

"So, we would've lost if I didn't tear my ACL. I thought it was the worst thing that happened to me but... it's why we're together and why I kicked *ass* on the bars today."

Everyone laughed because she whispered the word ass.

It makes me think of the change in her since the last week of summer. Adalee had this fortress built around her, thinking it was a show of strength, but when she let me help tear down her walls, there was an elegant, soft, strong woman inside.

THIS IS THE ONE DAY THAT ADALEE HAD HER gymnastics meet on the same day I had an early game, which is why my family decided to have the first official away game pajama party night.

And my family is staying in my house—all of them.

Pearse graduated in December and declared for the draft so Reggie and his family are using his room. Mac's spending the night at the baseball house after the party so Sarah Jane's family is sleeping there. My parents are staying in Logan's room. Archer and Megan are sleeping in the sunroom. Logan's sleeping on the couch, and I'm giving Harper and Adalee my bed, and I'm sleeping on the floor in my own house.

Adalee follows me to my room. It's time to change. She flies on to my back, slinging her arms around my neck. "We finally have sixteen hours together."

"Yeah, and we've been invaded," I say as I flip her off my back and onto the bed. "I wish we could spend the time in bed together, but we have to entertain our families."

Her hands run through my hair, which is shorter since I shaved it off two months ago. Her eyes tango with mine. She reaches down between us and says, "Quickie?"

Hopping off the bed, I lock the door. I shed my clothes, grab a condom, and begin working on her clothes. Leisurely, I peel her tight tank from her body like I'm opening a box with the perfect bow. When I have her naked, I nip her neck, gently rocking. My body slides through her folds, and I will never tire of this feeling. Our eyes stay locked as I make love to her, slow, easy and quiet.

There's no dirty talk, just hushed words and muted moans in each other's ear. Our mouths lock and explore as we hit our climax. But it keeps going like a hot air balloon flying just above the surface. It's been a week since we've held each other skin to skin, and we don't want to part.

"Thank you," she says. "I've missed this."

"Me too. Let's get cleaned up before Harper starts banging on our door."

She smiles. "Technically, this is her room tonight."

"Tell me why my parents didn't get the top floor of the hotel like last time?"

WE HAVE FOOD AND A HOUSE FULL OF PEOPLE IN pajamas. The kids play Twister while we eat in our blue and white pajamas Mom had made. The front reads, *families stick together*. It's her way of reminding all of us of how proud she is that everyone came together to help Adalee and me when Joe was in the hospital.

They realized in those four days that sometimes, all you need is for your family to show up. I knew they would do anything for me and to help me. I didn't need their words—I needed their presence.

Now it's Pictionary time. Teams are divided. Women against men.

Logan draws for our team. He's awful. He draws so fucking slow. Our times almost up before he finishes his first outline of what looks like a plane. Then he makes a sound while he's drawing a line down. I yell, "airplane crash!"

Harper stands up, shouting, "That's cheating. You're not allowed to make sounds."

"I don't play by the rules, sweetheart," Logan winks.

Harper's face reddens, her fists are balled up at her sides.

He clears his throat. "Sorry, I didn't know we were playing by the real rules. Who does that?"

My entire family, including Adalee shouts in unison, "We do!"

Logan and Mac look like they're watching a horror show before everyone laughs. Logan's wearing Stallions lounge pants and a white tee. Mac is wearing sweats and a Mario Bros. tee.

Despite the minor setback with unknown rules, the men make a comeback, winning the game.

Next is our family favorite, Charades, so we mix teams again. Adalee and I are on a team together this time. I pray this goes as planned. My mom made sure I got the right cookie.

I stand up and act like I'm putting a crown on my head, and I sit down very straight.

Adalee, yells "Proper." Archer says, "King." I gesture with my hands that they're on the right track and to keep going. Eventually, Reggie says, "Princess." I point and nod my head, then hold up two fingers, indicating the second word.

My nerves are rattling with emotion as I walk slowly, holding a pretend bouquet like Adalee did at my house. Adalee says, "Bride. Princess Bride."

"Yes. You got it babe." She stands up and hugs me. "Love you."

She presses her mouth against mine in a quick motion and says, "Love you for life."

This is my opening. I kiss her one more time. "Life's a long time Adalee," I whisper using her words from months ago and her brow creases. "I want longer than life. I want forever."

I bend at the knee. "Will you marry me?"

She knocks me on my back, kissing me. "Yes. Yes. Yes."

We kiss and I roll on top of her, pecking her lips a few more times. We sit up and Harper hands me the ring. "Would you like to see your ring?"

She nods and Harper hands me the box. When I open the black velvet box, Adalee covers her nose and mouth while elegant tears fall from her face. "Babe don't cry. It's *all your fault* we fell in love."

"We can debate whose fault it was later," she teases me, wiggling her brows. Adalee and I squeeze each other tight. Then we repeat our mantra at the same time. "Longer than life."

Logan says, "Can someone tell me how I can get a pair of these ridiculous pajamas?"

My family points at Adalee and me and says unison, "That."

I HOPE YOU ENJOYED READING HAGAN & ADALEE'S LOVE story as much as I did writing it. Hagan's been rattling around in my head since Scoring the Boss and he finally told me his story. Click here to review.

IF YOU ENJOYED THE ALL YOUR FAULT, GO BACK TO where it all began with the Sarasota Sharks Series. Start with Stealing A Second Chance. A brother's best friend, second chance romance. As many reviewers have warned—"Get your tissues ready for the emotional rollercoaster."

Scan the code to order your paperback copy.

Turn the page to read a BONUS EPILOGUE and a sneak peek into ON MY KNEES, Logan & Harper's story.

Bonus Epilogue

On My Knees - Chapter 1 - Harper

"No. Not happening." Hagan raises his voice.

I should have never moved in with my twin. He tries to control every move I make. My anxiety level was supposed to decrease when I decided to be roomies with Hagan. But nope, he's acting like he's my protector.

Tonight is the Stallion Awards. It's Kentucky's version of the ESPN ESPY Awards. Of course, Hagan and Adalee are nominated for Most Competitive Couple. She didn't win the Gymnastics All Around Title, but her score on the uneven bars propelled the team to win the Southeastern Conference title. And Hagan has the best on base percentage in Stallion history and the baseball team is currently playing in the regionals.

Mom took Adalee and I shopping in Chicago like she used to do for Sarah Jane and Megan. Magnificent Mile and then to a few smaller boutiques in the suburbs. We ended up buying dresses from the store Sarah Jane loves. Their selection for curvy girls was better but then again little, petite Adalee food her dress at the same store, Miss Princess. Their slogan is *"wear one store can fit all."*

Looking at my reflection in the full length mirror, suddenly I'm aware of all my curves. I need the best body shaper ever made. The last year has taken its toll. My shoulders slump and eyes fall.

"Hap, you can't go looking—"

From the hallway, a deep raspy voice interrupts, "Voluptuous," Logan says as his gaze coats my skin. I bite the inside of my cheek, desperate for our eyes not to meet.

One thing he can never know is how he gets under my belly. The way it knots up and flutters in his presence. My only defense is acting like he doesn't affect me. So I say, "What's that supposed to mean?"

Based on the red death rays shooting from Hagan's eyes to Logan's, my brother is about to go all alpha protector over me. But Logan seems unconcerned that these might be his final moments on earth. He shifts his weight, pressing his shoulder against the door frame. "What? I'm not allowed to say your sister is gorgeous."

Hagan walks chest to chest with his best friend. "Off limits, remember?" Hagan asks.

Logan is taller and thicker than Hagan, but I wouldn't bet against my brother when he thinks he's defending my honor.

Once, when we were sophomores in high school, a guy asked me out because there was a rumor going around about me giving blow jobs. Hagan placed an avocado green Tupperware bowl full of spiders in the boys' locker. I'll never forget Reed's face when a dozen albino creatures crawled all over his books and on his hockey hoodie. I wonder what happened to him.

"Got it. But I need a favor, but it's a fake favor." Logan stands straight staring at Hagan. "I need Harper to be my date tonight?"

At the same time, Hagan and I burst out, "What? Why?"

Logan responds, his jaw twitching. "Because you're my best friend and you don't want me to show up without a date. It will make us all miserable."

My body warms to the smooth confident tone of his voice. He's one hundred percent correct; I. Would. Hate. It. All these girls with athletic builds and without an ounce of fat would be hanging on him. It's bad enough to see women come and go out of the apartment. Although lately, it's been one older woman in her upper twenties.

The wheels turn in my brother's head. How do I know? Because his cheeks are smooth, not a dimple in sight, and one eyebrow dips as the other one raises. "Thought you were taking Josie?" Hagan asks.

"Nope."

Josie has evidently been Logan's go-to girl when he needs something other than nookie.

I push Hagan out of the way and now Logan's shirtless chest hits me square in my face, figuratively. That's when I realize he's in his tuxedo pants and nothing on top. The black material stretches across his thighs and my mouth waters. As I lift my head, each ridge and valley of his abdominal muscles sends dirty thoughts streaking through my mind. Somehow I manage to speak. "What happened? Did she finally get tired of being one of many?"

He steps back into the hallway and stuffs his hand into his pants pocket and sighs. "It's between Josie and me. I'm going to get dressed. You two talk about it and let me know."

When he walks away, I ogle his back while my mouth hangs open. Like my brother has any say in the outcome. As the thought appears in my mind, Hagan says, "You're not going on any kind of date with Logan."

"Hagan Chatham, you do not get to make decisions for me. He's your best friend. And tell me how many times he has asked you for a favor?"

Hagan, fully dressed in his formal wear, reaches for my hand. "He hasn't."

"I remember sitting downstairs after Joe's surgery and you said, 'Logan was your lifeline.' That was six months ago and maybe it's time we do something to repay him." My voice shatters thinking about those four awful days when Hagan wouldn't speak to me. It was the longest I had ever gone without hearing his voice. And when you're a twin it's devastating. "If he wasn't here looking out for you. Making you listen. I don't even want to think about..."

Hagan forces a laugh. "Come here." He pulls me into a hug.

"We'll call it a date publicly but it's just roommates who are both already going to the same Awards Dinner and sitting at the same table anyway."

He kisses the top of my head. "I love you Hap and I don't want you thinking you can change Logan Warren."

"I don't think of him that way." Lie. "He's way too... egotistical and argumentative. But Hagan, do you think I look bad in this dress? Mom and Adalee thought it fit me perfectly," I say, as my skin begins to itch and red waves wrap around my neck like a scarf.

His face softens and a half-smile appears framed by the dimples and bow tie. "Because you're my baby sister and—"

I cut him off. "By three minutes."

"I can't turn it off and on. You've always wanted me to lead. If that's not what you want anymore, I'll... I'll need some time to adjust." His voice sounds like he's falling off a cliff.

"I just want to have a fake date with my roommate to repay him for keeping you from jumping off of said cliff. What's the big deal? You'll be right there along with Adalee, Mom, Dad, Logan's mom, dad, sister and brother-in-law."

"You're right. Do you want me to tell him?"

I nod. "You can tell him that he can come and ask me. The first time he asked you and I'm not okay with that. If he wants me to be his fake date then he needs to ask me himself and we need to set ground rules."

He kisses me on the cheek before walking out saying, "That's my sister."

A few minutes later, Logan raps on the door. I reach into my dark walnut-stained jewelry box that my sister, Sarah Jane bought me a few years ago, when she said I was ready for real jewelry. I hve two pair in mind so I hold each up to my ear.

"The gold ones," Logan chooses for me.

I ask, "Why?"

"Because gold matches your complexion." His smile comes so easy.

I swallow hard as I continue to study each in the mirror but decide on the diamond studs. They don't overpower my face or dress. I push through the stem and anchor them in place.

Logan chuckles behind me. "Harper, will you be my fake date for the Stallion Awards?"

"Yes, but this is a one-time favor and you're going to owe me...BIG."

He walks over to my vanity. "Okay. Are you wearing a necklace?" I nod. "Do you need help putting it on, so you don't mess up your hair?"

"Please." I hold up the thin gold box chain necklace, handing him the ends. His fingers brush against my neck as he fastens it and my eyes close, loving his skin against mine. Thinking about Logan Warren in this way is not good for my heart.

"There. All set. Hagan left to pick up Adalee so your chariot awaits."

I feel like Cinderella as he opens the door to his Audi and waits for me to get my feet inside. His gaze stops on my strappy heels as he shuts the door and fire erupts inside me.

We park and come to the "Stallion Blue Carpet." All the athletes walk the carpet like Hollywood actors and A-list celebrities. His hand slides on my back as he whispers in my ear, "Just smile. I'll handle all the questions."

Fear licks at the base of my neck and I can feel a panic attack nearing. Lights flash all around and shuttering camera lenses. His hand is warm and comforting, it's as if he knows I need it to stay in place to keep me grounded. To keep the jitters in my veins at bay.

We pose or just stand there as reporters yell at him.

"Logan, what's the real reason you passed on the NFL?"

"Is she the reason you'll be back in a Stallions uniform next year?"

I try to smile but I'm not sure if it will be misinterpreted.

"You were going to be the #3 draft pick, why didn't you take it?"

"Those close to you say you've changed since losing the National Title Game. Is it true and if so how have you changed?"

Oh lord, do not bring up the only game he lost. How crass.

Suddenly, Logan draws me in closer, leans down and kisses my cheek. He says, "For what it's worth, I'm coming back because I can make plenty of NIL money, get my degree and continue to have fun."

Did he just kiss me? On the cheek? With cameras?

The reporters attempt to ask follow-up questions but Logan ushers me through the rest of the carpet where we take a few more photos and the last one in front of the University logo.

As we enter the lower level of the old coliseum, it's been transformed. The old gymnasium is mesmerizing. Blue crystal modern chandeliers hang from the ceiling casting a blue glow over the room. The floor is covered in round tables with white tablecloths and on each is a number. Logan keeps his fingertips on my back as we snake to table number one. Of course, we would be in the front, Logan is up for Male Athlete of the Year.

Nerves get the best of me, as nearly everyone stops to talk to Logan. "Goodluck. You deserve this. I'm so glad you're staying on campus," they say with a wink and fingernails dredging over his arm. It's rude, they have no idea this date is fake. He never removes his hand from my back and when he feels my body start to tremor, he places his other hand on my bare arm and keeps us moving forward.

Both of our parents are already seated, as well as Hagan and Adalee, with blue toile bows adorning the chair backs. Just before we get there, he lightly squeezes my arm. I turn to look at the face of the Kentucky Stallions, the person who would have gone in the first round of the NFL draft. His eyes are as beautiful as they are kind. The kind you can get lost in.

"Harper, thank you." He steps closer and leans down, whispering in my ear, "To answer your question from earlier, when I said you were voluptuous. I only meant that you're beautiful and the dress looks like God's seamstress made it especially for you."

He stares at me for a hot second and I'm speechless. His words tumble in my head and my legs feel like jelly.

Beautiful. God. Especially. For me.

Suddenly, I'm in his arms, on my knees and have no clue how I got there.

***

CLAIM YOUR COPY OF <u>ON MY KNEES</u>, LOGAN & Harper's love story.

Scan the code to order your paperback copy of On My Knees.

Join my newsletter for bonus chapters, sales, juicy tidbits about your favorite characters. www.kristinleebooks.com Scan the code to access quickly.

See Hagan's List on the next page.

HAGAN'S LIST

- [x] Airplane
- [x] Baseball Park
- [ ] Beach
- [ ] Camping
- [ ] Kitchen
- [ ] Hot Tub/Pool
- [ ] In her wedding dress

Also by Kristin Lee

Campus Stallions

A college spin-off series from the Sarasota Sharks.

All Your Fault (Hagan/Adalee)

On My Knees (Logan & Harper) Coming Oct. 2023

Sarasota Sharks Series

Stealing A Second Chance (Wils/Kenni)

Sliding Headfirst (Patrick/Avery)

Scoring the Boss (Archer /Megan)

Swinging for Love (Tackett /Talynn)

Welcome to Kissing Springs

Secret Santa

Sunshine & Saddles Coming 6.12.23

Bourbon & Brawn Coming 9.12.23

Anthologies Coming Soon

Ms. CEO A She's On Top Anthology Coming 5.2.23

Tough Call -A Sports Romance Anthology Coming 7.11.23

The Racing Hearts Series

Always With Me (Brandon /Gracie)

Let Me Love You (Ben/Mia)

Come On Baby (Nic/Kaylee)

Acknowledgments

I want to thank Cam & Kat, the real life couple that inspired this novel. This is not their love story but they did meet in the weight room similar to Hagan and Adalee. Cam and Kat helped me in understanding the time constraints between two collegiate athletes and how injuries affect athletes' frame of mind. Oh, and Kat admitted that Cam is the the "romantic" one in the relationship, so Hagan followed suit. Thanks again to both of you! I enjoyed all of our conversations.

Thank you to my readers. As a writer, I appreciate your feedback and reviews. It encourages me to write love stories that evoke strong emotions. Readers have become friends, and friends have become readers, which makes me grateful for such a rewarding career.

My family, even the ones that don't read, are behind me 100%. They're always asking if I met my goal or if I'm on track for the next book. My husband does most of the cooking at crunch time. My sister entertains my son or makes me leave the house. But most of all, my family experiences are bits and pieces of every book.

My beta readers are my lifeline and they deserve a standing ovation. Thank you to Kate, Casey, and Joan for helping me cultivate emotional, heart-melting romances.

Casey, you are there for me at every turn. If I need a picture of a character, you find the right one in snap. If I need to bounce an idea off of you, I know our talks will spark my imagination. Thank you for your friendship, skills and ideas.

I have PA's that work within different areas. Thank you to Riley who runs my ARC/ Street teams and does everything I ask and more.

But also Two Queens Promotions for giving me a beautiful website to promote my work.

My author groups are amazing!

There are too many to name but you know who you are! Thanks for sharing your tips and experience and answering my endless questions.

And my ARC team, they are the best. I love building relationships with them and chatting about books and life. My hope is that they value our friendships as I do.

Tori, my editor at Cruel Ink Editing & Design. She makes my work better and I love our working relationship. You're the best.

Thank you to Cady at Cruel Ink Editing & Design for producing a cover that reflects the novel. She worked through multiple changes on this cover until she designed this one and I knew instantly it was the one.

About the Author

Kristin Lee is a USA Today Bestselling Author and writes heart shattering, heart melting romances with a shot of humor and a twist of suspense.

Her books feature Forbidden, Second Chance, Friends to Lovers, Enemies to Lovers, Age Gap, Brother's Best Friend and Forced Proximity.

If she isn't writing or reading, you'll find her streaming her favorite shows, or attending sporting events. Did I mention she loves having a Bourbon cocktail while at the horse races?

If you haven't found your match, don't worry, you will. But for now, take a romantic journey in one of her romance novels, where you are sure to meet a swoon worthy book boyfriend.